The Thing About Feathers

Janine Edgeworth

For Mam, my silent cheerleader

With love and care

Chapter 1

I had just taken the lasagne out of the oven when my husband died. That's what I think anyway. I wasn't actually there but, when I obsess over it, I think it might have been when I was poking the scab of cheese on top with a knife. Conor would think that was gas. I couldn't even watch an episode of *Games of Thrones* when he was alive and here I was analysing his exact moment of death with the gore of a lumpy lasagne.

It had been a Tuesday, a day when I used to think nothing ever happened. I was making dinner while Conor was at football training. When I'd seen his friend Mark's name flashing up on my screen, I'd figured Conor's phone had gone dead. Mark was a joker. We all grew up in the same estate in North Dublin and, even at thirty, he was still fond of pranks. I'd answered the phone, balancing it on my shoulder while trying to rip open a bag of salad with my teeth. The line was muffled, like the phone had gone off in Mark's pocket, making his voice sound far away.

'Sammie … Sammie?'

'Yeah, Mark, what?' I turned the bag over, pleased to read that the salad was pre-washed. 'I can't hear you.' I stopped what I was doing, pressing the phone closer to my ear.

It was just noise, then I made out 'Conor's collapsed.' Mark had sounded so dramatic that I thought it was another one of his pranks. I rolled my eyes and was about to hang up. 'You need to get to the hospital, Sammie.' I could hear the wobble in Mark's voice, the shift of something enormous between us plummeting my stomach to my knees. 'It's … it's not good.'

I started crying like my heart already knew what I hadn't yet been told. Mark's words kept coming, morphing into gibberish before they reached my ears.

'Sammie? Sammie, are you still there?' His shouts turned to sobs and I can't remember much after that.

Sometimes during the night Mark's phone call plays on a loop in my head. My mind will play cruel tricks on me, making me believe it's happening all over again. Some days, I can lose hours folded inside my thoughts, dissecting the weeks before Conor died. Did I miss a sign? Was there some vital clue?

You see, I come from a long line of hypochondriacs. Mam and her sisters love nothing better than discussing their ailments over a large pot of tea. Nana Margo was the worst for it. Dad used to joke that she'd get a buzz out of dying. But with Conor we never got a chance to check anything. He was walking around with an underlying heart condition, his heart like a ticking time bomb waiting to go off. 'Sudden adult death syndrome' was what the doctor said. The younger one with the kind face and enormous engagement ring, who I'd say hugged her fiancé tighter that night

2

after meeting me. She had broken it down for me to its 'general term'. To something I had heard of. To something I'd never thought in a million years would become part of my world.

Four months after Conor's death, I was still moving around my house as if in a dream – in one place and then, somehow, all at once in another. One Sunday morning I found myself sitting at the dining table, my back stiff, hinting that I'd been there a while. The whole house was still. The sun squeezed through the cracks in the blind, lighting the kitchen in thin strips of yellow. I flicked on the kettle and tapped my phone to check the time. It was only 11 a.m. and worst of all I was off work, so the day at a glance, was already long and torturous. Hours squandered on social media were now a thing of the past. I couldn't bring myself to peek into other people's lives – even obviously staged photos still stung.

I made tea on autopilot and sipped it slowly, not quite sure what to do when it was gone. I was still hugging the cold mug when my doorbell rang.

'Sammie, hi. Sorry to disturb you. I, ehm … well, this came on Friday.' John from next door was standing in front of me, holding out a large brown box. 'I was away, and I'd had it in the hall and … ehm … here.' He placed the box in my arms and pulled his hand through his ginger hair, visibly relieved to have passed it over. 'All okay?' He looked at me, his eyes pleading for a yes.

'Yes, thanks, John. This is great.' I sort of hooshed the box up a bit, like I knew what was in it. I hadn't a clue. My days of internet shopping had come to a halt. I must have looked bad because John was staring at me, the corners of his eyes crinkling with concern. I smiled, making them smooth out a little.

'Sure, I'll, eh… leave you to it so.' He half-waved, sidestepping awkwardly over the low wall that separated our gardens. 'You know, if you ever need anything, me and Celine are right next door.' He pointed with his thumb like I might need clarification.

'Thanks, John.' I closed the door, slipping my smile back into my pocket.

I walked into the kitchen and placed the box on the table – only then did I see the name. *Mr Conor Keegan.* I ran my finger over each letter, feeling his name against my skin. I picked the corner of the brown tape, pulling it back across the box, my heart beating louder than the tearing sound. I didn't know what to expect, what Conor could have ordered that would have taken four months to get here. I opened the box and inside was a compliment slip. The words looked cheery against the silky cream paper. *Our apologies for the delay. With kind regards, Dawson Printing.* I pinched the slip between my fingers and the memories flooded in. Snippets of conversations. Conor at his computer, obsessing over artwork: 'Is that a lightbulb or a pear, Sammie? It's a bleedin' pear, isn't it?' I remember biting my cheek trying not to laugh as he held the piece of

4

paper up at different angles. He'd got straight back on to the printers and demanded it all be redone. I'd never heard him complain before.

Inside the box were stacks of flyers and business cards, each with the lightbulb logo – now perfect – above *Conor Keegan Electrician*. Conor's dream was in this box. Everything he had worked towards for the past two years was stacked within four cardboard walls. When he could have been out having fun, he'd chosen to stay in, to get ahead, to work towards his big future. Our big future.

In all honesty, we thought we were different. We believed the world was our oyster and, with a head full of shite about goals and positivity, we thought we could achieve anything. Little did we know that our lives weren't our own, that there was something dark lurking alongside us and we were never in control. My stomach twisted into a knot of anger and I clenched my jaw not to scream. I picked up the box, shaking, and threw it against the kitchen cabinet. The sides burst, spewing Conor's dreams on to the floor.

'You can't write "Ferrari" on it, Conor. That's just being ridiculous.'

'And why not? It's my vision board.'

'It's *our* vision board. Anyway, you sound like a knob saying "vision board".' I tried to grab the marker from Conor's hand, but he held it above his head so I couldn't reach.

'This was your genius idea, Sam. Now, what else do I wish for?' He tapped the marker off his chin. 'Oh yeah, a private jet.' He wrote it down in block capitals, drawing the dodgiest-looking plane, just to annoy me.

It had been just before my twenty-eighth birthday and I'd read a book on the power of positive thinking. I couldn't wait to tell Conor about it. 'All you have to do is think positive. Believe and you shall receive.' Conor looked at me like I was mental. 'Think of us as magnets, attracting everything into our lives.'

Conor wasn't usually into 'airy-fairy crap', as he'd called it, but he'd had a bad day in work with his boss being a pain. I'd kept on at him until finally he'd relented and admitted his dream was to work for himself. I'd already known this but having him say it out loud felt like an achievement. My dream was to become an interior designer. I'd written down 'style celebrity homes' and Conor had called me a stalker. He'd written 'have a couple of kids', which had made me smile.

Despite everything on our list, our ultimate goal was to be together. We didn't write it down because we didn't think we had to. Now here I was, a widow at twenty-nine, with nothing but memories and broken dreams.

I was still sitting, staring, when I heard what sounded like a child's toy. An odd melody that got more annoying as it went on. I followed the sound into my living room, where my house phone was flashing pale red under a layer of dust.

'Sammie, thank Jesus. Gerrrryyy!' Mam shouted, not bothering to move the phone away from her mouth. 'She's okay, she just answered the phone. I've rung your mobile three times. I was just about to get into the car to drive over to you, when your dad said to try the house phone.'

'It must be on silent, Mam. Sorry.'

'So, are you calling over today? You said you were.' Mam tried this most days, thinking I'd lost my memory along with everything else. 'I was going to suggest that we go shopping, but now Tasha's asked me to mind the kids. I don't know who'd want their bits waxed on a Sunday. Anyway, sure, she has to oblige them and don't get me started on …'

I'd gone back into the kitchen to search for black bags, thinking it was best to clean up the business cards and flyers while half-distracted by Mam's rant. I opened the press under the sink and pulled out the sleek roll, trying to rip a bag off with one hand.

'I thought seeing as you said you were calling over –'

'Mam, I can't … not today.' I stopped to concentrate on my excuse. 'I'm really busy. I've a few things to do in the house and –'

'You can't just go from work to home, hiding yourself away, love. It's June now – the bright evenings won't be around forever. Maybe we could take up walking? Doctor Ibrahim was saying it's the best form of exercise. Not that you need exercise – you're a rake as it is – but, well, me on the other hand.' I heard rustling at the other

7

end of the phone. 'I bought a blouse last week. I'm looking at it now – size eighteen. I'm mortified. I'll have to cut off the tags.'

I knelt down on the floor and started cleaning up the mess. In that moment it was just paper again, and for that I was grateful.

'Well?'

'I'm not hiding myself away. I've been working all week.'

There was a long, heavy sigh and I knew what was coming. 'Please, Samantha. Dad and me really want to see you. We worry, and if you don't come here, we're coming to you.'

'Right, fine then. I'll be around in a bit.'

I rinsed my cup and tidied around the kitchen, stuffing the black bag into the bin. I looked down at myself, and for a split second I was tempted to go to my parents' as I was. They only lived a ten-minute drive away, and it was something I'd have done loads over the years. I knew I couldn't do it now though – everything was different now and arriving in pyjamas would mean too much to them. So instead, I went upstairs and threw on my uniform of late: leggings and an oversized T-shirt. I redid my hair so that the bun sat in the middle of my head, rather than hanging off the side like a growth.

I pulled across my bedroom curtains and pushed the window open. The clear sky attempted to lift me. I could hear the faint sound of cheering in the distance from the green. The sharp blow of the whistle, the thump of a ball, the sporadic claps all filtered around the

8

room. I stood listening, taking comfort in the sounds that were once part of Conor.

Chapter 2

After Conor died I had gone to stay with my parents. I don't remember it ever being a choice that I'd made. One minute I was at Conor's funeral, the next I was lying in my childhood bedroom surrounded by lava lamps and Tasha's creepy porcelain dolls. I lay for days under a poster of Take That, only leaving to use the bathroom. I couldn't function on any level and spent most of the time asleep or half-dazed.

Conor and Dad were particularly close, united by their love for United. I think my parents thought they could look after me, and they did as best they could, but they were grieving too. They had lost not only a surrogate son, but also a good chunk of their daughter. Just looking at me was painful for them. In moments when they would regain some sort of normality, falling into chat about a neighbour or losing themselves watching a TV programme, I would walk into the room and suck the air out with my grief.

Now, as I pulled up outside their house, I felt lucky to have my own place, somewhere I didn't have to try so hard at being okay.

My parents' house hadn't changed much since I was a child. Each red-brick building sat identical to the next in a neat row of twenty. Personalities were expressed – or not, in some cases – through what could be done with the postage stamp of grass in the front and the windowsills. The windowsills were a big thing, which could go from being painted green, white and orange for match days to pink or blue for new arrivals. Dad had been ordered to paint ours regularly over the years. I could see today they were bright yellow under the overflowing window boxes. Our house could be in bits on the inside, but once each blind sat half an inch above the window handle and the window boxes looked like they were going to burst, then Mam was happy.

Each summer Mam and Breda Byrne two doors down had a 'garden-off' to see who could outdo the other in the flower or gaudy-statue stakes. Last year Breda got the chance of a life-sized statue of Our Lady, which she had propped proudly against her porch door. The statue had a blue plastic crown, like on the bottles of holy water we used to get in school, and red eyes that Breda had painted on – 'Purposely,' Mam had said, 'hoping to make the feckin' news if it rains.'

I got out of my car and noticed Dad straight away in the window with my niece, Aria. He was making her arm wave to me in floppy motions while Aria cleaned the window with her tongue. Mam would go mad if she saw her.

'Here ye are, Aunty Sammie.' Dad handed me Aria as soon as I stepped into the hall. 'Granda needs the bog.' Dad gave my shoulder a squeeze and was already halfway up the stairs before it could mean anything.

I walked into the kitchen where Mam was swatting a fly that was doing loop the loops above the cooker. I threw my keys on the table, making her spin around.

'Sammie!' She flung the tea towel into the air and it floated to the ground as dramatically as she was rushing towards me. 'Look at Aria all delighted to see you.' Aria nuzzled her face into my shoulder, which I took as a sign she was ecstatic, rather than because Mam was tickling her thigh. Mam pulled me in for a hug, which only stopped when Aria grabbed a clump of her hair.

'Where's Finn?' I asked, looking around for my nephew.

'He's in the garden searching for treasure.' Mam picked the tea towel up off the floor and gave it a shake.

I could see my nephew from the window, his mop of dark curls half-buried behind the rose bush as he examined something on the ground.

Mam flicked on the kettle. 'Do you want something to eat? A sandwich? I could do you a fry?' Her hand was already clasped around the handle of the fridge door.

'Just tea, thanks.' I sat down with Aria on my lap. I couldn't remember the last time I'd held her. She snuggled in and I held her close, thinking how she felt like a half-filled hot water bottle. She looked up at me with the same brown eyes as me and my sister.

'How are you feeling – *today*?' asked Mam. She'd learned from her Parents of Young Widows Group, which was 'conveniently' set up by Breda Byrne and Fr Brennan in the local community centre after Conor died, that the correct approach to take with the recently bereaved is to ask only how they are today, 'as grief can only be taken one day at a time'.

Mam gave me a sideways glance as she took two cups from the kitchen press. 'You look exhausted, love. Are you sleeping?'

I pretended not to hear her – instead I made a big of deal of untangling a strand of hair from Aria's fingers.

Mam was looking at me, holding the kettle mid-air. 'Would you not let me get you something off Doctor Ibrahim?' She poured some water into each cup, somehow managing not to scald herself, as she was still staring at me. 'It's nothing to be ashamed off, Sammie. Just a few relaxers to help you through.'

'I don't need tablets.' I pouted my lips and blew on Aria's nose, making her giggle. I wanted to say that Conor would still be dead when I came off them. Unless, of course, I stayed on tablets forever, which at times did seem appealing. Ah, a world of foggy bliss …

'They helped me after your Nana Margo died. I know it's not the same thing, but they let me relax a little.'

'A little? You were practically horizontal for the first six months.'

13

Mam clicked her tongue like she always did when she had something more to say but didn't want to. She squeezed out the teabags and poured in the milk, no doubt playing out the rest of the conversation in her head.

'Here you are now.' She put the tea down in front of me, spilling a little over the edge of the cup. It was my cup, the one with my name, now faded, down the side. *Samantha – Excited by change. Life of the party.* I watched as a thick brown dribble spread through the words, breaking them apart.

'I'll take Aria while you have your tea,' said Mam. 'She's due a nap now. Aren't you, pet?'

I watched Mam as she settled Aria into her pram. She looked tired, her body slower, her mouth twitching with concentration. I'd only ever noticed old people doing that before, and I wanted to tell her to stop. I picked up my cup and took a mouthful of tea, trying to wash down the fear of someone else I loved dying.

Mam walked over to the kitchen window and lowered the blind in an effort to block out the sun, which now hung like a giant medallion, pouring heat through the window. 'It's stifling today,' she said, ripping open a packet of Viscounts. 'I've had these in the fridge.' She shuffled a couple out onto the table and slid one towards me like a game of air hockey. She knew they were my favourite. She'd recently stopped trying to force feed me meals, in the hope that I'd call around more.

'Oh, I almost forgot, Sammie. Look what I found.' She picked up a wad of kitchen roll off the microwave and carried it over to me like a wounded bird. Carefully, she opened it out and I swore I was going to hear a chirp. I peered inside to see a raggedy white feather, making me swell with irritation.

'I was walking home from the shops thinking of Conor, as I often do when I'm passing the all-weather pitches, when a feather fell from the sky, just like that.' Mam wriggled her fingers in front of my face, like she was doing Incy Wincy Spider. 'It floated down and practically landed on my nose.' Her eyes were wide, trying to channel her enthusiasm. 'And before you say it, Sammie, there were no birds flying over. Sure, Conor was the height of a house – it was like he was standing there and dropped it so I'd know he was with me.' She took a deep breath and I looked away, trying to ignore the pink bleeding into her eyes.

'Yeah, it's nice, Mam.' I picked up a biscuit and slowly unwrapped the shiny disc. The sugary mint hit my nose, making my throat constrict in protest.

'It's a sign, Sammie. Isn't it? I told Tasha. Your sister agrees with me.'

I should mention here that I would have agreed with them too, not so long ago. That's the thing about feathers. I used to believe they were a sign from loved ones, along with butterflies and robins – a hello from the other side. When Nana Margo died, I'd kept a white

15

feather stuck to the sun-visor in my car. It had been comforting to look at as I imagined her with me.

But when Conor died, so did my belief in all that. He'd never been into any of it, and to think of him sprinkling feathers on Mam's head or anyone else's was just ridiculous.

'I'd give that toilet a good half hour,' said Dad, walking into the kitchen with the newspaper tucked under his arm.

'Gerry.' Mam shot him a dirty look. She wrapped up the feather and placed it carefully on the windowsill, tucking it in behind her ornament of a swan taking flight.

'Wait till you see this,' said Dad, unfolding the newspaper and licking his thumb. He shuffled through the pages and turned the paper around for us to see. 'Some aul' fella down the country found a Lotto ticket stuck to his shoe. Won thirty-eight million.' Dad said the last bit slowly, finishing with a whistle through his teeth. 'See that, Lil?' He jabbed the page with his finger, his hand like a shovel blocking out half the text.

'It's well for him, isn't it?' said Mam, pulling her glasses down from her hair to take a closer look. 'Doesn't look like he needs it, mind.'

'Nah … a big filthy-rich farmer, probably with his communion money still stashed under his mattress. I tell yis, if it was raining soup I'd be holding a jaysis fork.'

'And when would it ever rain soup, Gerry?' Mam took a sip of tea.

'I'm just saying. Nothing like that would ever happen to us. Some people are just born lucky – or even better, silver spooned.' He looked at me as he said this, purely out of habit. It was the first time I actually nodded back in agreement instead of rising to the argument that you make your own luck in life. *Life's just one long struggle* – my dad had been right all along.

We fell in and out of conversation, with Dad pointing things out in the newspaper and Mam and me pretending to be interested. Finn came in and out from the garden, lining up random bits of treasure in front of me. I arranged the twigs and pebbles around my placemat, making a fruit bowl for the grape and plum design.

Everything in my parents' house we've had forever. Mam is a hoarder and unless something was completely banjaxed it stayed. I traced my finger along the black line on the table, pressing down: it was like a button taking me back in time. Conor and I, sitting with a hundred names between us. He'd been joking about seating Mam's family down the back at our wedding meal. Mam had walked into the kitchen just after he'd said it, making him jump and mark the table, and we'd both burst out laughing. I'll never forget Mam's eyes, fizzy, as she stood watching us before saying, 'If you both can laugh doing a seating plan, you'll be together forever.'

'Here's Tasha now,' said Mam, interrupting my memory.

'No problem, Breda,' Tasha shouted from the front door. 'Tell Jade I've her booked into the salon for eleven … Yeah, no, the parking is terrible. Just tell her to put it out there to the angels.' Tasha laughed. 'That's what I do to get a car space.'

'Pity the angels can't bleedin' park it for her.' Dad shook his head. 'Whole arse of the car was sticking out on the path yesterday.'

'Did you know Breda's niece is getting married?' Tasha asked me, walking into the kitchen. 'Remember Jade? She was in your year in school.'

'Is she?' I said, trying to distinguish one frizzy-haired girl from another.

'Her and her girlfriend.' Mum looked at Dad, the whites of her eyes like two Polo mints. 'They're lesbians, Gerry.'

Tasha rolled her eyes at me before peeking into the pram at Aria.

'Well, now, seeing as we're all here …' Mam glanced nervously at Dad and Tasha. Not as nervous as I was now that she was sitting down beside me. Mam rarely sat down, and I was hoping she wasn't going to start rubbing my hand. 'Your birthday, Sammie …'

The word 'birthday' hit me, threatening to break my facade. I shifted about in my seat, trying to ignore the crash of thoughts that came with it. How could I have a birthday? How could I move on to another year and leave Conor further behind?

'I know you don't want to be celebrating anything, love, but with it being your thirtieth –'

'I've already told Mam that you won't want to do anything. Obviously.' Tasha raised her eyebrows at Mam.

I quickly drained the last of my now cold tea and hoped my silence would speak volumes.

'I know it's not for a couple of weeks yet, but I thought it'd be nice to do something small,' said Mam. 'Even dinner? Fr Brennan was telling me that the Craven Hotel do a lovely à la carte. He was there recently at a retreat –'

Dad gave an exaggerated cough.

'Have you got something to say, Gerry?' Mam narrowed her eyes.

'A retreat? A retreat called Larina.'

Tasha laughed, but quickly stopped with Mam's glare.

'Be very careful speaking ill of a holy man, Gerry.'

'Holy? More like he's running around getting his holey.'

Mam's face burned. 'You can be an awful eejit sometimes, Gerry – do you know that?'

Dad looked at me and threw his eyes up. He loved nothing better than taking the piss out of Fr Brennan and the Catholic

Church. He said that Conor dropping dead had made him certain there was no God. I had to agree.

Mam turned back to me. 'Anyway, love, what would you like to do for your birthday?'

'I'd forgotten all about it, to be honest, but I don't want to do anything.'

'Well, of course, that's understandable. I was just thinking something very small, like a family lunch, just us?'

'No, but thanks anyway.' I forced a smile, hoping Tasha would change the subject.

'How about a nice meal in the house? We can just invite Aunty Carol?'

I shook my head, not making eye contact, afraid that I might buckle and cry.

'What about the wax museum?' said Dad. 'You always wanted to go there, and it'd be something a bit different.'

'That was me, Dad, and I was ten,' said Tasha.

'How about a show or shopping?' asked Mam.

Silence.

'Or a girlie afternoon tea?'

'Just leave it, Mam,' said Tasha.

Mam opened her mouth to speak but closed it again. She looked at Dad, who forced a smile for both their sakes. I hated worrying her, but, more than that, I hated that she made me feel I was.

It was still bright out when I got home that evening, so I didn't have to panic about coming back to a dark house. But the downside was that it was longer until bedtime and more hours I had to fill. I opened my front door and the silence caught me. I swear for the rest of my life I will never get used to the emptiness in my home. I turned on the TV and it flicked straight to E! News. The glamour of the previous night's red carpet spilled from the screen in a weak effort to thaw out the room.

I pushed open the double doors that led from the sitting room to the kitchen. The smell hit me, a mixture of stale foods seeping up through the plug hole after another hot day. I'd been trying to ignore it, trying to push down the anger that the smell liked to taunt. It was mad how a stupid sink could make me feel so angry – angry Conor wasn't here to sort it. Angry he had to die. I chased the same thought around my head as I grabbed the bottle of bleach from under the sink. People die every second; children die; tragedies far worse than mine happen to people all the time. I unscrewed the bottle and squeezed the last few blobs into the plug hole, jerking the running tap backwards and forwards, helping it down.

I opened the fridge and reached for the half-bottle of wine. The sight of it alone stirred an undercurrent of something good. I had only started drinking wine recently. It never appealed to me before, but drinking it now made me feel like I was doing something. I was having a glass of wine, not just sitting, waiting for nothing. I would rather have had red, but I couldn't stomach it. There was something classier about drinking a glass of red wine, as opposed to the muggy-looking colour I'd become fond of.

The wine made a clunking sound as I poured, lapping off the side of the glass like a frothy sea. I enjoyed the sound – it tricked my senses and made my mouth salty, thirsty for more.

I felt a little antsy, like something was brewing and if I explored it, I'd fall in. I took a slug of wine and winced as the bitter aftertaste hit my throat. It always took a couple of mouthfuls to ease in. I looked around for something to do, something to tidy, but everything was as I'd left it that morning. There were no surprises living on my own. I missed the mess.

I noticed a couple of tops on the radiator and a pair of pyjama bottoms making a W. I folded them neatly and carried them upstairs to put them away. I laid out my work clothes for the following day and felt relieved that I could at least wake up with some kind of purpose. I took my time, trying to draw out the menial chores.

When I went back downstairs, the kitchen and dining room had dimmed to a menacing grey. I poured the last of the wine and drank it standing up. There was nothing left to do except go to bed. I switched off the TV and locked up downstairs. The silence of the house made my thoughts shout loud. I tried to think of the jobs on my to-do list for work the next day, lining them up like little soldiers ready to fight off the fear.

In bed was where I felt most alone. I physically ached for Conor's arms, for the hairs on his chest to tickle my cheek and the weight of his body warm beside mine. I felt anaesthetised slightly by the wine. The fear was there but it wasn't quite reaching me. I twisted down under the covers and scrolled through my phone until the glare of the screen stung my eyes and I felt I might possibly be able to sleep. I slipped my hand out of the covers and switched off the bedside lamp, before turning over into the dark.

Chapter 3

I arrived at work early the following morning, having stuck it out for as long as I could at home. I'd grabbed a coffee on the way in and was slowly sipping it as I listened to my boss, Dionne's voice message. The line was fuzzy, but I could just about make out that she'd be popping into the shop later.

Dionne and her husband Brian owned Haven Interiors. Brian had opened up a cafe in South Dublin that was doing really well and the only time I saw him now was beaming from Dionne's phone beside some foodie's five-star review. Dionne championed everyone, including me, quickly making me shop manager when she saw I shared her passion for home interiors. She had trusted me to order in brands and one-off pieces that I knew our customers would love. The thrill of it was what had made it so hard for me to leave over the years. Since Dionne had the twins three years ago, she relied on me even more to help with the shop.

A few months back Dionne had talked about creating a line of products under the shop's name. I'd jumped at the idea, even though I'd just finished an interior-design course and was eager to take the plunge to leave the shop. When she had said it to me, I'd taken it as a sign to stay put longer, convinced the universe was steering me in the direction of my dreams – like I'd read about in a bazillion motivational books.

I had been working on the product line right up until Conor died and had spent all my quiet time in the shop researching and sketching out ideas. I hadn't thought about them since and I surprised myself with the urge to look through them now.

I reached my hand under the counter, feeling behind the stapler, Sellotape and temperamental pricing gun to find my folder. I bent down and slid it towards me, pushing a line of dust along with it. The weight of it surprised me as it slapped onto the counter with a thud. It was thick with ideas. Fabric samples and pressed flowers poked out between the pages like an over-filled sandwich. I'd got a bit carried away in the beginning, thinking of myself as the next Laura Ashley. I flicked through the pages of all my ideas, and it gave me what I could only describe as a faint stir of enthusiasm.

Outside, the road was heaving with traffic snaking towards the city centre. I set the folder aside to show Dionne when she called later and thought I'd get to work on a new window display. Even when the shop was quiet, there was always something to do, something to stop me from slipping.

I was so busy trying to convert the rectangular space of the window into a convincing garden party that I hadn't heard a customer come in. It wasn't until she coughed and I jumped, almost dropping a Yankee Candle on my foot, that I noticed her.

'Hi, sorry.' I climbed around the patio set, still holding the candle. 'Can I help you?'

She was around my age, with dark auburn hair and green eyes that were set deep like she'd just taken off glasses. 'I'm just looking thanks.' She lifted her arm so her handbag slid into the crease at her elbow.

'If you need any help, just let me know.' I walked over to the shop counter to light the candle. The scent of jasmine and berries swirled into the air and when I turned around, she was watching me. I raised my eyebrows in a muted 'are you okay?' and she smiled, a quick flash of white, before dragging her eyes from mine to the dining-cabinet display.

I rearranged the jewellery dishes, changing the direction of the oval shells so they all nodded to the left. I could feel her eyes on me again, watching me, making me wonder if I should recognise her.

'This place is a real Aladdin's cave,' she said, picking up a pearl napkin holder and turning it over in her hand. She moved around the floor now like a child in a toy shop, stopping to examine whatever caught her eye. 'It must be great working here?' She looked over at me, popping the lid on and off a floral teapot. I was certain I didn't know her.

'It sure is,' I said, meaning it now more than ever.

She spent the next ten minutes walking around the shop, and each time I thought she was about to buy something, she'd place it back on the shelf. 'Is it always this quiet?' She picked up a compact mirror and flicked the catch open with her nail, holding it up, so she could admire herself in the square glass.

'Usually afternoons are busiest,' I said, chasing a blob of creamy polish around the counter with a cloth. 'I'll be hoping to lure them in today with my window display.'

She smiled at me over her shoulder, still holding the mirror in her palm. She was making me uneasy. I was just about to ask if I knew her from somewhere when she snapped the mirror shut and turned around.

'Oh, I just remembered,' she said, with a pathetic attempt at surprise, 'I've my friend's house-warming coming up and I need to buy her a gift. Any ideas?'

'Sure.' I walked over to the oversized throws and knotted rugs, pushing down the niggling feeling in my gut. She was following me when her phone rang.

'Hello, Jaclyn speaking.' Her voice was clipped and business like, far from the honeyed tone she'd used talking to me. 'I don't have it to hand. I'll call you back.' She shoved her phone into her handbag and tilted her head, looking at a printed throw. 'Oh, these are nice.' She walked over to the frames. 'Do you have anything with cute quotes? I love motivational ones.'

I held my tongue, along with a heart-shaped frame that I dangled in the air. 'How about *Home is where the bra isn't?*'

Jaclyn's phone rang again and she rushed out, promising she'd see me soon. The fact that she sounded like she really meant it made the whole thing even weirder.

I spent the rest of the afternoon perfecting the window display in between the trickle of customers. I'd got a bit obsessed with perfecting it and kept running in and out of the shop, much to the amusement of the butchers next door. It was almost closing time when I noticed Dionne's Land Rover pulling up outside. I watched as she unfolded herself from the driver's seat, her sleek, dark bob and model height making even her neon gym-wear look chic.

'Hi, Dionne,' I said, rushing over to the counter to get my folder. 'I've been working on a few ideas – you'll have to use your imagination: you know my drawing skills – but the drinks coasters are good. You can't go wrong with circles …' I looked up to see Dionne just standing there. 'Are you okay?' I stopped still to look at her properly. She was paler than usual, with the same greyish colour that Tasha gets in the first few weeks of pregnancy.

'Not really, Sammie.' She was fiddling with her keys, weaving a keyring with a photo of the twins between her fingers.

I snapped the folder shut and went straight into Clancy autopilot. 'Tea. I'll make some tea and you can tell me all about it.' Before she could say anything, I rushed past her and flipped the shop sign to closed. I locked the door and gestured with an over-enthusiastic smile and nod of my head for Dionne to follow me.

'Do you want tea, or maybe a glass of water? It is warm in here.' The window in the back room was the width of a sliced pan. I pushed it open and glanced at Dionne, who was plaiting her fingers together. I felt my stomach take a dive. Maybe she was sick? I couldn't bear it if Dionne was sick.

'I won't have anything, Sammie.'

We both sat down in the small room, which was furnished with two wooden stools and a kettle. A hall table with a design of Olympic-like tea rings had been our makeshift dining table for as long as I could remember. The room felt like an extension of my home.

'This is so hard, Sammie.' Dionne unlocked her fingers, flattening her palms on her knees. 'I'll just spit it out and remember, it's not as bad as it sounds. You'll still always have a job.'

'I'll have a what? Sorry?' I leaned forward in my chair, thinking I couldn't possibly have heard right.

'Brian and I are selling the shop. I'm so sorry, Sammie. I mean … with everything you've been through –' Dionne's voice cracked, making her inhale sharply before continuing. 'You've been the most amazing employee. You're more than an employee – you're a friend. I wanted to tell you sooner, but I couldn't. We weren't sure what we were doing and then …'

Her words floated around my ears. She was still talking, but I couldn't take it in. She reached over and rubbed my hand, her head tilted like she was stroking a puppy.

'Brian wants to concentrate on the cafe, and now that we're living on the Southside and with the twins, well, it just feels that I'm out of touch with this place.' She looked around like the walls we had sat within for the past eleven years had suddenly crumbled away, tainting the laughs, the tears, the work plans and gossip we had shared in them.

I couldn't speak. I moved my mouth, trying to feel for a word, but there was nothing.

'You know you can come work in the cafe. That's probably not something you want to do – you'd be wasted in a cafe. You've such an eye for interior design, and I really think you could –'

I burst into tears, making my chest heave, pushing out giant, noisy sobs. I was mortified. I'd lost Conor, which had been the worst pain ever, and now here I was crying over a stupid shop. But it wasn't just a shop. It had been part of my life for the past eleven years. It was a constant. Even after Conor it had been my comfort blanket, and now it was being ripped from around me.

'Oh, please, Sammie, don't cry.' Dionne hugged me, squeezing tighter, perhaps for her sake more than mine. 'I'm so, so sorry.'

The more I tried to stop crying, the more the tears kept coming.

'You'll be okay, I promise.' Dionne was shushing me like she would one of the twins after a fall. She grabbed a wad of kitchen roll from the table and dabbed my eyes. 'Listen to me, Sammie. The woman buying this place, she's only your age. She's coming from the Southside.' She folded the kitchen roll over and started dabbing my cheeks. 'She doesn't know anyone, and she doesn't want the hassle of hiring all new staff. She said she'd be happy to keep on anyone that I recommend.' She was smiling, hopeful, her eyebrows like two sides of a triangle. 'She's turning the shop into a clothing boutique and keeping a small section of homewares. You'd be great …'

I looked down at myself, at the person I no longer recognised. I was hardly a fashionista.

'You've always been into clothes – it might be a nice change for you. Her name is Jaclyn and –'

'Jaclyn?'

'Yes. Anyway, she is –'

'She was here, in the shop.'

'Jaclyn was? When?' Dionne held the now soggy kitchen roll mid-air, her eyes clouding with anger.

'Today.' I sniffed loudly, rubbing my nose with my sleeve. 'She was looking around for ages and asking questions.'

31

'Did she tell you she was buying this place?'

I shook my head, silently shouting, *obviously fucking not.*

'I told her that I still had to tell you. She's a pushy little –'
Dionne stopped herself.

I stood up. I felt hot, like my eyes and face were on fire.

'It's a lot to take in, I know.' Dionne stood up too. 'But you
do have options, Sammie. Brian and me, we'd never leave you
stuck.'

'I know.' I tried to breathe, to concentrate. My life felt like
one big endurance test, one I was undoubtedly failing. 'I don't want
to work for Jaclyn, Dionne. I couldn't.'

Dionne nodded. I knew she understood, and I knew she felt
genuinely awful.

'As for the cafe, let's face it – it wouldn't really be my thing.
You'd lose all your customers for a start.' I pushed out the joke so
that things would be left somewhat okay between us.

I drove home on autopilot. What would I tell my parents? Mam
would crumble, and Dad would be silently worried sick. The shop
was pulling me along – we all knew that. Without it, not even I knew
what I'd do. I parked my car in the drive and knew I needed to get
some air.

I preferred to walk with a purpose, so I headed in the direction of the newsagents at the front of my estate. I needed a drink. I needed something to smooth the edges. I walked to the end of the road and crossed over, cutting across the large green.

The green sat like a spider's body in the middle of the estate, with each road jutting out like a leg. The warm evening meant it was a hive of activity. I passed a group of teenage girls sitting in a circle, all eyeliner and fake tan, listening to music from a speaker the size of a postage stamp. The song sounded like a lifetime ago.

I kept walking, a little faster, twisting my wedding band with my thumb, around and around, trying my best not to think. Bursts of laughter and conversations darted around me. Kites snaked and flapped through the sky above my head. For a moment I felt invisible, like the world was moving without me in it. I was somewhere on the outside looking in.

Inside the shop, I went straight to the drinks section and picked up two bottles of Blossom Hill. There was a greasy-looking teenager behind the counter, engrossed in something on his phone. There was always a high turnover of staff – I presume because of the crap pay or because people like the guy I was looking at used it as a means to get through college. Only losers like me stayed working in the same place since school. Maybe I could apply here? I could do up a CV and leave it in. I smiled at him, even though I'd absolutely nothing to smile about, just in case this kid was the one who'd be taking in my application. Maybe I could do nice window displays and jazz up the deli counter with hedgehogs made out of pineapples dotted around the lettuce?

My enthusiasm for working there had fizzled out by the time I reached the end of the car park and the grimness of my life set in again. I walked home clutching the paper bag to my chest. I could feel the liquid swishing rhythmically as I walked, both cool and soothing in my arms.

My road was quieter than the other roads in the estate. Everyone liked to keep to themselves, which suited me fine. Apart from John and Celine next door, I rarely spoke to anyone. The younger neighbours around my own age all worked full time, running from their front doors to their cars in the morning, and doing the same in reverse eight hours later.

The couple directly facing us had a baby just before Christmas. I'd sent over a present – more of a karmic gesture for when Conor and I were going to start trying.

I opened my front door and went straight to the kitchen. I turned over the glass on the draining board and opened one of the bottles of wine. I poured greedily, making the wine spit over the side. I felt restless, my skin itchy, and I knew I couldn't sit at the kitchen table for the evening.

The sun was pressing against the patio glass, and for the first time it felt inviting. I unlocked the door and slid it across, remembering how the garden had always been Conor's place. I'd never got the whole relaxing outside thing and would sooner be curled up on the couch watching *The Real Housewives of* … well, anywhere, really.

Outside the sun was low, hanging lazily above the back wall. I pulled out a garden chair and wiped away a doily of silver cobwebs that hung from the armrest. Sitting back into the warm wicker, I rested the rim of the glass against my lips and listened to the faint chatter of family life from the gardens around me.

The garden had been a novelty when we'd first moved in. Having come from an apartment, it was nice to walk outside and into something that was ours. It was more wide than long, with a rectangular lawn in the middle. Around the edges were different types of shrubs with thick, glossy leaves and waxy flowers in yellows and orange. I hadn't a clue of any of the names except for the hydrangeas, which were the only remnants of the previous owner. The blue pom-pom-shaped flowers reminded me of my Nana Margo's garden as a child, where Tasha and I used to pick them and try to mash them into perfume. Morning glories were the ones that Conor had bought – purely for their name. The blooms looked like tiny fried eggs and mirrored the sun at each end of the garden.

Conor wasn't the gardening type, but I think he enjoyed creating something, knowing that the house interior would be my thing. Looking back, I think he wanted to make me proud: the little kid in him always basked in praise. He had spent hours making the rockery at the bottom of the garden. Dotted between the grey rocks were rubbery plants in deep purples and reds. It just about got some light through the branches of the large oak tree that stretched over from the house behind. I'd never been the outdoorsy type, so when Conor finally finished, he'd pulled me out by the hand and made me close my eyes. The garden walls were painted cream, where he'd hung tiny fairy lights to surprise me, and I remember looking at him and just loving him even more.

The decking was varnished a deep glossy brown, leading onto a winding stepping-stone path to the famous rockery. In the middle of the rockery sat the Buddha that we'd nicknamed Wayne. It smiled at us over rolls of fat, holding a tea light in each chubby palm.

The garden still looked good now, but the shed had seen better days. The roof had caved in a bit, having taken a beating during the winter. I was still examining it when my eyes caught a flicker of movement on the wall. A grey cat was tight roping towards me, his paws marking out his journey as his tail sliced the air behind. I froze, resisting the urge to clutch my knees to my chest and scream. Cats have always freaked me out – it's the way they stare like they're reading your mind and then judging you on it. I stayed still, clutching my drink, wondering for a second if I could throw it at him. He moved again, but this time in slow motion, each movement sending ripples through his light-grey fur. I stamped my foot in an effort to scare him, but he just stopped and looked at me, his amber eyes staring me down.

'You're funny.'

Holy shit – the cat was talking to me. Oh, please God, tell me it's not Conor reincarnated?

'It's only a cat, it won't hurt you.'

'What?' I looked up to see a young girl sitting in the tree overhanging our back wall. She was smiling at me, almost laughing.

'Hi.'

'Eh, hi,' I said, looking back at the cat.

'Are you really that scared of cats?'

'Ehm, yeah – well, a bit.' I was afraid to take my eyes off him in case he pounced or brushed off my legs. My skin broke out into tiny bumps at just the thought.

'He belongs to the old man two doors down,' said the girl. The cat's ears twitched with her voice. 'Relax, he won't hurt you.'

It was like something Conor would have said, and I really wanted to tell her to piss off.

'Shoo, go away,' she said, waving her skinny arm like a broom. The cat did what he was told and slunk down the opposite side of the wall into John and Celine's garden.

'Thanks.' I said, realising it was a legit fear of cats that I had and not just an overall weariness. I took a mouthful of wine with the girl still looking at me. I wasn't great at guessing kids' ages, but she looked around eleven. I quickly scanned the grass for a ball or whatever else she might have kicked over the wall.

'What's your name?'

'Mine?' I asked, pointing to myself with the tilted glass. 'Samantha – well, Sammie. That's what most people call me.'

'Most people call me Jojo.'

'I like your dress, Jojo.' The compliment fell out of my mouth, making me regret it instantly. If she hung around now it was my own bloody fault.

'Thanks.' She kicked a pleat of denim, making the tassels on her sandals twist together.

There were bursts of children's voices from other gardens and a dog barking in the distance. She was looking at me expectantly now, like Finn does when he wants to be entertained. 'Are you playing with your friends?'

'Nope, not today.' She smiled. 'I'm just chilling out.' She swung her legs like she was on a swing, her blue eyes dancing with mischief. She had a spattering of toffee-coloured freckles across her nose that looked freshly cooked by the sun. 'What are you doing?' she asked, leaning back, her blonde hair catching along the bark and making a fan. She was getting comfortable, like she was settling in for a chat.

'Just chilling out too, I guess.' The sun disappeared behind a cloud, leaving a breeze that put the garden into motion. Glimpses of white washing waved from over the wall and a plastic windmill spun a kaleidoscope of colours across the decking.

'I love those.' She pointed to the windmill, which was making a soft whistling sound. She was looking around at the rest of the stuff now, at the chrome gnomes and mushroom-shaped bird house. All damaged stock that Dionne had been throwing out. Mam's voice in my head had made me think it was a sin, so I'd ended up taking the lot.

'Who owns the bike?' asked Jojo. It took a second to cop what she was talking about. I'd forgotten Conor's bike was leaning haphazardly against the wall. Dad had offered to put it in the shed for me. I remembered I'd said no. I'd wanted everything the same.

'It was my husband Conor's,' I said, turning to look at it.

'My dad used to cycle to work,' said Jojo, 'but Mam always gave out because he wouldn't wear his helmet. He said he'd look stupid, but she said he'd look more stupid drinking his dinner through a straw.' She flicked a fly from her hand. 'Does your husband cycle to work?'

'No, well, no … not anymore.' I picked up my glass, swirling the puddle of wine around the bottom. I wanted her to go now. I wanted to drink, to forget in peace. She was looking at me, waiting for me to say more. 'He's … he's in heaven.'

'Oh.' Her mouth formed a perfect circle, making me wish I hadn't said anything. 'Do you really miss him?'

I swallowed the last mouthful of wine. 'Yeah, I do – a lot.'

'He must really miss you too.' She smiled, and I smiled back. I didn't know what else to do. Nobody had ever said that to me before. 'At least you're not wearing black. When my granny died, my grandad wore black for a full year.'

'Did he?' I said, feeling an overwhelming sadness for the poor man.

'Yeah, he went to Benidorm three times that year – he must have been sweating.'

I burst out laughing, shocking myself with the sound.

She was smiling, her eyes twinkling, and I couldn't tell if she was joking with me or not.

'Really?' I was still laughing as I put my empty glass on the table.

'True story,' she said, pulling her hair into a ponytail. She let it loose again, just as my eye caught a trail of purple bruising down her underarm. Out of instinct I rubbed my own.

'That looks sore.'

She shrugged and started humming a song I couldn't place. A belch of thick smoke carried over the wall, bringing a waft of barbecued chicken. My mouth watered, and I realised I hadn't eaten all day.

'Are you not answering that?' Jojo nodded to my mobile, which was flashing on the table.

I glanced at the screen. 'It's just my sister.' I pinched the side of the phone, sending Tasha to voicemail.

'Do you not like her?'

'Of course I like her.'

'Real-ly?' She raised an eyebrow, adding more years onto herself.

'Well, most of the time anyway.'

We both laughed. Jojo's laugh was hearty and unexpected from such a dainty little frame. It was a real belly laugh, which made me laugh even more.

'Jennifer!' a woman shouted from over the wall, her voice sharp, snapping the air and silencing both of us.

Jojo froze.

'Jennifer!' she shouted again, this time louder, making Jojo flinch in a way that seemed at odds with her personality.

'I have to go.' She jumped down, her blonde hair skimming the wall like a feather.

There were muffled voices and I leaned forward trying to listen, but they were soon cut with the slam of a door. A slur of music somewhere in the distance drowned out the slap I thought I'd heard.

Chapter 4

One of the worst things about Conor dying was that he was the one person I needed to help me through it. He had for so long been the person I turned to for everything. He made everything okay, mainly by just saying that it would be. Without him I felt vulnerable. Everyone kept telling me how strong I was. Well strong felt lonely – and pretending to be felt even worse.

I ended up blurting out to Dad on the phone about the shop closing down. I tried to sound breezy; thankfully he played along. When I'd asked Tasha how they really were afterwards, she had kindly diluted the truth. Mam thought that Dionne actually owed me her life for working in the shop for so long. I decided to ignore the nagging feeling that I was, yet again, the cause of my parent's pain.

I threw myself into the closing down preparations – reducing items, advertising the sale online, re-doing my garden display to show just about everything we stocked. This time with an ugly red sale sticker slapped across the front. I tried to block out what was actually happening and just worked hard like I always had.

Time whizzed past in those two weeks and before I knew it, the closing date was upon me. I woke up with a weight so heavy on my chest, that I thought I'd have to ring in sick on my last day.

Dionne had insisted on having a closing down party, inviting our regular customers and friends from the neighbouring shops. I couldn't think of anything worse. Despite wanting to ignore that this was happening, I managed to make somewhat of an effort with myself, if only to minimise the victim role I felt trapped in.

I got to the shop early, wanting to have a walk around and say my goodbyes. In my newly bereaved state, I thought maybe this could help. I could get the closure I didn't get with Conor. However, Dionne arrived just as I was about to have a one to one with the remaining candle display, and my moment was over. She burst though the shop door with more enthusiasm than I had seen in the past three years, arranging balloons and plastic cups, plates and goodie bags, all along the fold-out tables set up against the wall.

She tried softening the blow as I stood just watching her, throwing in sage one liners like, 'a change is better than a rest, Sammie,' and 'this is a new chapter for us both.' Brian was meant to follow her over but had got stuck at the café. It just went to show how he didn't care anymore. He didn't need to really; he was on to bigger and better things. They both were. They were one of those couples that Dad would say were 'pissed with luck'. There would probably be a chain of cafes, and then something else and something else … The world was at their feet.

Mam arrived to support me, even though she was still annoyed with Dionne. 'You lined her pockets these past ten years, keeping this place thriving, while she swanned around.' That wasn't completely true, but I was grateful for Mam's loyalty, even though I prayed she wouldn't get loose tongued and say something to Dionne.

I tried to keep busy by tidying around, re-arranging the neat triangle shaped sandwiches on their trays and straightening up the napkins. Mam was talking to the lady from the Spar a couple of doors up and Dionne was flapping about like the shop was filled to the rafters.

'Sorry, I'm late.' Tasha rushed over to me, still in her purple beautician uniform. 'That bitch Leona wouldn't let me out early. She booked me a client with a lady garden like a Brillo pad to wax. It took me an extra half hour and I think I pulled an arm muscle.' She flexed her forearm and looked around the shop.

'You're not missing much,' I said, as a couple of old dears shuffled past eating eggs sambos. Dionne stood anxiously checking her watch.

'You okay?' Tasha linked my arm.

'Sure.' I smiled. 'Onwards and sideways!' I repeated our family's mantra, that I used to always hate. Mam walked over, handing us both a plastic cup of wine.

'I'm not drinking, I'm driving. I've to collect the kids from Wayne's parents' later.'

I necked mine back, tasting the plastic more than the wine. 'Here, I'll have it,' I said, taking Tasha's.

'Mam, what the fuck are you wearing?' Tasha stared at Mam's feet.

'What?' Mam looked down at her khaki green hiking books. 'They're for walking. Doctor Ibrahim was saying that I need good ankle support.'

'If you're climbing mountains maybe, not walking down the

44

Malahide Road.' I hadn't even noticed them, which these days wasn't saying a lot.

'They're very comfortable.' Mam straightened her back, taking a sip of her water.

'Yeah, they look it. You're like Bear Grylls.' Tasha laughed, and Mam refused to look at her.

Slowly, the shop filled with familiar faces from the past eleven years. Despite the anxiety that curled like a cat in the pit of my stomach, I felt somewhat relieved that the shop had meant something to the locals. My hard work hadn't been completely in vain. Each person at some point made their way over to me, telling me how they'd miss me and the shop. I felt like I was going somewhere, that as soon as the shop door closed, I was going to evaporate too.

A glass clinked silencing the chatter and making us all turn around. Dionne was standing beside the counter, revelling in the scene.

'I'd just like to say a few words.' She looked around the shop.

A couple of late stragglers arrived, making us all turn around, and filling the shop with a blast of warm air from outside. The girls from the Hilton Hotel came in behind them, giving me a little wave as they bundled in the door. Terry and some of the other butchers from next door, brought a tray of cocktail sausages that Mam was helping herself to. A few mothers from the local mother and toddler group, complete with buggies and excited toddlers, made up the rest of Dionne's audience.

'When Brian and I opened this shop twelve years ago, we didn't know what to expect. We hoped it would be a success and, well, thank god it was.'

Mam fake coughed and Tasha elbowed her to shut up.

Dionne held out her hand for me to come over and I felt like an awkward school child standing beside her, my cheeks burning pink. 'I'm sure you all know Sammie, the manager, who really brought this place to next level.'

A couple of the butchers gave a whoop, and I had to stop myself from giving them the finger.

'Sammie came to work here when she was just eighteen …' I was only half listening to her. I just wanted to go, before what this all meant for me sunk in. 'I'm certain, I'm a hundred percent certain that you're on to greener pastures, Sammie.'

'Thank you.' I forced a smile and took a mouthful of warm wine.

'Most importantly, thank you to our amazing customers. You have been so loyal over the years, without you of course we'd have been nothing …'

I get embarrassed for people easily and I was cringing for Dionne. I could feel a film of sweat sticking my shirt to my back, and the plastic cup was now clammy in my hand.

'Here's to the next chapter.'

Dionne held her cup up and we all mumbled 'here, here.'

'Sammie and I have made you up some goodie bags. So, you can keep a piece of Haven Interiors in your home for many years to come.' There were claps and a bustle for the remaining bags. Even

Tasha looked excited for a freebie.

'Sammie.' I felt someone tap my arm.

I turned around to see one of our regular customers Mrs Wallace. She had, even during the recession, kept the shop afloat with her many business ventures. She looked flawless as always, with her blonde, curly blow-dry held back by designer glasses and her perfectly applied make-up, making her look much younger than fifty-five.

'Thanks for coming, Mrs Wallace.' I gave her a hug, inhaling a waft of orange blossom and freesia – her signature Jo Malone scent.

'Of course, I wouldn't miss it! But, to be honest, I wanted to speak to you, Sammie. Look every cloud and all that.' She waved her hand, distracting me with her heavy gold bangle that slid down her arm taking my eyes with it. 'I was thinking, would you be up for a little project? I'm doing some show apartments in Howth next weekend and I'm really stuck. My assistant interior designer didn't quite live up to her name. In fairness, she was utter shite. Would you be able to help? I would pay you obviously and I'd –' Mrs Wallace spoke a mile a minute, it was hard to keep up. 'You can have a think about it, but with all the help you've given me over the years – picking the perfect pieces just from my description of the rooms. Imagine what you could do if you were actually in them.'

'I'm really grateful, Mrs. Wallace –'

'Audrey.'

'Audrey. But I've no proper experience and I just, well, I just wouldn't be up for it.' I didn't want to tell her that whatever scrap of creativity I had left after Conor, well and truly died with the shop.

'But you helped me the last time. Your ideas were fab. A couple who viewed one apartment, complimented specifically the pieces you'd picked.'

'I'm sorry, Audrey, but I can't. Thank you though.'

'Okay, sure … no problem.'

She looked disappointed and I felt a pang of guilt, but there was no way I could do it. As much as I'd wanted to be an interior designer in the past, it had just been another stupid dream. And I knew now from experience that chasing dreams was pointless, when your life could be destroyed in an instant.

'Best of luck with everything.' She squeezed my hand before walking away.

'Sammie.' Tasha made her way over to me. 'Mam and I are going to head. I'm giving her a lift home, the less people that see her in those boots the better. Will you be okay?'

I looked over at Mam who was holding the napkin like a hotdog bun and filling it with the remaining cocktail sausages. 'Yeah, I'll be fine. Thanks for coming.' I hugged Tasha goodbye and gave Mam the evils, making her shove the sausages quickly into her handbag, and look away oblivious.

The shop emptied pretty much after them, until it was just Dionne and I left standing among scrunched up napkins and distorted plastic cups.

This place used to never feel enough for me. I'd been itching to step out on my own. Now it was another piece of my life gone. I felt lightheaded as I hugged Dionne goodbye, promising to meet for a coffee soon. As I was leaving, Dionne handed me a card with a bottle of red wine, and a cheque worth six months' pay. I wasn't expecting it, but I was grateful all the same.

My hands shook as I worked the shop key from my keyring, sliding it off the loop and handing it to Dionne. I couldn't look back and kept walking, my head down, my tears falling with every step.

That evening, I stood in my living room and opened Dionne's card. It was beautiful, with butterflies and swallows in silvery swirls around the front. Inside, the words stung from the page. *Thank you for helping to make our dreams come true – Love, Dionne and Brian.*

I placed the card on the mantel piece and took the bottle of wine out of the gift bag. Tonight, I was happy to drink red.

Chapter 5

I spent the next week sleeping – a lot. I've always felt more tired doing nothing and, well, that multiplied by a billion for me over those seven days. I felt slightly drugged and was hard pushed to wash a cup, never mind myself. I didn't step foot outside the house, except to grab essentials in the local shop. I just didn't know what to be doing, yet the days were still passing in stops and starts, one rolling into the next. I was having so many conversations with Conor in my head, ranting at him for leaving me and asking why he had to die, that I feared he'd left me insane.

Mam rang each evening, pleading with me to call around. Finally, I relented when she told me that Tasha had done up my CV and given it to Wayne's sister. As much as I no longer cared what people thought of me, the thought of Lydia reading my sister's glittered version of my past thirty years did poke at something of the old me and make me panic.

Lydia worked for a recruitment agency in the city centre: mainly for office workers, from what I could remember. I knew Tasha was only trying to help, but I was barely motivated to get out of bed, never mind hold down a nine to five. There was no stopping Tasha though, once she got something into her head, and I knew I'd have to go around myself to put a stop to her job search.

I decided to walk to my parents' house and use each step as a gear up to face my family. I used to enjoy walking when I was younger. We'd had no car and Mam would make us walk an hour each week to Aunt Carol's house. She'd bribe us by promising us ice-cream with the money we'd saved on bus fare.

Tasha would moan the whole way in, but I used to make up games like stamping on the cracks in the pavement, pretending that they'd open up and I'd fall down into another world. Mam used to love using Tasha and me against each other to add weight to her nagging. She'd say things like, 'Look at Sammie, not complaining,' if Tasha whinged, dragging her heels. When we got as far East Wall and the cracks on the ground were like a slab of marble, Mam would tell me to stop hoping about like I was simple and to look at how normal Tasha walked. When Aunt Carol eventually moved closer to us, I used to miss the walks. Then Dad got his first Fiesta and we never walked anywhere again.

On the walk to my parents' house, I couldn't resist stamping on some cracks, and trying to make believe there was a better world beneath me than the one I was stuck in. The game lasted all of two minutes, until I began to feel nauseous from walking with my head down. I got to my parents' house and was greeted with the smell of roast chicken and an oven that needed a deep clean. Mixed with the muggy weather, it made me feel weak.

'I'm just making a bit of dinner for Tasha and Wayne,' Mam called from the kitchen when I opened the door. 'They're on their way now.'

Mam was spooning the juices from the chicken over the roast

potatoes, doing her very best Marks and Spencer food ad impression, trying to woo me. 'I know you're probably not hungry, but I'll dish you up a little, just to be social.' She smiled, sprinkling a handful of thyme from a height, and giving the tray a shake.

I took a glass from the press and poured myself some water. As I gulped it down a mass of multi-coloured wool caught my eye. 'What are you doing with all that wool?' I asked, sitting down at the kitchen table. I leaned over and pushed open the widow, which only seemed to exaggerate the smell.

'I've taken up knitting again.'

I looked down at the pile, the colourful folds never ending. 'What are you knitting?'

'A feckin' carpet,' said Dad, walking into the kitchen. He put his cup in the sink and gave me a kiss on the head. He wasn't a kisser, but I think this was his way of acknowledging my shitty life.

'I'm not making anything, love. It's just for recreational purposes.'

'Oh right …' I sipped my water, not wanting to ask anymore.

'What time will Tony Soprano be here?' Dad glanced at his watch and sat down across from me.

'Now, Gerry, I mean it.' Mam stopped stirring the gravy to look at him. 'Tasha and Wayne are going through a rough patch. Nobody needs you and your schoolboy jibes making things worse.'

'What?' Dad shrugged. 'He thinks he's an Italian gangster, Lil. It's been a running joke for years.'

'You're happy enough to take that TV box off him – that he got from god knows where.'

'Too right. I don't have to like the fella to take free stations.'

'Here,' said Mam, handing Dad a bag full of biscuits. 'Put them in the hot press.'

'Ah for feck sake, Lil. You're not hiding all the goodies again, are ye?' Dad looked at me. 'In case Wayne fancies a biscuit with his tea, she's stashing the lot.'

'There's still biscuits.' Mam opened the bread bin to prove her point, where there were two packets of plain digestives.

Dad held up the bag, trying to see through the plastic. 'All because Wayne helped himself to a couple of chocolate bars, the last day he was here.'

'A couple? He finished off the whole packet. And I know he's family, but still …'

'Not technically,' Dad interrupted, pointing to the thick gold wedding band on his own finger.

'Still, you don't rummage around people's kitchen filling your face. Conor would never –' Mam stopped herself. She was obviously finding it hard to break her habit of comparing them. 'The feckin' size of Wayne anyway. I'm doing him a favour.'

None of us ever thought that Tasha and Wayne would last. He was from the area, living two roads away and fancied himself as a hard man. Conor was convinced, in his own words, that Wayne was 'riding rings around my sister.' I didn't know what to believe. I couldn't imagine him cheating and I knew Tasha wouldn't turn a blind if she knew. I guess we all thought she was just going through a rebellious phase by going out with him and when they broke up, she would find the nice guy she was meant to settle down with. That

53

she'd even appreciate him more, having been with Wayne. Then she got pregnant, and two kids later they were still together. They're not married, both insisting a piece of paper means nothing. But I remember only too well seeing my sister, in Nana Margo's wedding dress, practising walking up the aisle. I was always her bridesmaid, on cue throwing strips of peach toilet paper over her head and singing, 'Isn't she lovely'.

The front door opened and Tasha came in, carrying a sleeping Aria into the living room.

'Where's the Cod Father?' asked Dad, ruffling Finn's curls.

'He's getting your dodgy TV box from the boot, Grandad,' said Finn, making Mam tut loudly, while plating up the dinner.

'Good man.' Dad jumped up, rubbing his hands together. 'I'll see if he needs a hand.'

'Heya.' Tasha leant in to give me a hug. 'You look like crap.'

'Thanks.'

'I've emailed Lydia your CV. She said they're a bit quiet at the minute, but you'll have preference over whatever comes in.'

Tasha was talking as though I'd asked for her help. 'I'm not really ready to look for work yet.'

'You won't be looking. It's a case of Lydia ringing you when something comes in that she thinks you'll like.'

'Unless it's in retail, there's nothing much else I can do. And I only enjoyed that because it was interior stuff.'

'Maybe a change of career would be good for you. I told her you're good with numbers.'

'I'm crap with numbers.'

'What's seven plus eight?' asked Finn, jumping up and down beside me. I tried to think quickly, but my head was like mush.

'It's fifteen,' Finn shouted, a millimetre from my face.

'See?' I turned to Tasha. 'I'd have needed fingers for that.'

'Okay, no big deal. I'll e-mail Lydia and tell her no book-keeping jobs.'

'You can email Lydia and tell her no any job.'

'That doesn't even make sense.'

'You know what I mean.'

'Whatever,' Tasha mumbled, sitting down.

A few minutes later, we were all sat around the table with a mound of Mam's dinner in front of us.

'This is nice, isn't it?' Mam looked around the table. For no reason, I felt a lump rise in my throat. Looking around the table I felt Conor missing. The last time we were all sat together was at Christmas. Tasha had been fighting with her in-laws, when Wayne's Mam accused her of being a feeder. Wayne had always been on the chubby side and could eat his body weight in curry, but Mrs Reddy was convinced Tasha was the root of her son's weight problems.

'How've you been keeping, Sammie?' asked Wayne, hacking through the chicken with the side of his fork, his arm at a ninety-degree angle.

'Not too bad.'

'Our Lydia will find you a job. There's nothing worse than having nothing to do during the day. It can make you depressed.'

The gravy boat rocked, sloshing a thick brown blob onto the table. Wayne looked at Tasha and shrugged.

'I remember when I was laid off a few years back. I was moping around the house and –'

'I don't think it's the same thing, Wayne.' Tasha shot him a look he couldn't mistake.

'Oh right, yeah. I didn't mean to upset you, Sammie.'

'It's grand, Wayne, I'm not upset.' I skewered a piece of carrot with my fork, making a figure of eight in the mash potato.

'I know your situation is worse, much worse. I don't know how you get out of bed, to be honest.'

'Stop talking, Wayne.'

'Yeah, shut the fuck up, son,' said Dad.

'Anyone for more roasties?' Mam held up the dish.

'It's fine, Wayne, I know what you meant.'

'See.' Wayne looked at Tasha. Tasha rolled her eyes. 'Don't start,' said Wayne, rubbing his hand over the last of his dark curls. His hair looked like Ryan Giggs in the nineties, but with the middle bit missing. His balding was a real sore point.

'Start what?' asked Tasha, narrowing her eyes.

'You're always on my case.'

'That's because you're deluded for a start. You were laid off only last year, and you moped about – yes, but in the pub spending all your labour.'

'You go inside, lovey.' Mam said to Finn. 'You can watch the cartoons and I'll bring you in some ice-cream.' Finn went into the living room, delighted with himself.

'You're lecturing Sammie about work, when you're the laziest bastard around, Wayne.'

'I'm out working now, aren't I?'

'Yeah, the bare minimum. You know you could be doing more hours, but you won't. You'd rather be with the lads, sculling pints on a Saturday.'

'That was one Saturday.'

'Three last month.'

'What, are you keeping count now? You'd love that, marking them up on your little calendar.'

Dad cleared his throat. Wayne shovelled a mound of mash into his mouth. There was a film of sweat across his forehead. I wasn't sure if it was due to the tropic temperatures in the kitchen, or his temper flaring. I shifted around in my seat, glancing up at the clock. Either way, I knew my sister had touched a nerve.

'Are yis stuck for money, love?' Mam looked at Tasha.

'No, we're fine thanks.'

'I have a few pound in the Post Office. You're welcome to it, to tide you over.'

'Do you now?' said Dad, stopping his fork mid-air.

'It's my running away fund, Gerry.' Mam laughed.

'I need one of them,' said Tasha, taking a sip of water.

'I'm sure nobody wants to be listening to us talking about silly things, like money and that.' Wayne nodded towards me.

'Don't try acting all caring, Wayne.'

Wayne put his fork down, resting his palms flat on the table. 'I can't win.' He looked from me to my parents.

I pretended I didn't hear him.

'Let's change the subject, but before we do, it's all about

making ends meet,' said Mam. 'Cutting your cloth to suit your measure.'

'We're grand, Mam,' said Tasha, her cheeks reddening.

'If you stopped running to the Credit Union every five minutes, we'd be grand. Do you know she forged my signature on a loan last year?'

'Natasha Clancy.' Mam looked horrified. 'You could be arrested for that. It's money laundering.'

'No, it's not. And anyway, it was only a tiny loan. I've cleared it already. And I wouldn't have had to get it in the first place, if it wasn't for you only ever looking after yourself.' Tasha glared at Wayne.

'Remind me to invite you both around for dinner more often,' said Dad. 'This is lovely and relaxing. Just what our Sammie needs.'

The rest of our dinner was eaten in silence. I even managed to get down a few mouthfuls, just to have something to do.

When Tasha and Wayne finally left with the kids, I felt a ripple of sadness for my sister. I hadn't noticed how bad things were for her and Wayne.

'Your sister is right. He's a lazy so and so,' said Mam, unwrapping a dishwasher tablet and throwing it into the machine drawer. 'And to think of him giving you career advice.'

'I wasn't minding him,' I said, stacking the placemats in the middle of the table.

'Your dad was a lot of things, but he always handed up his wage. Do you think he gives Tasha nothing?'

'I don't know, Mam.'

Mam slammed the dishwasher door. It beeped, and the kitchen filled with the sound of gurgling water. 'If it wasn't for those kiddies, I'd tell her she'd be better off getting rid of him.'

'I don't think he's that bad.'

'Hmm.' Mam sprayed down the countertop, moving the j-cloth around in vigorous circles. 'God forgive me, but I think he took the wrong son-in-law.' Mam blessed herself as her words fell around my shoulders.

Chapter 6

I picked at the blistered orange paint on the wall, lifting slices under my nail and depositing them into my palm. I had a collection of tiny flakes all clumped together in my hand. I'd always hated the paint colour in the house, each wall was a different shade of custard. The whole house needed a make-over and it was always going to be my first big project. I'd had it all designed in my head and spent hours on Pinterest getting inspiration. On weekends I'd roam around different homeware stores, collecting paint brochures and eyeing up quirky accessories, while Conor played his football matches. My visions never got to leave my head, and so the house still looked like it belonged to an old granny.

I picked off another flake and thought of a woman Batty Patty, who'd collected rubbish outside our school. Always crisp packets and cigarette butts. There was a rumour she'd gone mad after losing her fiancé in a fire. Looking at me now, I didn't feel that removed from Patty and wondered had she started out picking paint.

I was trying to be constructive, occupy my mind, do what they tell you to do in the books. The ones with rainbows or a silhouette of a person looking out to sea. I'd started to play the 'this time last year' game. That was when my morning had taken a turn. It wasn't a fun game and held me captive, like spotting yellow car registrations as a child. I'd become obsessed. This time last year, we were getting ready to go on holiday. My biggest worry being, trying to find nice bikinis with enough padding to give me boobs.

I pushed back the kitchen chair, trying to push my thoughts back with it. The sun pressed against the window, highlighting the trail of brown tea stains and breadcrumbs from the counter to the bin, my journey of survival. I felt a sense of shame that swirled in, threatening to tug at something bigger. This was our home and I'd let it go to ruin the past couple of weeks, not so much as cleaning a cup after myself. Conor had never cared about how clean the house was, but at that moment it felt like all that mattered.

I spent the morning with a damp cloth and bottle of bleach spray, trying to push myself into the afternoon when I could sit outside and have a drink. I told myself three o'clock and had changed it to two by the time I'd finished hoovering. I poured a glass of wine and was just about to open the back door when my phone rang.

'Sorry for last night, Sammie.' Tasha's voice sounded strained on the phone. 'I felt terrible, how me and Wayne acted.'

'Don't be silly,' I said, a little too chirpy. 'How are things today?' I took a long sip of wine.

My sister let out a heavy sigh, and I could imagine her on the other end of the phone, winding her long dark hair around her finger like she did when she was stressed. 'We're all over the place with the mortgage and with Wayne's mam unwell, or at least, pretending to be unwell. You think our family are hypochondriacs, his mam is on the verge of a stroke every second week, so she can't help much with the kids. I can't leave them with Mam and Dad all the time, it's not fair, and the cost of childcare is mental. Like a second mortgage; I'm not even joking. And then well … there's that loan Wayne was talking about.' She said this last bit really fast, I barely caught it.

'The loan from the Credit Union?'

'From a loan shark.'

'Tasha, you didn't?' I held my glass mid-air.

'I know, I'm an eejit. I've taken a couple of small loans out with him before, for Christmas and that, and well it just kind of escalated and now he's being a prick.'

'But … Tasha –'

'I had no choice. I didn't want to be coming to you or Mam with my problems – but Wayne, he hands up barely anything each week. His money just seems to disappear. Then I had so much on with Christmas and everything breaking, like my car and the stupid boiler, all my problem of course. Wayne didn't seem to give a shit if I couldn't get to work or the school, or we'd no hot water.'

'That's really unfair –.'

'Tell me about it. We have so many rows over it, and you all think he's just a bit thick, well, he's not that thick let me tell you. And he … well … it doesn't matter.'

'He what?'

'Nothing, just he can be nasty with his words.'

'Eh, so can you.'

'I'm just fed up.'

'How much do you owe the loan shark?' I felt a wave of relief, remembering I still had the money Dionne had given me; I could help Tasha.

'Three.'

'Hundred?'

'No thousand.'

'Three thousand? Jesus, Tasha.'

Tasha was silent.

'Look, it's only money it doesn't mean anything.' I was trying to make her feel better, but I couldn't help feeling panicked. There was a loan shark years ago who'd set fire to our neighbour's car when he didn't pay up. We didn't know what the point of doing that was, until we saw the note saying 'next time you'll be in it.'

'I know it's only money. I feel bad even talking to you about it.'

'I didn't mean it like that.' I took a mouthful of wine and sat down at the kitchen table. 'Can you afford the repayments?'

'Just about, if I do lots of overtime in the salon.'

'How has Wayne not seen him calling?'

'I leave the money in an envelope behind the wheelie bin and he collects it every Thursday, when Wayne's at the gym.'

'I don't want to know anymore.' I waved my hand as though she was sitting in front of me.

'It's bad, isn't it?'

'You just need to pay him off quickly, but you should also tell Wayne it's a loan shark. Like you said, it's his bloody fault you needed to get a loan in the first place.'

'Yeah, but he just doesn't get it. He thinks because we have free childcare that I should have plenty of money. And I'm not great with budgeting, he just turns the whole thing around on me.'

'Still, Tasha. You need to say it. You might not be the best at budgeting –'

'Don't throw in me over-spending my pocket money and having to get subs off you for the ice-cream van –'

'I'm not. I'm just saying that you spend all your money on the kids, not yourself.'

'It's not worth the argument. And the kids are starting to pick up on us fighting. Well, Finn is anyway.'

'I'll help out with the kids, so you can do extra hours.'

'No, no way.'

'I want to, Tasha.'

'Thanks. Anyway, enough about me. Will I pop into you later?' The last bit was impregnated with false enthusiasm and I knew she'd want to get back to the kids after work.

'No, I'm okay.'

'Are you sure? Wayne will be home to babysit his own kids, so I can come over straight from work.'

'I'm fine … really. I'm just going to have an early night.' I took a long sip of wine and knew if I kept going that could actually be true.

Outside in the garden, I rested back into the wicker chair, stretching my legs out into the heat. I looked up, clutching the stem of my glass like a balloon that might float away. The sky was a clear blue, the perfect kind that could make you excited for the day. An aeroplane rumbled above me, leaving a white powdery split in the sky. Its grey belly sailed low above the oak tree. The airport was only ten minutes away, and the aeroplanes were as common as birds. When I was little, I used to give them a wave, imagining a hundred smiling faces waving back at me.

I could hear kids playing, girls squealing and a ball bouncing against a wall. I listened trying to pick out Jojo's voice. I had thought of her a couple of times since we chatted but had been so distracted by the shop and my own misery that I hadn't even sat outside to see her. Just as I looked down the garden, she was climbing the tree.

'I was just thinking of you,' I said, putting my glass on the table.

'You were?'

'Yes, I could hear you playing.' I couldn't think how to mention her mam and what had happened the last day, without sounding like a nosy neighbour. Was it really a slap? Or a ball or a door banging from another garden?

'Are you okay?' I asked looking at her face trying to read for signs of abuse, which seemed completely absurd now she was sitting in front me, smiling. Her legs were tanned and so slim they were like an extension of the tree, two branches dangling as she swung them. I was just about to ask would her mam be mad at her for climbing the tree, when she tilted her head and spoke.

'Are you sunbathing?' She looked at the table where my glass was.

'No, I'm just –'

'Relaxing?'

'Yeah, relaxing,' I said, knowing I was no longer capable of such a thing.

'Wouldn't it be cool to have a tree house?' She looked up at the branches, like she was sizing one up.

'I always wanted a tree house when I was little,' I said. 'My sister Tasha and me, had to make do with a bedsheet thrown over the washing line.'

'You could make one now. Have you got any wood?' She scanned my garden, squinting her eyes against the sun.

'No.' I laughed. 'I don't even have a tree to put one in.'

'You can make one for this.' She patted the bark, like an old man patting a bar stool.

Everything was so simple for kids. I smiled, not wanting to quash her enthusiasm. 'I wouldn't know where to start. Maybe you could ask your dad to make one?'

'He's ... not really the tree-house making type.'

I could hear John's lawn mower starting up next door, spluttering before breaking into a hum.

Jojo was examining the ends of her hair, holding them up like a fan, her lips pursed in concentration. I watched her for a few moments. She was a waif of a thing, who looked like she'd blow away in a strong breeze. She was wearing the same denim dress she'd had on the last day.

'What's your star sign?' she asked, dropping the piece of hair and brushing it through with her fingers. 'Mine's Scorpio. It means mature and strong.' She looked pleased with herself.

'I'm a Gemini. The twin one.'

'There's a twin one?' She looked at me.

'I think it just means twin in Latin, and possibly a split personality.' She didn't get my crap attempt at a joke, instead, she repeated the word again, as kids often do.

'I don't know much about star signs.'

'My dad's a Leo and his name's Leo, isn't that mad? He isn't into star signs or his birthday … Why do adults always hate their birthday?'

'Because they're getting older, I guess.'

There was a bang like the lid of a wheelie bin slamming, making Jojo jump. She looked behind her, ducking her head under a branch to see if it was coming from her garden.

'Do you hate your birthday?' She turned back to me before I could ask what was wrong. 'Or do you just hate everything since your husband died?'

'Ehm, well …' I took a sip of my drink, not expecting her bluntness. I wasn't going to tell her that I was trying to forget it was my birthday next week. 'I don't hate everything.'

'Oh.' She looked at me now, like she wasn't completely convinced, like she was allowing me the lie.

I picked up my glass, surprised it was empty. 'I'm just going to get a drink,' I said, standing up.

'You must be parching?'

This kid was relentless. 'Yeah, it's the heat.' I went inside and quickly poured the last of the bottle of wine into my glass as Jojo waved at me from the tree.

'Me and my best friend Cassie were fighting for her birthday and she cancelled her whole party,' said Jojo as soon as I sat back down. 'Wasn't that so dramatic? She told me afterwards, she didn't want to have her party without me, but that just made me feel really sad.'

'Oh … right.' I put my glass on the table, my head slightly spinning.

'We're still best friends, even though she has a new friend, Kara. I'm not mad on Kara …'

I laughed at her expression and listened to her ten reasons why. She finally stopped talking and when I looked up to speak, she was gone. I could hear laughing and a bright yellow ball bounced into my garden, hitting Wayne – the Buddha. I picked it up and threw it back over the wall.

Chapter 7

Tasha once told me that a parent's pain is like your own, multiplied by a billion. She explained that when a kid doesn't want to play with Finn in the park, it's like a dagger through her heart. Literally. She'd gestured this, and I couldn't help but remember her words when thinking of my parents. I think that was the reason I'd finally relented and agreed to do something with Mam for my birthday. Also, thanks to Jojo's story about her friend, I didn't want to think of Conor sad that I hadn't done anything.

It was Saturday afternoon and I'd spent the past hour following Mam around Brown Thomas on Grafton Street. I trailed behind her as she circled each cosmetic counter, streaking her hand with different shades of coral lipstick and chatting to doll like girls that spritzed her with perfume. I felt like the journey in on the 27B was a time machine, throwing me back to the nineties when I followed Mam for hours each Saturday around town. Unlike my child self, I tried to summon up some enthusiasm each time Mam asked was I enjoying myself, flashing her a smile, which was no doubt transparent.

Mam was using her running away fund to treat me to afternoon tea in The Shelbourne, one of Ireland's most famous hotels. It sat grandly, opposite St Stephen's Green Park, and Mam always spoke of wanting to go.

'Smell that.' Mam thrust her wrist under my nose. 'Sandalwood. I was expecting Mr Sheen, but it actually smells quite nice.'

'That's lovely, Mam. You should get it.'

Mam tutted, linking my arm and leading me out the door. 'It's the price of six bottles from the Avon. Sure, it would be a waste.'

We made our way up Grafton Street, through the throngs of shoppers and tourists. Mam insisted on stopping at every busker on the street, waving her hand in front of the man painted head to toe in silver and stroking the dog carved out of sand, before emptying her purse of coins to throw into his cap. She was having such a great time, which made me relax a little. It didn't feel so much like a birthday, but more Mam's big day out, which suited me fine. It wasn't that I was feeling particularly worse, just nowhere felt familiar, not even the streets I'd walked a hundred times before.

'Isn't Dublin a lovely city all the same?' said Mam. 'I can see why tourists like to come here. They think us Irish are great craic.' Mam hot tailed it over to a Japanese woman, who was about to take a selfie in front of Phil Lynott. 'Will I take that for you, love? Mum reached over to grab her phone.

'No, no, thank you. It's okay.' The woman smiled at Mam, clutching her phone to her chest.

'Mam, she's taking a selfie, the whole point is that she takes it.'

'Oh, sorry, love.' Mam stepped back. 'He was a fine thing,

wasn't he?' She nodded to the statue. 'I went to see him once in concert, he was even better in the flesh.' She winked.

I can safely say I never saw Mam wink in my life and could only presume she'd gone a little crazy caught up in the buzz of town.

'Come on, Mam, we'll be late for our reservation.'

'Reservation? We sound real posh.'

I linked Mam's arm and led her up towards Stephen's Green.

'Ah look at the Disney shop, isn't it magical? We'll have to bring Finn and Aria in sometime. We could take the bus, they'd love that.'

'Yeah, it'd be great.' I made a mental note to be very busy that day, possibly with an imaginary interview. Mam had spent the bus journey in going through each email that Lydia had sent me over the weekend.

'You don't want a job to be discovered in, just something stress-free, where you can leave your brain in the car.' Mam's career advice was awe inspiring. I gave up telling her that I couldn't bring myself to go to an interview, let alone do a real job, no matter how idiot proof it was.

We turned the corner at the top of Grafton Street towards The Shelbourne. A shiny black Bentley pulled up outside and the doorman hot footed it down the red carpeted steps, to open the car door. A silver haired lady stepped out in a cream cashmere suit, that made Mam turn and mouth money to me, rubbing her fingers together in case I couldn't lip read. We watched as she made her way through the doors and Mam followed, attempting to strut behind her with her Penneys bags.

Inside, we were seated by the large bay windows facing the park. The seats were bucket style and I sank into the plush suede, glad to finally sit down. Mam looked around taking mental notes on everyone, who all surprisingly, as she said, looked just like us.

She sat back smiling, as the waiter poured her tea through a strainer. Looking at her, I couldn't help but think how she'd dedicated her whole life to me and Tasha, missing out herself.

'I'll have to buy one of these.' Mam turned the strainer over between her fingers. 'Your Nana Margo used to have one years ago, when we were kids. Back then, the older women sipped their tea from saucers …'

I was only half listening. The array of cream cakes and smell of rich chocolate fondant made me queasy. I just wanted a cold drink, maybe a half glass of wine. I shrugged my cardigan off and hung it on the back of the chair. I saw Mam glance at the tops of my arms, which made me, out of guilt, pick up a mini banoffee pie.

'Has Conor's Mam been in touch?' Mam picked up a scone, slicing it carefully along the side. 'The last time I spoke to her, I got the feeling that she was staying in Spain for good.'

'Yeah, I'd say she will.' I picked up my cup, taking a long sip of milky tea.

Conor's dad had died when Conor was twelve after a short battle with cancer. I think his Mam, Alice, got some comfort in thinking of Conor and his dad together. I couldn't think too much about it or my chest would constrict, and I'd have to push the thoughts away as quick as they'd come.

'Conor's brother and Alice's sister live over there. There's nothing keeping her in Ireland anymore.'

Mam nodded with a mouthful of scone, the crumbs sitting in the creases of her pink lipstick.

'Maybe you could visit them sometime? You always got on so well with Alice.'

'Yeah, maybe,' I said, humouring her.

'It's a pity your dad doesn't like to go foreign, and me with my plane phobia, we could have gone with you.'

'Yeh, it's a pity alright.' The thought made me shudder.

'Imagine staying here!' Mam looked around her. 'I bet the rooms are amazing.'

We enjoyed the rest of our afternoon tea. Mam kept telling me she was proud of me for agreeing to come. I think, no matter how old you are, hearing your parent say they're proud of you makes your inner child smile.

'Now, I've gotten you a little pressie, it's only something small.' Mam bent down to pick up her handbag.

'Mam, you shouldn't have. Coming here was enough –'

'Shh, I can treat my eldest daughter if I want to. Sure, you deserve it. You deserve the world, Sammie.' Mam looked at me for a moment before rummaging in the ten different pockets of her handbag. She flicked through bills, pulled out a medicine bottle – which I presumed had an emergency antibiotic from Doctor Ibrahim, in case whatever she went in complaining about didn't clear up in a couple of days. Then she took out a small package wrapped in pink tissue paper, held with a neat silver ribbon.

'Here, love.' She handed it to me, putting her bag back on the

73

floor. 'It's just something small, a keepsake really. It's probably not up to your interior standards.'

I could tell she was nervous, as she folded and unfolded the edge of the cloth napkin in front of her.

I untied the ribbon and the paper fell away, revealing an array of coloured glass. Pinks, yellows, purples and blues all morphed together to give an oil spill effect. I picked up the tiny, knotted rope and pulled it upwards, unfolding the wind chime. It swayed catching the light, making it dance pockets of colours across the table. 'Mam, it's gorgeous. I held it for a moment, listening to the soft clinking of the beads. Along the top, I spotted the tiny lemon tree, making my heart flip.

'I only noticed the lemon tree as I was paying, love. It's the brand that makes them. I hope it's okay?' Mam bit her lip.

I nodded, opening my eyes wide so not to blink open the floodgates.

The first birthday card Conor had ever gotten me had a lemon tree on the front. Not a quirky drawing but an actual photograph of a lemon tree, complete with ceramic pot. It looked like something you'd get for an eighty-year-old granny. I'd given him so much stick over the card, that he swore he would get me something with lemons every year just to annoy me. And he did. I'd gotten lemon soap sets, lemon shaped slippers and even a plastic necklace with a lemon segment. I thought this birthday would be the first one lemon free, the one year I really wanted one. I looked up at Mam who smiled, before she called the waiter over to box up what we hadn't eaten for Dad.

When I got home that evening, there was a man standing in my drive. He was looking over the wall at John and Celine's house like he was contemplating knocking in there next.

'Can I help you?' I asked, walking up the path. Conor usually dealt with the random cold callers who wanted us to change gas company or get our votes in the local elections.

'Ah, I was just about to give up,' he said, smiling, standing back.

He was tall with dark hair shaved tight, his face and overalls had splashes of white paint. No clip board or leaflets in sight.

'I'm doing work on a house at the front of your estate and I've run into a bit of electrical trouble …'

I felt my stomach drop. He didn't know. He must be an old friend of Conor's, who didn't know he was dead. I looked around, for what I didn't know. Maybe Tasha or Mark, or someone to just appear and tell him so I wouldn't have to.

'I saw this address on the internet for an electrician. I was trying the mobile number, but no joy.' He pulled out his mobile from the side pocket of his overalls as though it was proof he had rung.

I felt a wave of relief that he didn't know Conor, which was quickly replaced with the awkwardness of the situation. I fumbled with my keys, trying to locate the one for the hall door. 'Sorry, but there's no electrician here.' I glanced at him, before turning back to the door. I wasn't going to start telling the whole story to a random workman on my doorstep, so instead I repeated 'sorry.'

'Oh right, no worries. He looked at the door number, rubbing

75

the back of his head with his hand. 'Sorry to have bothered you.' He walked a few steps backwards, still clutching his phone. I noticed there were two little girls on the cover, their faces pressed together, smiling with ice creams.

'I can give you the number of another electrician, if you're stuck?'

His face broke into a smile again. 'That would be great, thanks. I'm doing an attic conversion and the couple are due back from holidays next week, we're already running way behind. Electrics are not my thing.'

I would never usually invite a stranger into my house, but the picture of the kids on his phone and the fact I didn't operate from a sharpened perspective lately, made me not think twice.

I opened the front door and gestured for him to follow me into the kitchen.

'My phone battery's almost dead. I'll just plug it in and get the number for you.'

'Great, thanks.' He smiled, rocking on the balls of his feet. 'It's a cracker out, isn't it?' He wiped his forehead with the back of his hand. I noticed a tattoo with the names Sophie and Erin in swirly writing on the inside of his forearm. 'Great weather for a party?' He looked at the bottles of wine, lined up beside the bin. 'I'm a Cider man myself. Bulmers and ice.' He smacked his lips. 'Roll on next week when I'll have my life back and this bloody attic finished.'

I plugged in my phone and waited as the Apple icon swirled around the screen. 'It's a guy Rob, he's a friend of my husband's. He's a really good electrician and he's local.'

'That's perfect, thanks.'

My phone sprang into action pretty rapidly – thank god, before my brain processed the fact there was a strange man in my kitchen. It felt odd having someone in the house. I quickly leaned over, opening the kitchen window and apologised for the smell from the sink.

'I'm not a plumber, but I could sort that sink out, if you want? I reckon it's just a blockage in the U pipe. It will take me five minutes.'

'No, it's fine. Thanks.' I quickly scrolled through my phonebook for Rob's number, before scribbling it down on the back of an envelope. I noticed my hands were shaking, making my writing loose like a child's.

'Are you sure? As a thank you for the number.'

'No, my husband can do it.' I blurted the words out, before I realised.

'Sure, of course, well thanks for this.' He folded over the paper, shoving it into the pocket on his overalls. I probably could have just called it out for him to type into his phone, like a normal person from the twenty-first century.

We walked out to the front door, just as John was pulling into his drive.

'Work man from up the road. I gave him one of Conor's friend's numbers,' I said, as John opened his car door.

'Oh right, hello.' John smiled, before leaning over to the passenger seat to get his briefcase.

I don't know why I felt awkward, but I did, and I just wanted this man gone from my door.

'Thanks again for the number,' he said.

'No worries, bye.'

I smiled at John, who was now at the boot lifting out a bag of groceries with his briefcase still sandwiched under his arm. He closed the boot with his elbow. I was just about to go back inside when he called me.

'Sammie, actually I meant to say.' He rested the shopping bags on the wall. 'I saw your dad last night in the Bailey. I waved over, but I wasn't sure if he saw me. I didn't want him to think I was rude, after he kindly fixed up our side gate during the bad weather.'

It took a moment for his words to register. The words 'dad' and 'pub' hadn't been said in the same sentence for at least twenty years – well, not in my family.

'Are you sure it was my dad? He's never usually in the pub.' I tried to sound casual; it wasn't a skill I'd acquired.

'Ehm, yes. I think so. He was standing outside in the smoking area, chatting to a couple of other men. I'm almost sure it was him anyway.'

'I'd say he didn't even see you, so don't worry.' I tried to relax my face into a smile as I said goodbye, before closing my hall door.

Dad hadn't been in a pub in twenty years, unless for family occasions, when Mam would be with him. He didn't trust himself around drink. He was probably just passing by on his way to the bookies, or maybe dropping something off to one of the men from work. I settled on this theory as I walked into my kitchen. Opening the kitchen press, I took out the bottle of bleach and squeezed it down the sink. Half for the sink and half for the lingering smell of aftershave in my kitchen.

Chapter 8

I had gotten myself into a bit of a routine, which I was proud of. I woke each morning and had a cup of tea, and a half slice of toast when I could face it. I would then clean the morning away, quite literally. I scrubbed the shower, feeling a sense of satisfaction as the suds foamed around my hands, and I removed grime that I'd never noticed before. I hoovered, polished and just generally scrubbed at everything with a cloth and cleaning spray until afternoon, when I could nip to the shop and grab milk, bread, wine – the essentials. The greasy teenager, whom I had since found out was called Kai, was there each time, even greeting me some days with a smile. He was on his summer holidays from college, he was studying to be teacher.

I would never have put him down as the schoolteacher type; it made me think that you never know what people truly desire. His eyes had shone as he told me he wanted to teach History and English and how he couldn't wait for the teacher's holidays, so he could travel the world. I had the urge to tell him that your life is mapped out for you, and nothing's in your control, no matter how hard you work. But I didn't want to go all heavy on his head, and there was a queue behind me, so instead I said that the teacher's hours were great. Sometimes he looked at me, the pity for me on his face like a mirror. I'd crack a joke quickly like the old me and make him laugh.

Other times his eyes would be glued to his phone and I was just another annoying customer interrupting his life.

Lydia had called a couple of times about jobs she thought I'd be interested in. I found this out through her voice messages, because I couldn't face answering the phone. The last was for a job doing hospital admin. It had excellent career prospects and educational opportunities, said the voice message, her flat Dublin accent forced into a high-pitched business tone. My head spun just listening to her explaining the job role. When I didn't return her call, she rang again to apologise for suggesting a hospital, that it was probably the last place I'd want to work 'after everything'. She then suggested a secretarial job in some PR company. She mentioned a few Z-listers who they worked for but even then I – once the celebrity stalker, who could tell you the star sign and middle name of every Kardashian and Jenner sister in order of shoe size – still couldn't muster any enthusiasm for the job.

I was doing good though, for someone who'd had a lifetime of crap thrown at them in a matter of months; I was doing bloody great. That's what I was telling myself anyway. I was getting up. I was cleaning my house, really keeping on top of things. I was getting a daily walk in to the local shop and fresh air in the back garden. I had a colour on my face which helped hide the mauve circles under my eyes. I found that a couple of glasses of wine before bed was helping me sleep and I didn't have to rush getting up for work in the mornings, so if I had a couple more I could lie on an extra hour.

Overall, I was coping well, considering. I even thought about getting a part-time job cleaning offices or schools. I had it all planned out in my head. My hours would be flexible, and I could work on my own, not having to bother with idle chit chat. This enthusiasm usually lasted the length of my first cup of tea.

When Tasha phoned on the Thursday asking me to mind the kids, I'd thought she was ringing to talk about Wayne. I wanted to be able to listen and give her advice, to prove to myself how well I was doing. I was giving my sister relationship advice – I couldn't ask for better than that. When I hung up the phone it dawned on me that I'd never minded both the kids on my own before, Tasha always called on Mam first. I felt confident though and was on such a roll lately that I knew I could handle it.

I arrived at Tasha's house early. She lived a five-minute drive from my parent's house in the opposite direction to me. Her house was a small terrace and I remember thinking, when she bought it, that my house was bigger. It's amazing how sibling rivalry can pounce on you when you least expect it. I felt terrible for ages after thinking that.

Maybe karma had me where I was. Maybe I'd had so many evil thoughts over the years, that the universe stored them all up and then bitch slapped me over the head with them when I'd least expected it.

I'd always wanted the best for Tasha though. I was the only one out of our whole family, who'd told her that her dyed red 'Rihanna' hair looked horrendous on her. Dad had called her Bosco behind her back and Wayne said there was no fear of any fella giving her the eye with a head like a beetroot. I was thinking all this as I walked to my sister's house. I couldn't face the drive, so I took my time, sipping a bottle of sparkling water that I bought from Kai on the way. I ended up shaking the bottle before unscrewing the lid and letting the gas hiss out; the bubbles were making me queasy. I think if I'd thought enough about it, I'd have realised I was hungover.

Tasha's house was in the middle of a cul-de-sac, where parking was like gold dust and even a millimetre of a car bumper across a neighbour's driveway, could cause all-out war. Tasha was regularly arguing with neighbours and I presumed it was Mrs Miller's turn as I waved, and she ignored me, closing her front door.

'You're a star,' said Tasha, opening the door. 'Did you pass Wayne? He only left a couple of minutes ago.'

'No, I didn't see him.' I stepped over a large lump of yellow plastic in the hall and followed Tasha through to the kitchen.

'He was meant to be in work a half hour ago. I swear, if he loses that job for being a lazy bastard, I won't be responsible for my actions … Don't mind the state of the place. I hadn't a minute all morning.' Tasha picked a pile of washing off the table and plonked it on the ironing board, which was set up against the wall.

I'm not going to lie; I was a little shocked. My sister was usually quite organised, and I didn't ever remember her house being like this. Then again, I couldn't remember the last time I was in her house. I looked around, trying not to stare. The most anticipated kitchen island in North Dublin was now a clothes horse. Speckles of black shiny granite glistened between dirty dishes and cereal boxes.

'Where're the kids?' I asked, thinking they could be here, hidden under the mound of toys and mess.

'Aria is upstairs napping. She'll sleep for another hour or so. Her lunch is in the fridge and her sippy cup is …' Tasha looked around.

'It's grand, I'll find it.'

'Finn is in his room on the PlayStation. Give him another twenty minutes and then throw him out the back garden to play. I'm off at one, so the morning should fly for you.'

'Take your time, go shopping or whatever afterwards. It's not like I have anywhere to be.' As soon as I said it, I regretted it.

Tasha stopped still to look at me.

'It was a joke, Tasha. I'm fine.'

'Ah.' My sister raised her finger, her zebra print nail distracting me. 'You know what fine stands for? Fucked-up – insecure – negative – emotional.'

'Then I'm definitely – fine.'

We both laughed.

'I'm going to make tea, do want one before you go?' I quickly scanned the counter to locate the kettle.

'No, I better go,' said Tasha, picking up her handbag and beauty case.

I flicked on the kettle and took a cup from the rack. They were the ones I'd bought her when she first moved in. They were sky blue with dancing silhouettes around the side, and my stomach danced a little with them. I quickly pushed the thought of the shop from my mind and smiled at my sister. 'Go on or you'll be late too.'

I made myself a quick cup of tea and ran upstairs to check the kids. Aria was lying on her back, her chubby arms resting above her head. I pulled the blanket from under her chin and she stirred, her eyelashes fluttering before relaxing again.

Finn was in his room, blowing up monsters and squealing with delight as their guts ran purple down the screen.

'You okay, Finn? I'm just downstairs if you want me.'

He nodded, not taking his eyes off the TV.

I couldn't help but clean the kitchen, scrubbing the floors and the kitchen counters. I was even going to do the ironing, until I saw what I thought was a superhero pillowcase, was in fact a pair of Wayne's jocks, and decided against it. I polished the angel statues on the windowsill, and the Archangel Michael figure instead.

Tasha had always been into angels and healing. She had talked about doing a Reiki course before Finn was born, but never got around to it. Mam was convinced she had a gift when she was kid, even though it was me who had seen Grandad Joe after he died, something Tasha never forgave me for.

We couldn't remember our Grandad Joe. He was Mam's dad and died when Tasha was two and I was four. Mam had a picture of them both on her wedding day. He was a stout man, with a wide smile and a wisp of black hair that was mid-air in the photo along with Mam's veil. The photo had hung in our hall for as long as I could remember. Even though it was sun damaged with a yellowy hue, making them both look a bit jaundiced, Mam refused to take it down, or even bring it somewhere to get restored. So I knew what he looked like and recognised him instantly when I saw him walk across our landing in the middle of the night. I was ten and had gotten out of bed to have a wee. I wasn't scared, I remember thinking – oh there's grandad – and it only sank in later.

Mam never took me seriously when I told her that story; if it had been Tasha who'd seen him, she would have. We weren't allowed to cross over to each other's patch. I had an eye for interior design and putting outfits together. Tasha was the beauty expert and spiritual one. Even as kids Tasha was the sporty one, I was good at drama: Mam praised us accordingly.

I finished my tea and was rinsing the cup when I heard Aria cry. I raced up the stairs and found her standing in the cot with her blanket tangled like a snake around her legs.

'Come here, sweetie.' I picked her up, letting the blanket fall as I held her close. 'You're roasting. Where's your sippy cup?' I looked around the room.

'Finn, can you help me find Aria's cup, please?' I called, walking out on to the landing.

Silence.

'Hello, earth to Finn …' He was fixated on the game. The colours bounced off the screen, highlighting his face. 'Finn, it's time to turn that off now.'

Aria squirmed in my arms and began to whimper. Finn was still ignoring me.

'Finn!'

Aria started crying.

'Come on, Finn, we can go outside to play.'

'You shouted at me.'

'Sorry, I didn't mean to.'

'Mam said only she's allowed to lose the head with me. And Nana Lil, but not Nana Sue.'

'Okay, I'm sorry. Just come on and turn that off. I have to sort your sister out.'

'That's her hungry cry.'

'Is it?' I looked at Aria, who had a chubby fist stuffed in her mouth.

'I'll give her some lunch. Do you want something to eat?'

'Five more minutes on this, for helping you out?' He looked up at me with a cheeky grin.

I rolled my eyes. Feck Tasha and her rules, an extra five minutes wouldn't hurt. 'Okay, five more minutes.' An arm combusted, hitting the screen and I left the room before reconsidering.

Downstairs, I spotted the sippy cup. The pink plastic handle was poking out from behind a stack of letters on the hall table. 'Here you go.' I handed Aria her cup and she guzzled down the purple juice in one go.

In the kitchen, Aria continued to cry but softer now, which I took as a sign I was in the right vicinity.

'Are you hungry?' I opened the fridge. There were lunch boxes stacked with what looked like salads and silver take-away containers, which I presumed belonged to Wayne. Surely Aria didn't eat salad or left-over Chow Mein. I took out a yogurt and Aria bounced on my hip. 'Yogurt it is. Come on, let's sit you in your chair, good girl.' I strapped Aria into her pink highchair, pinching the side of my finger twice with the catch. Her hands opened and closed at the sight of the yogurt. I grabbed a pink plastic spoon from the drawer and pulled out a kitchen chair to sit down.

Aria practically inhaled the whole pot and began to cry again. 'They're only tiny little pots,' I said, opening the second. I scrapped off the creamy yogurt from the lid and popped it into Aria's mouth. I was enjoying feeding her. We had a system going, spooning in the yogurt and wiping the excess off her mouth with the side of the spoon. 'Here comes the aeroplane.' Confident now, I whizzed the spoon around Aria's head, making her wriggle with excitement. I scraped around the bottom of the pot, popping the last spoonful of yogurt into her mouth.

'Good girl, eating all your yummy yogurt,' I said, balancing the empty pot on top of the already full bin.

'Oh, look what I've found. Will we read a book?' I waved the book in front of Aria and was rewarded with a big tic tac smile. I was feeling a little cocky now, this whole 'kids' thing was actually quite easy. Finn was playing away and Aria was content.

'Where's the apple?' I pointed to the picture, feeling like Supernanny. 'Apple. Can Aria say apple?' How impressed would Tasha be, if I had Aria talking by the time she got home.

'A.P.P.L.E. Big red A.P.P.L.E.' Aria made a funny gurgling sound.

'Nearly. Try again – A.P.P.L.E.' Aria gurgled again, this time projectile vomiting across the rosy apple. 'Shit,' I said, jumping up. 'It's okay. You're okay.' Aria went again, spraying pink lumpy liquid across the floor and table. She began to cry, rubbing sick into her eyes. 'Finn,' I shouted. 'I need your help.'

Finn ran down to the kitchen. 'Eww gross.' He stopped at the door, holding his nose. 'Girls are disgusting.'

'Grab me the kitchen roll off the counter and the baby wipes from the living room.'

I tried to hold Aria's hands away from her face, which was hard seeing as she'd suddenly developed bionic strength. Finn did what he was told, quickly grabbing the stuff. He then stood back, watching in disgust as I tackled the mess. I peeled the sick soaked clothes off Aria, who cried even louder as her top was pulled over her head. Her eyelashes were glued together with regurgitated yogurt. Her blonde curls, now pink, stood on end.

She felt slimy and I held her tight, so as not to drop her on her head. Awkwardly, I continued wiping her down, trying to ignore the smell that was making my own stomach turn.

'Mam always baths us after we get sick,' Finn piped up.

'This is fine. Your mam can bath her when she gets home.' I swallowed down the build-up of saliva in my mouth, trying hard not to puke.

Finally, Aria was dressed and in her bouncer chair with two red eyes. I washed my hands and checked the time, 2:15 already. Tasha must have taken up my offer of going shopping, which I was glad about. But still, I didn't want to be solely responsible for too much longer. I picked up the yogurt carton to check the use by date.

'Uh oh,' said Finn.

'What?' I put the empty carton on the table. It was a week off its best before, no mess up there.

'Silly Sammie. My sister is not allowed yogurts.'

'What? Of course, she's allowed yogurts. They were in the fridge.'

'You're in trouble …'

'A dairy allergy?' I said, half an hour later. 'I thought all babies drank milk, Tasha. Oh God, I'm so sorry; I've totally wrecked her.'

'Relax. She'll be fine once the rash settles down.'

We both looked over at Aria in her bouncer chair, who had since broken out into a rash, making her resemble a red cornflake. I swallowed hard, not to cry.

'You're the worst minder ever, but I still love you.' Finn came over and rested his head on my lap, making me feel a million times worse.

'I'm such a bad aunty. How did I not know she's allergic to milk? I see her drinking milk in Mam's all the time.' Shamelessly, I wanted to land Mam in it too.

'That's her special formula; I leave it in Mam's for her,' said Tasha. 'We only discovered the milk allergy when she was a couple months old. I thought she had reflux like Finn had.'

I shook my head. I was in complete shock, not to mention feeling like a complete gobshite.

'Sure, how would you have known?'

'I feel terrible. You'll probably never want me minding them again.' I picked up my cup of tea and took a sip, feeling a jab of self-pity. I wasn't even capable of minding my own niece and nephew.

'Will you shut up! The amount of stuff I've done to them –

and I'm their Mam.'

'Remember the time you were swinging me around and let go and I bashed my head,' said Finn. 'I had a huge purple bump.'

'See,' said Tasha, looking at me.

I smiled meekly.

'And remember the time you cut Aria's nail with the clippers, and nearly chopped the top of her finger off. There was blood everywhere –'

'Okay, Finn, that's enough: Aunty Sammie gets the message.'

I was glad to be back home that evening and out of my sister's happy chaotic home. There was such a lovely feel to her house, a warm feeling, one I no longer had here. Or maybe that warm fuzzy atmosphere only came with children. I had stayed to help with dinner, playing with the kids and even feeding Aria her mashed potato, so she wouldn't associate me with food trauma. Tasha and Wayne had managed to be civil to each other and by the end I felt like a spare part, an outsider watching the perfect family. I couldn't help but think that my sister had it all.

It was chillier in the garden that evening. I sat outside with Conor's hoodie, his old navy one that I'd told him loads of times to throw out. I tugged the front, so it sat high on the back of my neck, blocking the cool breeze that was creeping in everywhere. A plump grey cloud sat above the garden threatening to burst. I didn't think I could get fed up with the recent sunny weather but I was starting to.

With each day the air felt stuffier and I'd have welcomed a downpour. I took a long sip of wine and heard my phone beep from the kitchen. I went in to grab it and it was Tasha, thanking me again for minding the kids. When I came back outside Jojo was there. She was picking leaves from a branch and shredding them, scattering them through her fingers like confetti.

'Are you not cold?' I asked, noticing she was wearing the same denim dress. The sight of her made me fold my own arms across my chest.

'Nope.' She plucked another leaf and let it go, watching it twist and turn in the wind. 'Any news?'

'No ... well apart from almost killing my niece.' I told her the story about Aria, and had her laughing, almost falling out of the tree.

'Babies can be gross, especially pukers. Oh look.' She pointed over my head to three magpies on the wall. 'One for sorrow, two for joy, three for a girl ...'

'Four for a boy.' I pointed to another one on the shed.

'My cousin Jen might have a boy so. She's only fifteen and her Mam went mental. Jen thinks babies are even more gross than me.'

'Really?'

'Yeah. She wanted to be a vet, but her mam said she's ruined her life now. They live on a farm, so she would have been good.'

'She could still be a vet.'

'That's not what my Aunt Meg said. I heard her on the phone to Dad a while back. She said Jen's thrown her future down the toilet, and that she's reared her own kids, she won't be rearing Jen's.'

I tried to keep a straight face as Jojo imitated her aunt's accent, who was presumably from somewhere in the west of Ireland.

'What would you like to be when you're older?' I asked, trying to steer the conversation away from teen pregnancy.

'I did want to be a doctor, but I hate blood. I like acting; I like pretending to be someone else.'

The birds took flight, squawking like machine guns into the sky. There was nothing tranquil about magpies.

'What do you work at?' She asked, plucking another leaf.

'I'm not working.' The words sounded foreign even to my ears. 'I used to work in a shop that sold household things. But the owners have just sold it.'

'Did you sell irons and stuff?'

'No, it was a bit more interesting than that. We sold candles and gifts, and one-off pieces of furniture.'

'Did you like it there?' She tore the leaf down the middle and let it go in two halves.

'Well yeah, I worked there for a long time.'

'Why didn't you buy it then?'

'I don't think I'd be a very good shop owner. I like decorating.'

'Really?' She scrunched her nose.

'I liked decorating even at your age.'

'I bet your house looks really posh.'

'I wish. I was waiting to do it up, and then, sure … now, I

just don't have the time.'

'You'd think you'd have loads of time, with not having a job and all.' I drained the last of my wine, not sure what to say. 'No offence,' she said quickly, flashing a smile. 'When my sister and me shared a bedroom, I thought I'd have no choice but to get into decorating. Dad wasn't going to do it, and Mam wasn't bothered that I had to sleep in a snot-coloured room with a plastic kitchen and giant toy box. See through,' she raised an eyebrow. 'So, no hiding anything, which was pretty embarrassing seeing as she was still into playing with dolls.'

'So, you don't share anymore then?'

'No, no not anymore

It wasn't all bad,' she said a moment later. 'We used to chat and tell secrets and sleep in each other's bed.' She brushed a leaf from her dress. 'It was just annoying cause I liked things neat, and she was messier than me, so ...'

'It just wasn't to be?'

'Yeah. It just wasn't to be.'

I went inside to refill my glass and Jojo was still there when I came back out. I sipped my drink, listening to the muffled sound of a radio in the distance.

'Are you okay?' I asked, after a few minutes, conscious she'd gone quiet.

'Yep.' She blinked, breaking out of a trance.

'You could always share again.'

She looked at me blankly.

'With your sister. You could maybe ask your mam?'

'Eh, yeah. Maybe.' She stretched her mouth into a smile, which was straight and unlike her own. 'I better go, bye.'

'Bye, Jojo.' I smiled, hoping if there was something bothering her, she would open up to me. 'I might see you tomorrow.' And I really hoped I would.

Chapter 9

Tasha had asked me to mind Finn and Aria again a couple of days later. I think she likened my last babysitting stint to falling from a horse and felt that if she took too long to ask again, I wouldn't agree out of fear. I wasn't particularly in the humour for minding kids, but I didn't want to say no, knowing she needed the extra hours to pay off her loan. I tried to broach the subject of the loan again but she cut me off, telling me it was under control and not to be worrying. I was happy to believe her.

We agreed I'd bring the kids out this time for a walk to the local park. I tried not to take offence when I pulled up outside the house to collect them, and they were both dressed head to toe in neon.

'Finn really wanted to wear his road safety vest that he got in school. Didn't you, love?' Tasha nudged him and he nodded unconvincingly.

Aria was wearing a smaller frayed version that looked like it had been hacked up to fit.

'She loves to copy her brother,' said Tasha, noticing my confusion. 'At least they won't be hard to miss.'

I wanted to point out that Aria didn't walk and the chance of me putting her down somewhere or losing the whole buggy with her in it was slim, even for me. Instead, I smiled and nodded, steering the two kids out of the garden.

The park was a ten-minute walk from Tasha's house, tucked away off the main road. It was where we had spent most of our teenage years. Our first pull on a cigarette, swig of cider and sloppy first kisses, had all taken place in the park's bushy outskirts. From the outside, the oak trees surrounding the entrance and walkway made it look more picturesque than it actually was. Inside was still the same with a large football pitch, a rose garden and a small playground tucked away in the corner. There was a small pond with ducks and the odd abandoned shopping trolley under the bridge at the far end.

'Can we feed the ducks first?' asked Finn, tugging the bag of bread that Tasha had secured to the buggy.

'If you want.'

'No, the swings.' He hopped from foot to foot in that random way kids do.

'Okay, then.' I turned the buggy in the direction of the playground, while trying to muster up some enthusiasm. I was on the verge of a headache and wished I'd had the savvy to take two painkillers before I'd left the house.

The playground was surrounded by multi-coloured bars and had undergone a major revamp since the nineties. It looked more like a military assault course than a playground and my stomach dropped as I looked around at the steel contraptions, complete with hand ropes and zip wires. 'Be careful,' I shouted after Finn, who was already scaling a rock wall with ease. 'Please God, don't let him hurt himself,' I thought automatically, forgetting I was no longer friends with God.

Thankfully, in neon yellow Finn was easy to spot among the bundle of colours darting around. I watched, holding my breath as he weaved in and out of ropes, before jumping from heights that made me sure he'd shatter both his ankles. I'd wanted to be distracted and, well, this was doing it for me. I was rooted to the spot, with no thought other than getting Finn home in one piece. As I stood on my tip toes to catch the back of Finn's curls slip down a slide, I felt someone touch my arm and I turned around to see a woman, who looked like she was rearing ten kids on a mountain. Her thick, bushy plait slunk over her shoulder like a python, and her patterned skirt reminded me of a rug Nana Margo used to have in the parlour.

'There's only one way in and out, pet – and the ground …' She stamped her foot with a navy Croc. 'It's like sponge, he'll bounce right up again.'

I smiled a thank you, trying not to take my eyes off Finn.

'And it tires them out something mighty.'

'Yeah.' I kept looking forward. I was finding it hard to talk and keep an eagle eye on Finn at the same time.

'Are you an au pair?'

'Me?' I turned around. 'No, I'm their aunty.'

The woman gave a little laugh. 'Ah, just you'd know they weren't your own. Tessss …,' she shouted, walking over to the climbing frame. 'I told you already, no hanging by your ankles. Come on, it's time to go.'

I pushed Aria's buggy over to an empty bench, trying to

figure out what she'd meant. Aria looked just like me; anyone with half decent eyesight would know that we were related. I watched the woman as she rounded up three kids (surprisingly, not ten) who looked nothing at all like her. I couldn't remember the last time I'd dissected someone's words, trying to weave out the insult. I used to spend days over thinking conversations, worried I'd offended someone, or that I'd given too much of myself away and thinking they were judging me. Nowadays all that seemed irrelevant, and I'd no room for silly trivia in my head.

Motherhood was something that I'd taken for granted. Conor and I had hoped to start 'trying' on our two-year anniversary, six weeks from now. I'd taken the whole *A goal without a plan is just a wish* mantra to a new level. I'd been taking folic acid daily and trying to eat a bit healthier – as in two, rather than three bars of chocolate a day. I would regularly take a detour through the baby section on the way to the homewares and could hold a conversation with anyone about how boys' fashion had really come on in the past few years. I'd even panic when I'd hear someone liked 'my' baby names. I didn't want too many Pippas or Reubens in my future child's class. I truly believed that I'd have children, that I'd be someone's mum. My heart twinged with my reality: like everything else, that dream died along with Conor. And my belief in quotes and mantras, that all meant nonsense now.

'Aunty Sammie, look.' Finn's voice broke into my thoughts, shooting my heart into my throat. He was hanging by his knees on the climbing frame, his face going from pink to puce as he waved upside down.

'Don't be swinging like that! You'll break your head.'

He gave me a thumbs up, which was actually a thumbs down, and plummeted headfirst before catching himself by the ankles. I threw up a little in mouth and was left with the sour taste of wine.

'I learned myself that trick.' Finn flipped himself back upright like a gymnast. 'The man on *Britain's Got Talent* did it with a knife in his mouth.'

I'd no words. Instead, I turned to Aria who was bum thrusting to get out of her buggy. I unstrapped her, my hands still shaking, and managed to get her into a baby swing without dislocating her foot. I copied the professional beside me and stuffed her blanket in front so she wouldn't somersault face forward.

There was nothing relaxing about parenting, I thought as I pushed Aria gently, while still trying to watch Finn.

After Aria got bored in the swing, we watched Finn attempt and fail nine times to pull himself across the monkey bars. He made it as far as the second last bar each time, before losing his grip. I have to say, I expected more from him and was a little disappointed.

'Just leave it, Finn, it's too hard.' I shouted over to him. This caused me to get a few judgy looks from the parents standing around. I stood out for two reasons, one: I wasn't shouting words of encouragement from across the playground – 'You can do it, buddy, good job' – and two: I wasn't taking a million pictures. Every child under five was being papped by an over enthusiastic parent, no doubt to be plastered on social media under #familyfunday or #parklife.

After Finn gave up and having finally prised him from the tyre swing, we made our way across the park to feed the ducks.

'Can a swan really break your arm?' asked Finn, tearing a piece of bread apart.

'If they're angry enough,' I said, hoping it would keep him from the water edge. A man was ahead of us holding a dog on a lead, while two little girls stood on the bridge throwing lumps of bread through the bars.

'Erin, not too close,' he shouted, before gesturing for the dog to sit down.

As I got closer, I recognised the builder who I'd given Rob's number to. Finn ran ahead joining the girls on the bridge. I slowed down, not sure whether to say 'hi' if he would even remember me.

'Eat up swans. Eat up,' Finn shouted, now in competition to out throw the girls and drawing attention to us both. I had little choice but to say something.

'Hi,' I smiled, walking off the gravel path onto the grass beside him.

He looked at me for a moment, trying to figure out how he knew me, then his cheeks filled with two spots of colour. 'Hey, how's it going?' The dog jumped up barking frantically, running in circles around the lead. We both looked at him, eager for the distraction.

'Lockie, sit.' He tugged on the lead, making the dog jump even higher. 'Sorry, he's mental. I mean, I think he really is mental; if he doesn't settle down I'll have to bring him somewhere to get checked.'

Aria was squealing and clapping her hands with delight. Every 'dog savaging a child' story I'd ever read, tumbled into my head at that exact moment, making me pull the buggy backwards.

'I'm not really a dog person.' I kept my hand firmly on the buggy.

'Either am I, funny enough. The girls begged me to get him. Their mam wouldn't even consider it. I can see why now. Come sit, boy,' he said, trying to push the dog's back legs into a sitting position. 'Don't let your two talk you into it. Especially this little one when she gets older.' He looked down at Aria who was waving her hands at Lockie.

'Oh, no Aria's not mine; she's my niece. I'm minding her and my nephew for a couple of hours. I don't have children.'

He was patting the dog. 'She looks very like you.' Before he could say anything else, Finn ran over to the buggy, grabbing two more slices of bread from the bag.

'Five more minutes, girls. We have to get lunch.'

Aria was still cooing over the dog, making it harder for me to walk on. It was a little awkward with nowhere to go, unless I wanted to stand on the bridge with the kids.

The dog finally settled, flopping down on the grass. The silence was surprising.

'Did you get in touch with Rob?'

'Oh yeah, yeah, he's great. Thanks.' He rubbed his head, glancing nervously at the girls. 'I eh, I'm really sorry if I upset you calling in. I'd no idea about your husband; I felt awful when Rob told me.'

'Not at all, it's fine.' I waved my hand as if he'd just apologised for stepping on my foot.

He looked at me for a moment and I could see a flash of pity cross his eyes. The kids were laughing together on the bridge, Finn loving life, no doubt taking after Wayne for the flirting. 'I know it's not the same, but when I split from the girl's mam, I had lots of awkward moments with people constantly asking after Carla. It's really horrible, but obviously, nothing compared to what you're going through.'

I wasn't sure what to say, so I pulled the buggy back a bit to check Aria.

'At least she's agreed to talk things through, finally. Maybe even give us another go?' I don't think he realised he was still talking aloud. 'All I can do is hope for the girl's sake that she will, or that we can even be friends.' He was looking down at the ground, kicking a tuft of grass with his shoe. It was endearing to watch him, making me think pain is just pain, no matter how big or small. He looked up like he'd just remembered I was there. 'Sorry, I eh …' He looked embarrassed and bent down to pat the dog. 'Since the break-up, I can't shut myself up from blabbering on. I'm now one of those annoying guys I used to avoid on nights out, who'd burn the ear off you about their ex. And there was Carla telling me I had issues opening up.'

'She'll be happy to see the difference in you so.' I laughed, trying to make light of the conversation.

'I hope so.' He smiled. 'Thanks –' He stalled, like he was waiting for me to fill in my name.

'Sammie.'

'Sammie,' he repeated. 'Thanks, Sammie. I'm Max.'

The dog leapt up, barking frantically at a fluffy Maltese running past. I said goodbye as I walked on, with Finn falling into step beside me.

'Do you fancy him Aunty Sammie?'

'Who?'

'That man.'

'No Finn. Of course not.' I looked at him to see if he was joking, but he was serious, just walking, holding the side of the buggy like it was the most normal question ever.

'Oh yeah.' He laughed. 'Uncle Conor.' He took off as he said his name, skipping ahead leaving it floating back towards me.

'Yeah, Uncle Conor,' I said after him.

He turned around, now skipping backwards. 'I'm hungry. Can we go to Mc Donald's?'

Chapter 10

'Is that a famous person?' asked Finn, pointing to the brand-new white Mercedes parked outside his house. He was trying to look through the *Minions* telescope that he'd gotten free with his Happy Meal.

'If gangsters are famous,' said Mrs Miller, taking a long drag of her cigarette. She was leaning against the pillar at the end of her garden, staring up at the car.

'Excuse me?' I said, stopping beside her.

'Well, it's hardly Rod Stewart, unless he's loaned your sister a few bob.'

'Eh, do you mind?' I nodded towards Finn.

'I do actually.' She turned to look at me, her hand on her hip. 'Your sister has all sorts coming onto this road, with her –' She stopped herself and looked at Finn, her eyebrows raised.

'There's your friend, Finn.' I couldn't think of the red head kid's name who was kicking a ball at the top of the cul-de-sac. 'You can have a few minutes out to play, go on.'

Finn ran off.

'Loan shark, isn't it?' said Mrs Miller, sucking on her cigarette and blowing out a thick cloud of white smoke in my direction. I looked down at Aria, who was asleep in her pram and back at Mrs Miller, trying to make her feel bad. I knew well from Dad that you can't shame a smoker.

'What my sister does is her own business.'

'Is it, yeah, until her business is driving onto our road every week and intimidating us neighbours.' She must have seen the confusion on my face. 'That's it. When your precious sister leaves them short, it's us they start interrogating. What time will she be home at? Make sure you tell her to ring me. Mrs Kenny two doors up almost died when the fella approached her, a big six-footer with a skin head.'

'Six-foot, skin head?'

'Well, maybe not six foot. Mrs Kenny can be a bit of an exaggerator, unlike myself, but she needed a strong whiskey after the encounter all the same. Anyway, that's not my point. The point is that sister of –' before she could say anymore the car door opened making us both turn around. A man looking more like a dodgy car salesman than a thug, with slicked back hair and a pinstripe suit, stood out on the pavement.

'Where's Tasha?' he shouted over to us.

I quickly walked over to him so Mrs Miller wouldn't hear us. 'Sorry, who are you?' I asked, trying my best to sound polite and a bit dim at the same time.

'Don't.' He held his hand up. 'I'm not in the humour for bullshit.' Up close he had a darkness to his eyes that made him look sinister. His eyes slide from me to Aria, making me grip the buggy tighter without realising.

'Who's in the house now then?' He looked up at the bedroom

window, squinting against the sun.

'No-one, well, I mean just her, her … dog. He's a, eh, guard dog … a big, horrible thing.'

His eyes narrowed.

'He minds the house when they're not in you see.' My heart was thumping along with the ball that Finn was kicking against the wall.

He smirked. 'Can he put out a fire?'

It took a second to cop what he meant.

'Finn, are you okay?' I called over to him, hearing the wobble in my voice.

'Don't try that shit either,' he said. 'I've kids myself, and if you want to play that game, your sister owes me money, which in turn is taking food from my kid's mouth.'

'Look, please.' I turned to face him, feeling Mrs Miller's eyes on my back.' Just let me speak to Tasha and we can sort something out. I know you probably can't discuss her personal business with me, but –'

'Nine grand. She owes me nine grand.'

'Nine?' I almost threw up with the word.

'And with interest it's going up every day.'

He held up a white envelope in his hand and I recognised Tasha's bubble handwriting on the front, the cute circle for a dot over the i – what was she thinking?

'She keeps leaving me short with her repayments. I let it go the first couple of times, but it's taking the piss now, and leaving me letters. Does she think we're fucking pen-pals?' He closed his fist around the letter scrunching it into a ball. 'That shit doesn't work with me.'

'Aunty Sammie, I need to go the toilet.' Finn shouted over.

'Please. Let me speak to Tasha. I absolutely promise she'll not leave you short again. I have money,' I lied. 'I can help her. Please, just leave it this one last time.'

Finn ran over. 'The baby's awake.' He looked into the buggy. 'Hey, Ari, Ari goo.' He sang into the buggy, making Aria whine with irritation having just opened her eyes.

I looked at the man and managed a convincing smile as he glared at me.

'Last time. I mean it.' He ruffled Finn's hair making me shudder. He turned and got into his car, slamming the door.

'Nice, isn't he?' Mrs Miller shouted over.

'Piss off,' I mumbled under my breath, making Finn giggle.

'I heard you the first time, Sammie.' Tasha took another mouthful of tea.

'I don't care. I'm going to keep telling you. You're a gobshite. This man is the real deal, he doesn't give a crap, Tasha. You'd know by him.'

'Can you not curse in front of the kids please.' Tasha bent down to pick a toy up off the floor and handed it back to Aria in her highchair.

Tasha always cursed in front of the kids, but it wasn't worth the row now. 'Sorry.' We sat in silence for a few minutes watching Aria suck on a plastic block.

'Let me help you, Tasha. I can help with the repayments?'

'No. And as for that aul' witch Mrs Miller, the cheek of her! She has the hamper man calling all year, she owes him a fortune and I don't comment.'

My head was banging at this stage and I just wanted to go home and have a drink.

'Leona was only saying that she has lots more hours for me in the salon. And I'm going to tell Wayne.'

'You are?'

'Yeah. It's his fault that I had to get the loans out in the first place, squandering all his money. He can help with the repayments.'

I couldn't believe her change of heart and tried to hide my surprise. 'Right, well that's good. I'm glad.'

'Once you're glad, Sammie.' I narrowed my eyes at my sister's sarcasm. 'Do you want to stay for dinner?' asked Tasha, getting up to clear the cups.

'No, I better go.' I practically raced out of Tasha's house, eager to get home. I don't think I'd relaxed properly since Conor died, but being away from my family's dramas was definitely the closest thing to it.

Chapter 11

There was no end to the rain when it came. I lay in bed listening as it beat in sheets against the window. I dozed on and off, eventually throwing back the bedcovers and making my way downstairs. The smell in the kitchen was worse and, for a second, I regretted not having taken Max up on his offer to fix it. I flicked on the kettle and made myself a cup of tea. Although it was bright out, the rain was still pouring and opening the window to let some air in wasn't an option.

Instead, I searched the kitchen drawer for a lighter and, when I found one, I bit the bullet and lit my designer candle on the windowsill. There was no point in waiting for my dream kitchen; that day would never come. Instantly the kitchen was filled with the smell of lime and mandarin, completely contrasting with the bleak background.

The kitchen drawer that housed the lighter was home to everything random. The customary middle drawer – one down from the cutlery, above the pots – was filled with everything we might need at a moment's notice.

Under a pile of take-away menus I found a bag of candles, which I'd forgotten Dionne had given me. They had been a gift from a Wexford lady who handmade all her own products. I'd always been obsessed with candles and emptying the bag onto my kitchen table made me instantly want to house them. They were different shades of blue, labelled – sea salt, fresh linen… I pressed one to my nose and inhaled the sweet smell of blueberry.

When we were first shown around the house, the estate agent had opened the door under the stairs. 'A closet? Harry Potter's bedroom? Nah, ha – a secret toilet,' he'd said. Looking back, he should have won an Oscar for his acting, as if a downstairs toilet was not a given in most houses in the area. He'd looked about twelve and had only come up to Conor's elbow. He was wearing a suit shinier than my wedding ring. We'd already fallen in love with the house within the first five minutes exchanging knowing looks behind his back, but we humoured him anyway with his enthusiastic display.

Opening the door now, I was right back there with them, laughing as Conor folded himself in half to fit in. It had since been neglected and I'd often walk past it, preferring to use the bathroom upstairs. Standing inside I was surprised at how roomy it was compared to what I remembered. Everything had felt smaller with Conor towering next to me. I placed a navy tea light on the windowsill and felt an old habit nudging me to coordinate the rest.

Upstairs in the hot press, I had a towel bundle that we'd been given as a moving in present. I took out the hand towel with cream and navy stripes and bundled it under my arm. I opened my wardrobe, remembering Tasha had given me samples of hand creams from the salon in gold and blue packaging. They were covered in dust behind an old pair of Uggs but would do the job.

Back downstairs, I organised the toilet rolls into a wire basket on the floor next to the sink. I folded the hand towel neatly, looping it through the holder. I popped the hand lotions into a glass jar on the empty shelf, placing a fake plant pot on the other end to balance it out. I closed the door and opened it again, a habit I used to have when adding something to any room. I used to make Conor do the same and guess what had changed. He usually wouldn't have a clue, unless it was hanging an inch from his face and even then, he'd be unsure.

I couldn't believe how different the room looked. The blue gave it a hotel feel – albeit a hotel for elves. My family and I would be fine, but anyone over five foot four wouldn't appreciate it.

I checked my phone and an hour had passed. An hour with me absorbed in something other than my own thoughts. I looked out the window and it was still raining, lighter now with small drops puncturing the massive puddles in the garden.

I made myself another cup of tea and sat down at the kitchen table with my laptop. As it clicked and hummed, I wiped the screen with my sleeve, blowing a layer of dust off the keys. I felt like I was on a roll. I didn't want to jinx myself and think too much about it, but I allowed myself to be carried on autopilot into my favourite websites. I scrolled through photos and more photos of cushions, candles, quirky decorative accessories to sofas and tables. I put pieces together in my head, forming rooms and settings.

The rain stayed for the rest of the evening, but I hadn't noticed until my eyes became heavy and my fingers slightly numb – a piece of me was back. A piece of me had survived all this and my new pimped out elf toilet was proof of it.

One thing people don't know – well maybe they do, but there's not much focus on it – is that grieving is a rollercoaster of moderate highs and very low lows. My life was quickly forming a pattern, of one step forward and ten steps back.

It eventually stopped raining the following morning, which was Tuesday. The sun was a watery lemon in the sky, doing its best to dry up the soggy earth.

My morning had been a bad one. Having woken up early, the air in my room was thick and heavy luring me back into a groggy sleep. When I fell back asleep, I'd dreamt of Conor. People often asked me had I dreamt of him? Mainly Mam and my aunts. It was seemingly a big thing to dream of a loved one after they'd passed. It meant it wasn't a dream but a visitation, them letting you know they are still with you. Well, I didn't want the dream and after it, I knew why.

In my dream/nightmare, I'd walked into the kitchen and Conor was there. He didn't look at me at first, just continued what he was doing, filling two cups with boiling water. He moved around the kitchen and I stood watching him. He was alive again, and I didn't question it. He turned around and hugged me, his arms heavy on my shoulders as I wrapped my arms around his waist. He was wearing his hoodie, the navy one, and I sank into it, holding him tight. Everything felt normal and right. Eventually, he let go and handed me a cup. His smile creased around his blue eyes, he was so handsome, and he was mine. The dream was so vivid that when I woke, I'd expected to be holding a full cup of tea. I expected him to be with me. The realisation that it was a dream, dragged me back down into the pain. The physical jolt in the beginning, the raw ache, the pain with no softened edges, just sharp corners of terror had caught me again.

I lay in bed and felt so helpless that ringing Mam even seemed an option. But the fear broke itself down, passing slowly in loose chippings and, eventually, I got up, a part of me wishing I had never woken.

The following morning, I bypassed the kettle and went straight to the fridge. I needed a glass of wine. I needed the boost after my rough night's sleep. I poured a glass and set it down on the counter before pulling up the kitchen blind. I saw Jojo through the window. She was wearing her usual denim dress with an off-white cardigan that looked like it had seen better days. Although who was I to judge in my old, faded pyjamas – again. I slid open the patio door and stepped outside. The air smelt of damp grass and mud, a complete contrast to the fruity smelling wine. I inhaled slowly before taking a mouthful.

'You're out early,' I said to Jojo, who looked like her night had been rougher than mine. 'You look tired.' As if on cue she yawned, rubbing both her nose and eye at the same time. 'Mind you don't fall out of that tree,' I said sitting down.

'Mind you don't fall drinking that juice.' She didn't look up. I felt my cheeks blush with the jibe. 'Bea, what a stupid name for a stupid bitch. Buzzing around us, being a pain.'

'Sorry, what?' I asked, thinking I'd misheard.

'Nothing.' The expression on her face assured me that I'd heard right.

'Did you say Bea? Is that a person?' Her jaw clenched and I was surprised to see her pretty face contort with anger. 'Is it short for Beatrice?'

'I don't know what it's short for. I just know I hate her.'

'Is she your friend? Is she giving you a hard time?'

'She's giving *us* a hard time. She's needs to just mind her own business.'

I put my glass down on the table as if that alone would give me some clarity. Had I missed something. I'd never heard Jojo swear before. 'Are you okay? Has something happened?'

Jojo shrugged.

'Can you speak to your parents?'

'Mam can't do anything. Ugh, it doesn't matter.'

'I've no clue what you're talking about, Jojo, but I can try to help if –'

'I just want to be left alone.'

I didn't want to tell her that she was sitting facing my garden, so if she wanted to be left alone, perhaps moving somewhere else would be a good idea. 'Could you speak to a friend? Does Bea live on your road?'

'I don't want to talk about it.'

'Okay, no problem,' I said, worrying I'd upset her. I picked up my drink and turned to go inside.

'Sammie.'

'Yes.'

115

'Sorry for being mean.'

'You weren't. It's fine.'

By the time I got inside and looked out my kitchen window, she had gone. I thought of the only Bea I knew. Beatrice Lyons who I'd gone to school with. She had been nicknamed Beatrice 'Lies' because she was always telling fibs. She'd even convinced us once that her dad was a famous musician, and she'd toured the world with his band during the summer holidays. Turns out they were on holiday in Donegal. The last I'd heard she was working as a social worker. Even that, we were convinced was a lie.

Chapter 12

'What time will the conman be here?'

'He's a reputable psychic medium, Gerry, and he'll be here shortly,' said Mam, smoothing her hand over her hair and checking her reflection in the oven door, again.

'I thought you were going out, Dad, or do you want to get a reading too?' asked Tasha.

Dad jumped up, grabbing his jacket. 'I'm going for my walk. You can ring me when he's gone.'

'Well, it better be just a walk and not a trip to the bookies. I'll be asking the psychic where you really are,' Mam joked.

Dad laughed and I found myself analysing it. Was he nervous? Was he sneaking to the pub? If I decide to get a reading, will I ask the guy out straight – Is my dad back on the drink? I pushed the question from my mind, already convincing myself of the answer. I was being stupid. John had seen Dad for a fleeting moment and could have confused him with anyone. My dad didn't stand out and could be mistaken for any other dad out there, with his receding grey hair and polo shirts in varying shades of blue.

I took a mouthful of tea, still not quite believing I'd agreed to come. Tasha had been so excited on the phone, telling me she'd booked a medium. She'd said he was the real deal. I attempted to give out to her, telling her she should be keeping her money to pay her debts, but she cut me off, insisting it was all sorted and it was a gift for minding the kids. I didn't have the heart to say no to her, but she understood that I might change my mind at the last minute and she wouldn't try to force me to see him. I also thought, if he was good, I could ask him to speak to Jojo's gran. I could find out what was going on with her.

Mediums were a big hit with my family, so it wouldn't be a wasted trip for him either way. Mam had been cleansing herself and the house with sage all day in preparation.

As Dad left Aunt Carol arrived, eager to speak to the dead. 'Oh, I'm all excited, girls,' she said, clutching her rosary beads, a Buddha and a handful of angel cards. Her hair was dyed a deep plum that bled onto her forehead, making it look like she was wearing a matching headband.

'Where are ye going with all that, Carol?' asked Mam, putting a fresh pot of tea on the table.

'Since I had the health scare last year, I'm keeping all me options open. I'm praying to anyone and everyone out there.'

Tasha rolled her eyes, sighing heavily.

'How are you, love?' Aunt Carol gave me a hug and sat down. 'Please God and Angels and Buddha that your Conor comes through. I'd say he will.' She squeezed my arm.

'She still doesn't know if she wants a reading,' said Mam, leaning across us to put a plate of custard creams and Viscounts on the table. 'She'll see how she feels, won't you, love?' She looked at me, giving me a smile.

I sort of shook my head and gave a shrug, hoping it would suffice as an answer.

Seanie Star (that was apparently his real name) finally arrived, half an hour late. He went straight into the living room to set up, where we'd each go in to see him, one at time. Mam went in first while Tasha, Aunt Carol and I, all sat in the kitchen whispering and half trying to listen. Twenty minutes and sixty euro later, Mam came out sniffling.

'Amazing,' she mouthed to Aunt Carol. 'He told me that Mammy is with us, she's watching over us all and your Denise is going to have twins. And she won't need the IVF. It will save her a fortune.'

'Oh Jesus.' Aunt Carol put her hand to her chest, closing her eyes. 'Oh, she'll be thrilled, Lil.'

'You go in, Sammie, go on; he's lovely. He's real down to earth.'

'I can go in with you?' Tasha offered.

What had I got to lose? I stood up. 'No, it's okay. I'll go in by myself.' Mam squeezed my arm as I walked past, and I felt myself fill with anticipation. If this man could speak to Conor, if he could tell me he was okay, he was happy, how would I feel? If he told me he was still with me, I think my heart would combust.

Mam had the front room dimly lit like a brothel; she was only short of having Barry White playing in the background. There was a row of tea lights along the mantelpiece, giving off an overpowering smell of lavender, and two large church candles on the windowsill, threatening to set the fringing on the blind alight.

I sat down opposite Seanie Star, who had his eyes closed and was taking slow, deep breaths. I was surprised he was so young looking, no more than early thirties, and I was even more surprised when he uncrossed his feet and I noticed he was wearing a pair of Gucci trainers. He must be making a fortune. He was chubby with tight brown hair and when he opened his eyes, I was glad to see they were a warm brown that looked kind, making me care a little less about the Guccis.

'I'm just cleansing the room after the last lady, allowing spirits to leave with her or stay, whatever they choose.'

My heart was hammering so loud in my chest, I was sure he could hear it. I wiped my clammy palms in my leggings and took a long deep breath. He gave me a quick spiel that I didn't listen to, instead I willed Conor to come through. Please Conor, I know you don't believe in this sort of stuff, but please give me a message. Please, just let me know you're here.

'I have a person here with the initial P?' Seanie was staring at a spot on the wall above my shoulder. He rested his wrists on his knees, facing upwards like he was levitating around the room, rather than sitting on my parent's battered couch. 'Now remember these might be spirits that aren't necessarily close to you, so you need to really think.'

I tried to think of all the P people I knew, but I was struggling. 'I can't think of anyone, I'm sorry.' I twisted my wedding ring with my thumb, hoping it would be a magnetic force attracting Conor through.

He filled his lungs with exaggerated deep breaths and tried again. 'The letter R or T?'

I shook my head, thinking for a moment could he mean my Uncle Ray, then I remembered everyone knew him as Jack, he would never have introduced himself as Ray, not even in the spirit world. I looked at Seanie blankly.

'The letter A – a lady, older … Annie or Angela?'

I shook my head again. 'I'm sorry.' I was really trying.

'Now really think, I can feel you're a little tense, try to relax.'

I wanted to speak to my dead husband, of course I was a little tense. 'I can't think of anyone. Sorry.'

'Okay, don't worry.' He studied my face for a moment. 'Is there someone that you're hoping to speak to?'

I nodded, surprised that my eyes were beginning to fill.

'Try and be open to it. We'll see who else we can get through.'

Seanie closed his eyes again, and I tried to ignore the disappointment I could feel setting in. I felt foolish for even agreeing to this.

'Okay.' He sat up straight, confident now. 'There's a male coming through. A big, burly man.' He tapped his chest. 'Died from something to do with the heart?'

I nodded my head so hard I thought it might fall off my shoulders and roll on to the floor. 'Yes, yes, he did. It was his heart.'

'He's an older man, wearing a suit.'

Thirty wasn't old. I bit my lip and stayed quiet, hoping he'd correct himself.

'Not old, old, but early sixties when he died. A heavy smoker,' said Seanie.

My heart sank with his words. Conor never smoked, he hated cigarettes even more than me. There was no way it was him. I racked my brains trying to think. 'It could be my Grandad Joe?' I said. 'But he didn't die from his heart.'

'Something to do with the chest area.' He made circle motions with his stubby fingers, his thick gold identity bracelet slide down and stuck in the crease of his wrist. 'He was like a father figure. He had a stroke. Yes, a stroke. He was a funny man; he hasn't lost his sense of humour.'

'I was only young when he died. He wasn't really a father figure to me.'

'Yes, a grandfather.' He chuckled, shaking his head. 'He's a gas man.'

My disappointment quickly shifted to frustration. 'Is he?' I said, trying hard to stay polite. I glanced at the time on the TV box. I'd already been in there fifteen minutes.

'I sense a child, female – a baby? Went before her time.'

I shook my head, trying to hold back my tears. I wasn't letting Tasha pay him that was for bloody sure.

'I think maybe this child wanted to speak to the last lady too. Is she your mother?'

I nodded not trusting myself to speak. Surely the family photos dotted around the living room would have told him that.

'This child is happy, she's very like you. Is this a sister? Did you have a sister pass to the other side?'

'My mam lost a baby before she had me and my sister.' I heard myself say.

I saw his shoulders relax and I think he was just relived to have told me something that was sticking.

'Right – okay.' He moved forward, sitting on the edge of the couch. He pressed his palms on the coffee table like he was trying to channel more, or at least look like he was. 'She is with you all.' He looked at me, smiling, delighted with himself. 'Your relatives on the other side are looking after her.'

'My Mam will be happy to hear that.' There was an edge to my voice, and it wasn't that I wasn't glad the baby had come through, but it was never something we talked about. Mam had only mentioned a few times that she'd lost a baby a couple of years before she had me. She hadn't known she was pregnant, until she miscarried at six weeks. It was never made a big deal of, and something I never thought about, not really since the time she told me in my teens. I knew Mam obviously thought about the baby, but as a family, we still always felt complete.

Seanie reached down and picked up a stack of cards, shuffling them, he fanned them out onto a piece of blue silk. 'Have you any questions you would like to ask – maybe career, money, love?'

'No.' I shook my head. I'd had enough. I wasn't going to spoon feed him information, nor did I want to hear I was going to win the lotto. If he started trying to make up things about Conor, I'd end up force feeding him the deck of cards.

I reached into my pocket, pulling out three twenty notes, letting him know we were finished. There was no way I was letting Tasha pay for that, treat or no treat. 'Thanks.' I said, placing the curled-up notes on the table.

'You're a very spiritual person yourself.' He looked at me, stuffing the money into his shirt pocket. 'Have you ever tried to read cards?'

'No. I don't really believe in all that.' I couldn't help myself. I was pissed off with him, and even more at myself for getting my hopes up. As if Conor was going to come through a man in a pair of Guccis. I stood up, telling him that I'd send Aunt Carol in next.

'Well?' said Mam, pouncing on me as I walked back into the kitchen. 'Did Conor come through?' Her face looked so full of hope, that I felt worse for her saying 'no'. I shook my head.

'Oh, love.'

'But Grandad Joe came through, and your baby. Conor must have been too busy up there.' I smiled trying to sooth her disappointment.

'It was probably too soon, love. They go through a transition period. He's probably still transitioning.'

I didn't even want to think about that one, instead I sat down beside Tasha and let her pour me a cup of tea. Mam's eyes looked far away, like she was only digesting what I had told her about the baby.

'He said the baby's happy, that she's with our family, Mam.'

'I know, love. I never doubted it.'

124

Enduring Seanie Star had been worth it, to see the look on Mam's face.

After everyone had gone, it was just Tasha and me in our parent's living room. We'd opened the bottle of wine that I'd brought along and sat side by side under Mam's knitted throw.

'He was a load of aul bollocks,' said Tasha, 'and the state of him. He was like something off *Love/Hate*. Imagine me winning the lotto and Aunty Carol finding love in Turkey? She hasn't even got a passport.' We both laughed.

'But then again, he did tell you about the baby and he knew Wayne's cousin had drowned.'

'I think a lot of it was guess work,' I said, topping up my glass. 'At least Mam's happy.'

'Hmm …'

'And Aunt Carol, she's delighted with herself.' I laughed.

'Are you disappointed?' Tasha looked at me over the rim of her wine glass. She took a sip, rubbing her thumb along the stem.

'Yeah … a bit.'

We sat for a few moments sipping our drinks, lost in our own thoughts.

'I have an idea,' said Tasha. She turned to face me on the couch, tucking her feet under her bum, which made her taller than me, giving her somewhat of an advantage on whatever crazy idea she was about to propose. 'What if we tried to talk to Conor?'

I should have seen it coming.

'He's not going to come through Nidge, is he? Maybe if we really try, we could channel him ourselves.'

'Eh … no Tasha. I'm probably clinically insane as it is, if I were to be examined. This would tip me over.'

'Come on Sis, pleeeeeease.' Tasha did that little sister thing she'd perfected over the years. Like a little talent, her eyes wide, her voice cutesy and it was like she was begging me to swap troll dolls again, after she'd cut a lump of hair off her one.

Softened up slightly by the wine, and clearly in an already vulnerable state – I eventually agreed. So, my sister and I sat with our legs crossed, the tea lights now smoking in puddles of purple wax and TLC singing *Waterfalls* on MTV in the background.

'Just try clear our minds first, and then we'll ask Conor to give us a sign when he's here.'
I was definitely tipsy, my sister's words having no effect on me. I just listened, going along with whatever she was saying.

'Conor, please give us a sign. We're not afraid …' Tasha continued talking. I closed my eyes, swaying slightly. I felt relaxed, tired even, listening to her voice.

'Say something to him, Sammie.' She held my hand, and I felt my heartbeat picking up. Tasha was the spiritual one, if Conor was going to come through to anyone, maybe it would be her.

I opened my mouth to speak, when Dad's voice boomed from the kitchen.

'Girls, will I fry yis a rasher?'

I jumped and my eyes shot open.

'Jesus Christ,' said Tasha, taking my hand again. 'No, Dad, we're grand,' she shouted. 'Now close your eyes, Sammie.'

'Are you sure, girls?'

'Yes, we're sure. Thanks. Just ignore him,' Tasha whispered. 'Just think of Conor's face, his eyes, his –'

'Sammie, will you have a rasher, love? They're from the butchers; they're the real deal.'

I tried to concentrate, to block Dad out.

'Girls, can ye hear me?' Dad's voice was louder now, the noise from the kitchen behind him.

'Dad, shut up talking to us. We don't want anything,' shouted Tasha.

'Will I put a couple on and yis can make a sambo?'

'We don't bloody well want rashers.' Tasha's face was now puce.

'What are yis doing in there anyway?'

'Nothing.' We both shouted.

'Sammie, are you not hungry? Sammie?'

'Jesus Christ, Dad,' I shouted, 'I'm trying to channel Conor here.'

'You're what?' The door opened and Dad popped his head around, waving a small butcher's bag.

'I am trying to speak to Conor,' I said slowly, through gritted teeth. Dad's eyes widened in horror as he backed out of the room, clicking the door shut behind him.

Chapter 13

Not surprisingly, Conor never came through to Tasha or me. Instead, we both ended up eating burnt rasher sambos and listening as Mam casually mentioned bereavement counselling, listing the benefits in alphabetical order.

As I hung my clothes on the washing line, wiping each peg to get rid of the cobwebs, I thought how the back garden was fast becoming my favourite place to be. It was the one place that didn't shift and become unfamiliar each time I stepped into it. Although, there were lots of new discoveries to make with different flowers blooming, adding new colours and scents to the garden, ones I hadn't known were hiding, waiting to surprise me. I even googled some of them to find out their names. The ones that looked like it had just snowed were nicknamed goat's beards. The snap dragons were the colour of my bridesmaid's dresses, on long spindly branches, their trumpet like blooms were a mixture of peach and orange. With my world zapped of colour without Conor, everything could feel grey and lifeless, but the garden remained cheery with little effort.

I could hear laughing and giggling coming from Jojo's garden, punctured by the squeak of a toy. I hung around for a couple of minutes in case she climbed the tree to say hi, but she didn't. I was glad to hear her playing with her friends and hoped she'd sorted things out with Bea.

Later that afternoon my phone rang and, when I saw Rob's name appear, I was tempted to let it ring out. I hadn't spoken to any of Conor's friends, trying my best to avoid them. Conor had been the first one to settle down; the rest shagged their way through north Dublin. Any girlfriend I'd become friendly with over the years always ended up being dumped, leaving me the awkward job of the go between.

'Hello.' I forced my tone to be as normal, as much old Sammie as possible.

'Hey Sammie, it's Rob.' There was an awkward pause, which thankfully gave me a second to remember that I had given his number to Max.

'I heard Max has been in touch,' I said, walking up and down my kitchen.

'Yeah, thanks for that. I've gotten a few jobs off him.'

'I'm glad; that's great.'

'I eh ... rang and removed that ad. I hope that's okay. I didn't think you'd be up for doing it, or having anymore random callers.'

'I hadn't even thought of it, Rob. I should have done it, thanks.'

'No, it was no problem. I was glad to do it, I was, I mean, I was glad to help.'

I always prided myself on being a doer, on making things happen; I felt vulnerable, even more unlike myself because I hadn't thought to do it. Conor had harped on about that ad for ages, it cost a fortune, but he was happy to go the whole hog. *'What you put in, you get back,* Sammie.' The only quote he'd loved.

'Anyway, the reason I'm ringing is that me and the lads want to do a fund-raiser for Conor. A five-a-side football match with all the proceeds going to SADS. We looked it up and there are lots of charities we could donate to, depending on how much we get. We could even split it between a few. It's kind of last minute, but we want to hold it next Saturday. It's the only weekend in the summer that everyone will be around.' He continued talking like he'd the words written down in front of him and was reaming them off to cover everything. 'The whole club is getting behind us and of course, we don't want to put you under pressure, but if you wanted to come along or even meet us after in the Bailey, we'd love that. If you're up for it of course?'

A million excuses sat on the tip of my tongue. How could I face all his teammates and watch from the side lines, knowing it was where Conor had died? 'I'm not sure I could watch the match Rob, if I'm honest.'

'Of course. I understand –'

'But I'll pop in afterwards.'

'You will? Brilliant.' He sounded relieved. 'I'll have the Jäger bombs ready, or was it Sambucas you banned Conor from drinking?'

'Both,' I said, pretending to sound cross.

The old joke ended things nicely. When I hung up the phone, I didn't know what had made me agree. The thought of a night out made me ill.

I drove around to Tasha's house to fill her in and ask her would she come with me.

'Going out twice in one month, who am I?' Tasha laughed. She was standing at her hall mirror.

'Where did you get the dress? It's lovely,' I said, as she turned to the side to examine the back of the floral maxi dress.

'It's years old, but I've never worn it. One of the girls in work is leaving, we're just going for an early bird – Do you want to come, to get out?'

I couldn't think of anything worse. 'I'm okay, thanks.'

'I'm only going for an hour. I'm in work early tomorrow.'

A key twisted in the front door making us both turn around.

'About time,' said Tasha as Wayne walked in. 'I told you I was going at six.'

'Alright, Sammie,' said Wayne, ignoring Tasha.

'I thought you were off at four, Wayne?'

'I was but one of the lads needed a lift and then –'

Tasha put her hand up, stopping him mid-sentence. 'I don't wanna know.'

'Dad.' Finn ran down the stairs. 'Did you remember the Match Attack cards?'

'They had none, all sold out. Sorry, buddy.'

'Aww …'

'Two packets tomorrow, buddy, I promise.' Wayne ruffled Finn's hair.

'Okay.'

Tasha mumbled something under her breath that I didn't hear, but it made Wayne mutter back, 'fuck off!'

'Where are you going, Mam?' asked Finn. 'You're all dressed up.'

'In your Nana Sue's tablecloth, by the looks of it.' Wayne laughed.

'Nana's tablecloth.' Finn was laughing now too.

'It's a bit mad looking, Tash.'

'Yeah, it's mad looking, Mam.'

'Do you hear the fashionistas,' I said, noticing Tasha's shoulders sag. 'They haven't a clue.'

'Make sure you eat your dinner, Finn. I made a casserole so plate some up for him in a half hour, Wayne.'

'I'm not hungry, Mam.'

'I don't blame you, son,' said Wayne, taking off his coat. 'Your mam's casserole is muck.'

'That took me ages to make,' said Tasha. 'I stopped off especially on the way home from work to get the ingredients.'

'Nobody asked you to,' said Wayne, slinging his hoodie over the bottom of the stairs.

'Yeah,' said Finn, 'nobody asked you to.'

I could see Tasha glance at me, before looking back in the mirror.

'Do you want a lift?' I asked trying to sound chirpy. 'Where are yis going?'

'Well, if Tasha's outfit is anything to go by, it's nowhere extravagant.'

Tasha grabbed her phone off the hall table and threw it into her handbag. It wasn't like Tasha to bite her tongue, but I could see her look at Finn and force a smile which made me fill with pity for her.

Wayne, oblivious to it all, mouthed 'crazy' behind her back.

'A lift would be great, thanks. One of the girls will drop me home. Wake Aria up in ten minutes, Wayne, or she won't sleep tonight.'

'She'll be grand.'

'She's in a routine. If she sleeps now, she won't go down later and she'll be unsettled during the night. You're not the one getting up to her if she wakes.'

Wayne kicked off his shoes making them land under the hall table.

'You're crazy, Mam.' Finn laughed, walking back up the stairs.

'What's the story with Wayne?' I asked when we got into the car. 'He didn't seem himself.' I didn't want to embarrass Tasha by letting on I'd noticed too much.

'Eh, that's Wayne being himself. He manages to rein it in when he's in Mam and Dad's house.'

'I never noticed him that bad before. I've seen him joking about, but not –' I turned the key starting the engine, not quite sure how to word it.

'Putting me down?'

'Well, yeah … a bit'

'Oh, that's his new thing. By new, I mean the past year. Since Aria came along all we do is fight over money.'

'But you lived together before you had kids. What's happened?' I asked, driving to the end of the cul-de-sac. Mrs Miller was at her door and I instinctively held Tasha's hand down, stopping her from giving the finger.

'Kids are what happened, Sammie. You can't hide your money when you have kids; every penny needs to be accounted for and all thrown into the one pot. It wasn't so bad with just one, but with two ... Wayne resents having to part with his money. Like I told you already, he's a selfish bastard.' She pointed for me to drive straight on. 'And did you see Finn? He thinks the sun shines out of Wayne's arse.'

'Well, he is his dad ...'

'Who has no time for him and would rather spend his time and money on himself. Those Match Attacks are a euro and have been out the past year. He hasn't bought him one packet. Turn right at the next set of lights up here.'

I did as I was told not even thinking where I was driving to.

'And he's setting a bad example. I'd never want Finn to think it's right to put a woman or anyone down the way Wayne does; his banter goes too far.'

'Hmm,' I said, agreeing but not wanting to add fuel to Tasha's bonfire. I could see her stiffening in her seat thinking about it.

'The sooner he helps you with the loans the better, he'll have no choice but to help out, unless he wants that creep at your door again. What did he say when you told him about the debt?'

'Yeh, anyway, enough about Wayne –'

'You did tell him, didn't you?' I turned to look at her. I never thought to ask before now. I could feel the shitty sister guilt creeping in.

'Eyes on the road, please.'

'Tasha?' I changed gear, slowing down behind a bus.

'I didn't get a chance to yet, can we just not talk about it right now.' I could feel the weight in her words and didn't want to push it.

Chapter 14

'Sammie, hello weirdo. I've been watching you for like ten minutes and you haven't noticed. Are you bird watching?'

I had noticed but didn't know if Jojo wanted to be left alone like the last day.

'It's really fascinating to watch,' I said, not taking my eyes off the tiny sparrow. 'It's like he's looking for something under the decking or sharpening his beak.' I squinted to see him better, shielding my eyes from the fizzy orange sun.

Jojo coughed 'loser' into her hand.

I was on my hunkers holding my wine glass and tried carefully to stand without scaring him away. 'Do sparrows sharpen their beak? I'll have to look it up.' I glanced at Jojo thinking she was just like this little bird. One wrong move and she was gone.

I took a sip of my drink, hoping she might open up again. I was drinking some French muck thanks to Kai, who'd messed up the shop's wine order. Each sip vacuumed the saliva from my mouth leaving my throat dry and scratchy.

'So how is – is your friend Bea still being annoying?' The sparrow took flight, his wings flapping wildly like he'd just realised he was late for something.

Jojo looked at me blankly.

'Bea. The girl you were talking about the other day. You seemed really annoyed.'

'No, I wasn't.'

I sat my glass down on the table and pulled out a garden chair. 'You said that she needed to mind her own business, that your mam was annoyed with her too.'

Jojo twirled her fingers beside each ear mimicking I was crazy. I actually felt crazy in that moment.

'I think the wine is making you loco.' Jojo laughed.

'Right, well, I'm glad you're feeling better,' I said, trying to hide my annoyance. My hand moved to pick up my glass, but I stopped myself.

'It's all about silver linings.'

I must have looked as confused as I felt, Jojo repeated herself slowly.

'Silver linings – as – in – the – clouds.' She pointed to the sky with her index finger. 'I read a story about them once in school. Every bad thing has a good thing.'

'Yes, I know what silver linings are.'

'After Gran died, my grandad said, him getting the widow's pension was a silver lining.'

I couldn't help but laugh.

'But I think dying is bit easier for old people to handle, especially when the person who died was old too.'

'Maybe,' I said, humouring her.

'They see the silver lining, that's the difference. They say things like, the person had a good life which is code for long, and they were lucky to get to a good age, which is code for ancient. We heard that a lot when Gran died; she was seventy-seven. My mam said that wasn't even old, 'cause she didn't drink or smoke and took cod liver oil every day. And she's no longer in pain, that's another silver lining. Not everyone is good at looking for silver linings.'

One thing I knew for sure, there was no silver lining to Conor dying. Not a single one.

'Jennifer.' Jojo's mam shouted in a normal shouty voice, no erratic undertone. 'Jennifer' she called again. Jojo didn't move.

'Your mam's calling you.'

Jojo looked up at me, confused.

'She just shouted Jennifer.'

'Did she? I better go.' Jojo hopped down behind the wall. It was only when she had gone that I realised she was wearing the same denim dress and sandals. I knew kids could be odd when it came to clothes. Finn had a thing about his socks feeling funny that had Tasha threatening to chop his feet off, but still, it was a little strange.

When I went back inside, my phone was ringing on the kitchen counter.

'Hiya Mam,' I said, rinsing my glass under the tap.

'Sammie, Breda's son's mother-in-law's dog had pups. Little … What are they called again Gerry?' Mam shouted.

'Shitting machines,' I heard in the background.

'Oh, Cocker Spaniels, that's it. Those lovely shiny dogs,' said Mam.

'That's nice; and?'

'You should get one, love. They're beautiful; I saw a picture on Breda's phone. They've been microwaved and wormed, and are ready to go … Okay, Gerry. Jesus. Microchipped, Sammie, not microwaved as the dog expert himself just corrected me.'

'I don't want a dog, Mam.'

'But these are lovely little things.'

'I'm sure they are, but I've never wanted a pet.'

'It would be a bit of company for you.'

'I don't want a dog to keep me company.'

'Well, security then, whatever. I think it's a great idea.'

'Why don't you get one then?'

'I don't want a feckin' dog, are you joking me? It's bad enough running around after your father without cleaning up after a dog too. Anyway, I'd be afraid with the kiddies here. You have the room and you could take it for nice walks.'

'Eh, it's grand, thanks. I don't need something to walk.'

'Have a think about it, love.'

'I don't want one –'

'I told Breda I'd let her know tomorrow. The woman said she'd keep one for you no problem, and to tell you that they're very healing, Cocker Spaniels …' I held the phone away as Mam harped on. She was just as bad as Tasha, if not worse, trying to fix me, trying to make everything better. When would they both realise that I was permanently broken?

139

Chapter 15

It felt surreal, getting ready for a night out. I was in a sort of haze, going between my bathroom and bedroom. I wanted to look well for their sakes. I didn't want pity or to make Conor's friends feel uncomfortable. I hadn't seen most of them since the funeral, when I was not a sight for the faint hearted. I would never be the fun-loving Sammie they knew, but still, I wanted them to recognise some part of me.

Tasha had phoned a couple of times to confirm plans. I knew she was half expecting me to back out. I had contemplated it, thinking that maybe a donation would suffice, and that I could just drop Tasha to the pub to deliver it. Although, since talking to Jojo, I had thought about silver linings, and, well, if this fundraiser managed to help save even one life, it would be a good thing. A positive even, and I wanted to be a part of it.

I walked into the back bedroom or my 'over-spill wardrobe' as Conor used to call it. I had claimed the wardrobes when we moved in, stuffing them with my good coats, handbags and heels. I quickly found my old reliable clutch bag and walked over to the window to pull the blind down. I usually didn't bother, but knowing I was going out – a rare occurrence these days, it could be dark by the time I got home. I could see Jojo's house from the window. It was the mirror image of mine except with white pebble dashing and the oak tree shadowed half of their garden. I had never noticed Jojo's family before. There was so much I hadn't noticed when I had a life of my own.

I could see into their kitchen clearly and through the patio doors I could see Jojo's family sitting around the dining table. Jojo's mam was blonde too, her hair scraped into a low ponytail. Jojo's dad was beside her with his head low to the plate, and at that moment he looked up to pass something to Millie, Jojo's sister. She was a younger version of Jojo with long, blonde hair spilling onto the back of her chair. They looked like a frozen food ad. The kind where the family sit around the kitchen table, grinning at each other with a half-moon piece of chicken on their fork, a puddle of mash and peas for good measure. There was no sign of Jojo. A light was on in the upstairs bedroom and the curtains were drawn even though it wasn't dark out.

My phone beeped pulling my attention away from the window. It was Mark: *Looking forward to seeing you Sammie, we all are!* My stomach dipped with nerves.

I checked myself again in the mirror. I'd let my hair dry naturally, which thankfully it did kindly. My hair needed a cut, but the extra weight made the curls hang loose, giving it a salon job look. Usually, I spent hours applying false lashes, perfecting the season's smoky eye with my phone blaring a tutorial from my dressing table. Instead, tonight I put on some tinted moisturiser, mascara and a couple of coats of nude lipstick. I was tanned from sitting in the garden, so when I threw on a pair of skinny jeans and a white top I'd bought a couple of years back, I looked healthy at least. Tasha and I arrived at the Bailey a half an hour early. The pub had recently undergone a refurbishment and looked nothing like I'd remembered. I stood for a moment, admiring the new plush purple seating and white painted stone walls. It was quite busy, and I looked around to see if I recognised anyone, wondering for a split second, would I see Dad among the older men at the back door to the smoking area.

The round tables along the wall were filled with couples all silently sipping drinks, while looking around at other couples. Under each plasma TV there was a gathering of men watching a football match, open mouthed like hungry birds chirping for food. There was R&B playing low in the background, and the smell of cider mixed with bleach brought me back to the great times I'd had there.

There was an area reserved for us at the front along the windows. Tasha went to the bar to get the drinks and I sat down, trying to ignore the nervous feeling that was settling in my stomach. Now that I was here, I wasn't sure I was up for it.

'We don't have to stay long,' said Tasha, putting a glass of vodka down in front of me. There was a lot to be said for sisterly intuition. 'Even an hour, okay?'

I nodded. 'I'll see how it goes.' I poured my diet Coke into the vodka, mixing the two with a straw. The ice splintered and spat making my mouth water. I took a large gulp. I had managed to build up a bit of stamina for drinking the past few weeks. I knew tonight a pretty coloured alcopop wasn't going to cut it.

The double doors opened, and a swarm of yellow jerseys poured through them like a spilt jar of honey. The sight took my breath and I felt Tasha squeeze my hand. Each face was familiar, their laughing, the boom of their voices filled the pub and every inch of my head. In that second, I felt Conor could walk out from among them. If he did it would be normal, it would make more sense than him not. Tasha waved, catching Mark's eye and he came straight over to us.

I stood up as he approached the table. Mark was known as 'wee man' on the team. He was only my height, so in heels I was taller. I hugged him, feeling a comfort that I didn't know I'd get.

'Did you see the back?' He turned around to show us the back of his jersey. 'Keegan' with the number six was written in thick, black bold. 'We got them made up especially. No one has been allowed to wear Conor's number, but today we all went out in it.'

I could see Tasha dab her eyes and I tried not to look at her.

'That's lovely, Mark,' I said. 'Conor would have loved it.'

'We've made eleven thousand so far.' His eyes lit up with pride. 'And we still haven't collected all the money.'

As each team member hugged me, they told me again how much they'd raised. Their excitement was infectious. I knew doing something worthy had brought them some peace and I felt genuinely happy for them.

One thing about sitting among a football team is that there's no room for wallowing. I'd feared they would tip toe around me and that a shadow would hang over our night – I couldn't have been more wrong. I had never been so grateful for men not to be in touch with their emotions and turning everything into a joke.

'So, Tasha, ye still with Wayne?' Rob asked, taking a sip of his pint. 'I saw him down the Chinese last week, ordered a black bag of curry. No mess, he was like bleedin' Santy.' Rob stood up, pretending to throw a sack over his shoulder.

'Sure, I'm madly in love,' said Tasha, sipping her drink.

'Yeah, when you were fifteen and seeing me. I can still taste your cherry ChapStick.' Rob smacked his lips together.

'Do you hear him?' Another one of the lads, Carl, pipped up. 'Katy Perry crooning there.'

'I never wore ChapStick, Rob. You must be confusing me with someone else?'

'I think Greg Gleeson was fond of a bit of ChapStick, so the rumour was before he came out.' Carl laughed.

'Thinking back, it was probably your ma!' said Rob, 'good aul Maureen was a great kisser.'

'Still on the sunbeds?' Tasha teased. 'Oh, and you're booked in for a facial next week.'

'It was a full body massage actually and I requested you.' Rob winked.

The banter was flying, and I laughed along as they tore into each other, each joke a lower blow than the last.

'I heard about Haven Interiors closing,' said Jay, who was one of the quieter lads on the team. His dad was Terry, the butcher who worked next door to the shop. 'Dad was telling me about it. He couldn't believe it when it went. He says he misses seeing you every day and you'd better drop in to the butchers.'

'Awh, tell Terry I said hello, and that I don't miss the slagging.' I tried to keep the conversation light as he asked what my plans were for work, and if I wanted him to put a word in for me in his accounts firm.

I now had a train of vodkas in front of me with everyone buying Tasha and me drink. I paced myself, conscious that I might lose my grip with too many. The fact that Tasha and Rob were deep in conversation the past twenty minutes also had me feeling sober. I knew my sister and I knew she always had a soft spot for Rob. They had gone out together on and off as teenagers. It was nothing serious, but I think everyone wondered would they have gotten together properly, if it wasn't for Wayne coming along.

Rob was handsome with dark hair and brown eyes. The lads joked that he fell straight from God's pocket, and Conor used to say that when Wayne looked in the mirror, it was Rob he saw.

I was just about to give Tasha the eye to come to the toilet, so I could throw water on her face and remind her that she was as good as married with two kids, when the blonde girl who had just arrived, sat down beside me.

'Hi, I'm Amy, Mark's girlfriend.'

'Hiya, I'm Sammie, nice to meet you.' I moved up, making room for her on the couch.

'I've heard a lot about you, and of course about Conor from Mark. I'm so sorry.'

Usually when people say they're sorry for what happened it would irritate me, but this time it didn't. Amy was soft spoken, and each word sounded sincere. She was pretty with doll like features and unexpectedly green eyes. She looked nothing like the girls Mark usually went for.

'Thanks,' I said, stirring my drink with the straw. 'So, how long have you and Mark been together?'

'We met here a couple of months ago. It's going really well.' I knew she didn't mean to add the last bit, and her cheeks blushed slightly. She took a sip of her Bacardi Breezer. 'I usually don't bother coming on boy's nights with Mark but, obviously, tonight is different and I've heard so much about you, I really wanted to meet you. Mark really wanted me to meet you.'

I glanced over at Mark who was walking in from the smoking area.

'I really want him to quit smoking, his apartment smells like an ashtray.'

'You've been in Mark's apartment?'

The shock in my voice must have hurt her. In my defence, Mark never let a girl set foot in his apartment, even the ones he was crazy about in the past. I think he was afraid they would leave tampons, or toothbrushes or refurnish the whole place pink while he slept.

'I stay over most nights,' said Amy, straightening her drink on the coaster.

'Of course, sure why wouldn't you.' I rolled my eyes, like I was a complete idiot.

Mark had smoked since he was twelve. He was proud of the fact he carried an inhaler in one hand, a box of Silk Cut in the other, and could still manage to score a hat trick. He gave up smoking a couple of years ago, when his dad was diagnosed with lung cancer. The lads called him Patch Adams as he wore that many Nicotine patches. This struck somewhere deep within me.

Conor's death was like a web, catching everyone, spreading to not just me but affecting those around him. Those who I have never even thought about. I felt a mixture of guilt and sadness.

'He's trying to cut down, but I think after your husband passed away, he needed them. I understand that. It's affected him really bad.'

'It has?'

'Of course.' She nodded and I couldn't help but feel naive. 'They were lifelong friends, Mark told me. Don't tell him I said anything, but he gets panic attacks now, he never had them before.'

Mark walked over and sat down beside me. He put his arm around my shoulder, and I swallowed down the lump in my throat.

'Does she pass the test then?' He nodded towards Amy. 'I said to her, if Sammie doesn't like you, you're blanked.'

I smiled, hitting his leg. 'She's gorgeous and way too good for you.'

'Thanks, Sammie.' Amy laughed.

'Shut up, she hasn't copped that yet,' Mark joked.

The rest of the night I laughed like I hadn't in a long time. The lads shared their own stories of Conor and a side of him not even I knew. Pranks he played on them, ways he helped them that he never even told me about, and white lies he told me, silly things that made me miss him in a somehow lighter, less intense way. I was getting on so well with Amy that we even swapped numbers, agreeing to meet up again.

The night was a success and I was just about to say so to Tasha, when I noticed she wasn't there and neither was Rob.

'Be right back,' I said to Amy, who was telling me why she didn't trust the Kardashians. I was eager to hear her reasons.

I went straight to the toilets, calling my sister's name outside each cubicle. I knew the chances of her and Rob needing the toilet at the same time were slim. I walked through the smoking area, and cursed Tasha for making me look for her. Outside, the road was busy. There was a queue for the night club next door and a line forming at the chipper across the road.

I was just about to go back inside to ring her phone when a shimmer of gold sequins caught my eye. There they were: her and Rob sitting in deep conversation on a wall across the road. Their knees were touching, and their faces were inches apart. I squinted my eyes, and thought for a moment could I have imagined them kiss? If any of Wayne's family were around there would be murder, considering her and Rob's history. He had forty-two cousins in North Dublin alone, so the chance of someone seeing them was pretty high.

'Tasha,' I shouted, walking across the road.

She looked up and Rob hopped off the wall, like it had just been set alight.

'Tasha, are you ready to go?'

'Just give me a minute.'

She didn't seem drunk, neither of them did, which worried me even more.

'Rob and I were just catching up.'

I bet you were, I thought looking at Rob. He was looking at the ground, like a schoolboy caught smoking behind the sheds. I didn't want to pull out the widow card, but if it saved my sister from breaking up her family then I would.

'I really want to go, Tasha. I've had enough. It's getting a bit much for me.' I dabbed my eyes for effect.

'Of course, no problem.' She jumped down. 'I have to go with my sister, Rob. I'll see you again.'

We grabbed our bags inside the pub and said our goodbyes. Mark and Amy promised to call around, and I promised to answer the phone to arrange it. We hugged and I knew I'd look forward to seeing them.

Tasha was quiet in the taxi home, staring out the window as the streets blurred past. I didn't need to ask if she'd kissed Rob. The answer was written all over her face.

Chapter 16

'When life gives you lemons, make –' Mam looked from me to dad, before turning to stick her new calendar onto the fridge.

'Would ye get lost, Lil.'

Mam smiled at me. 'Come on, Sammie, it begins with an L. Oh, actually it doesn't …' Mam squinted to read the small print. 'Gin?' Mam tutted. 'We'll ignore that one and skip on to tomorrow.' She pulled off the slip of paper and scrunched it up. 'Alcohol is never the answer.'

'What's with the quotes, Mam? It's not very you.'

'Nothing wrong with a few motivational words. Although I ehm, I got it for the drawings – really, and it was reduced with it being the Summer…' Mam busied herself around the kitchen, re-filling the tea and sugar canisters, even opening up the un-used coffee and giving the loose grains at the bottom a shake. I had a feeling the calendar was more for my benefit than hers.

'Oh, and the quotes are written in Chinese too, see.' Mam flicked through the pages.

'Well, that's handy, isn't it, Sammie.' Dad shook his head.

We heard a key turn in the front door.

'What in the name of jaysus have you done to your lips, Tasha?' Dad's attention turned to my sister when she walked in.

'What?' Tasha touched her top lip with her fingertip.

I raised an eyebrow and Tasha shot me a warning look.

'You look like a feckin' blow up doll.' Dad shook his head. 'I don't know what goes through your head – if aitin.'

'They do look a bit OTT, love,' said Mam. 'You'd want to watch you don't get addicted, like those celebrities.'

'It's not plastic surgery. They're just lip fillers. They'll go down in a couple of days and I'll be fab.'

Dad sighed loudly.

'Has Wayne seen you yet?'

'No, why?'

'I'm just asking,' said Mam, raising her eyebrows.

'It's my face, I can do what I want. Besides, I got them done for free off a girl in work, so at least he can't throw that in my face.'

'I don't think he'll be able to throw anything at your face, it will bounce right back,' said Dad.

I couldn't help but smile and felt bad when Tasha eyeballed me, like I'd broken a sister code. It was her fault I was sitting there, listening to their stupid conversation and cheesy quotes. I was meant to be watching the kids because Mam had to bring Aunt Carol to the hospital and Dad was driving them. Turns out Aunt Carol had wind, not a hernia, and they didn't need to go to A&E after all. Tasha had forgotten to call me back to say I wasn't needed, after I'd already rushed over.

'Did you see the hideous water feature in Breda Byrne's garden?' asked Mam, looking at me.

'It's kind of hard to miss.'

'She had to run an extension lead in through her front window.' Mum shook her head. 'It's a feckin' eyesore, and she

151

won't be able to keep up with the cost of it. She's forever topping up her meter as it is with the girl's sunbeds.'

'Is it not for charity?' I asked, remembering I saw a sign for something or other, stuck to the front of it.

'She wants people to throw money into the fountain and she'll fish it out at the end of each week. She's donating it all to St Helen's nursing home.'

'Like a down payment,' Dad joked.

'She's an attention seeker, is what she is, Gerry.'

'You should get one too, Mam,' said Tasha. 'A water feature would be lovely in the garden, maybe with a few little fish?' Tasha bit her lip, not to laugh. 'The kids would love it.'

Mam pursed her lips, like she was contemplating it. 'No, sure I wouldn't know where to even look for one – not that I'd copy Breda anyway, but she got hers off the back of a lorry.'

'I think Wayne's uncle was selling one a while back, a big cherub having a wee,' said Tasha, egging her on.

I kept looking at Tasha from the corner of my eye. She didn't look like someone who was guilt ridden for kissing another man. If anything, she looked happier.

'Don't even think about it, Lil,' said Dad. 'And you stop your messing, Tasha.'

'You'd have to ask him yourself though, Mam. I'm not talking to him.'

This seemed to bring Mam back down to earth and I saw a flicker of worry cross her eyes. Before she could say anything there was a knock on the front door.

Dad got up to answer it and walked back into the kitchen followed by Wayne.

'I thought you were working late,' said Tasha, any trace of happiness dissipating from her.

'I was but we finished early. My gym gear is in your boot, so I was just stopping by to get the key.'

'Ahem … gym.' Dad fake coughed into his hand.

'Wayne likes to sit in a Jacuzzi three nights a week for an hour and pretend he's working out.'

'Of course I work out.' Wayne grabbed a handful of belly. 'I'd be much bigger than this if I didn't go to the gym.'

'You should have rung to say you were finished. You knew Mam had the kids. I raced here from work so they'd be in their own house for bedtime.'

Wayne glanced at the clock. 'You're hardly going to be home for bedtime now.'

Tasha's face flashed with colour, and I knew she was trying her best to keep calm with us all watching. 'What time will you be home at?'

Wayne shrugged. 'It's open late tonight.'

Tasha picked up her handbag and threw him the keys.

'How did he not notice your lips?' Mam whispered to Tasha, after Wayne had walked out.

'Because he's too worried about keeping his mates waiting at the gym to notice anything. But I'm sure he'll notice them later and will have something to say about it. I don't care though. I don't give a fuck what he says anymore.'

Mam looked at me, her eyes wide.

Wayne shouted in to say he was leaving the keys on the hall table. It hadn't gone un-noticed, that he'd never stepped foot in the living room where Finn and Aria were watching TV, even though he wouldn't be home until after their bedtime.

'I'm going home,' said Tasha, bringing her cup to the sink.

'Tasha …' Mam put her hand out to touch her arm.

Tasha shrugged her off. 'I'm fine, Mam, I've got to get the kids sorted for bed. I'll give you a ring tomorrow. Sammie.' She gave me a quick hug and was gone.

'Will I heat up your dinner, Gerard?' Mam ripped the tinfoil from the plate and threw it in the microwave before he answered. She wiped her eyes with the back of her hand.

'Lil, will you get it together for god's sake.'

'Mam, are you alright?' I asked.

'I'm fine, love,' she smiled at me, her eyes red rimmed. 'It's the onion gravy, it's like acid.' She sniffed and Dad sighed.

I have to say it was little weird not to be the cause of Mam's worry. It had become my place in the house for the past four months, now it was Tasha's turn. I think they'd forgotten I was even there as they discussed my sister's relationship.

'I don't know what to be telling her anymore, Gerry. If it's not meant to be for them, it's not meant to be.' Mam sat down next to Dad as he ate his dinner. She knew she had him trapped, having a conversation he'd rather avoid. 'Tasha always went for the wayward ones.'

'Hmm.' Dad made an effort to answer, as he filled his mouth

with pork chop.

'Except for young Robert Campbell, he was a lovely kid. Always so polite.'

I felt the heat rise in my face with the mention of his name. I was always a crap liar and I knew if Mam looked at me, my forehead would turn into a billboard with the words 'Tasha kissed Rob' flashing across my head.

'Was Robert there the other night, love?' Mam looked at me.

'Ehm … yeah, I think so, there was loads there.' I tried my best to sound casual and picked up my cup like I hadn't realised it was empty.

'Of course, sure everyone would have shown up for our Conor.' Mam brushed some crumbs off the table, into her hand. And just when I thought she was about to drop the subject, she started up again.

'Why did she have to end up with Wayne, though? We should have put our foot down in the beginning Gerry and told her to steer clear … But then of course, we wouldn't have little Aria and Finn.'

'We'd still have gotten them, just they'd have a decent father, and possibly more normal names.'

'I wonder if Robert ever married?' said Mam.

I rubbed at a non-existent mark on my hand, pretending I didn't hear her.

'Oh … I don't know.' She let out an exasperated breath. 'It's all just a mess.'

Dad finished his dinner, mopping the last of his gravy up

with a slice of bread. 'It's up to them what they do, Lil, we can't get involved. Whatever will be, will be. We've more important things going on anyway.' Dad glanced at me, but Mam didn't seem to notice. She got up and looked out the kitchen window. It was only a matter of time before she launched into the whole – where did it all go wrong for us? And questioning her mothering, which had nothing to do with anything. I couldn't listen to it all from her perspective, so I quickly made my excuses about having to be somewhere and headed for the door. Dad was right behind me, shouting that he was going for a walk to get some fresh air. I hoped only one of us was lying to her.

When I got home, I saw Jojo from the kitchen window. She was sitting in the tree wearing her denim dress but this time with a pair of grubby trainers. I was surprised at how much this annoyed me. Surely, she had other dresses to wear. If she was my daughter, I'd have her wardrobe bursting with clothes. My head was everywhere, the anger spinning back onto itself. Who was I to judge anyone, let alone Jojo's mother? I needed to mind my own business before I turned into my own.

Chapter 17

I had always been close to Mam growing up. She was a typical Irish mammy, full of love and slightly suffocating. She'd made sure we had all the 'proper' childhood memories – trips to the seaside, days out on the dart. She made our Halloween costumes by hand, spending hours so they'd fit us perfectly. She kept our baby photos in albums filed in chronological order, and we both had a baby box complete with the black stump from our belly button, neatly labelled in a jar. She was never overly strict, but still kept us in line because we didn't want to upset her.

Mam was easily upset and like most things about your parents, they only start to annoy you as you get older and see their character flaws as weaknesses. Mam's was that she had a habit of making everything about herself.

When it came to Conor she couldn't, although I'm sure she milked it at her bereavement support group. But, with me losing my job and Tasha and Wayne on the brink of killing each other or separation, on top of Conor gone, it was all too much for Mam.

Each time she rang now, it was to discuss Tasha and Wayne. I was glad to be off her radar, but the analysing was tiring, especially when I didn't have the answers. By the end of her last phone call, I was so tempted to say 'Aren't they lucky neither of them is dead?' just to shut her up, and – if I was totally honest – to be a bitch. Of course, I didn't really think this, but Mam had that effect on me. Her phone calls wore me down. They used to be about old neighbours sick or dying, most of whom I didn't know. She would drag the story out for as long as possible with lots of pauses for effect.

Even Tasha was starting to bug me. She sounded distant on the phone, and I knew she had a lot going on, which was why I wanted her to drop the whole job-hunting conversation. It seemed to make her feel better, like it was her way of fixing my life and ignoring the new mess that was her own.

It was five weeks to our wedding anniversary, which I'd accidently calculated from the date popping up on my laptop. I tried my best not to think that we would have been two years married, and what had been the best day of our lives, would forever be a thorn in the calendar. Our vision board now lay in the back of Conor's wardrobe like a skeleton.

Tasha had taken on the job of sorting through Conor's wardrobe after he died, leaving me with a couple of hoodies, football jerseys and his wedding suit. On the top shelf were his books on being successful by Jack Canfield and the likes, and his special rock – another one of my stupid ideas.

Conor had that rock lodged in his jean pocket every day, insisting it brought him luck. He would rub it like a child with a lucky marble, and I remember thinking he had the whole 'Secret' thing down to a fine art, moving mountains from Artane. He never washed his jeans, wearing them for months on end, until they smelt of wet dog. Tasha never commented on the vision board or any of Conor's things. There wasn't a lot to make fun of, now he was gone.

It had been a full week without human contact – aka my family, and I was feeling better for it. Jojo was climbing into the tree when I pulled open the sliding door and stepped onto the decking. I was happy to see a smiley face, one that wouldn't ask me about my progress on the job front or draw me into a discussion on the Tasha and Wayne saga. I was also going to return the favour and mind my own business about the fact that Jojo was wearing an off-white dress that looked two sizes too small.

The sun was everywhere, squeezing through branches and between furniture. I sat back into the chair, sliding my feet out of my sandals. The ice cubes in my drink had already melted, now two white pips bobbing along the top of the wine glass.

'I think you need to water your plants,' said Jojo, as I stared into the glass.

'Really?' I asked, pushing my sunglasses up to have a look.

The flowers looked okay, not droopy or off colour, but then again what did I know? I could wake up tomorrow and all Conor's hard work could be shrivelled up and gone. I felt an unexpected panic at the thought and stood up.

'I never even thought about watering them. Do you think they'll be okay?' It didn't occur to me that I was asking a kid, waiting for her answer like it was gospel.

'Yeah, it's been raining … but still, they need to be watered.'

I chewed my lip looking around, feeling stupid. I heard Celine's flip flops slap across her decking, drifting down the garden before rustling on the grass. I was tempted to shout over and ask if she had a loan of a watering can.

'There's a hose behind you,' said Jojo, reading my mind.

I turned around to look. 'Oh, yeah,' I said, as I unwound it from the wall. The tap was stiff and wouldn't budge.

'Put a bit of muscle into it,' said Jojo.

'I'm trying.' I twisted harder, feeling the burn in my palm, the water choked and spluttered onto the decking.

'Conor would be so proud.'

I smiled hearing his name, surprised she'd remembered it. 'Conor, if you can hear me, I'm saving your plants,' I said, humouring her. I pulled the hose behind me like a stubborn pet.

I moved around the garden under Jojo's watchful eye, as she pretended to narrate a TV show.

'The plants were gasping, until Sam came along …'

I looked up at her calling me Sam, something only Conor had ever called me. She didn't seem to notice and was instead talking into her hand that was curled into a fist like a microphone.

'… here in Artane, North Dublin, the blooms are being hydrated. Thank the Lord, this woman who was on the brink of being done for plant murder, has saved herself by unleashing – the hose.'

'Hey,' I said, jerking the hose so it splashed the wall underneath her feet. 'Quiet or I'll water you too.' I was laughing, moving backwards towards the decking to reach my drink. I picked up the wine glass and looked up to see a head of mousy brown curls over the wall.

'Hi Sammie,' said Celine, her voice extra chirpy. She looked around the garden and then back at me. I look a sip of the now warm wine, it tasted sour and I threw the rest into the grass.

'I was just ehm …' She looked up at John, who was presumably at their back-bedroom window and waved. 'I was just wondering if you'd like to pop in for a coffee … if you wanted, if you're not busy?'

'Thanks, Celine, but maybe another time. We're just busy watering the plants here. I'm being accused of plant murder and all sorts.' I pretended to splash Jojo again, who stuck out her tongue.

Celine looked from me to Jojo. 'Oh … well … okay. If you're sure? You know where we are if you need anything or just want to chat.'

'Okay, thanks, Celine.'

'Now, where were we?' I turned back to Jojo.

'The little yellow guys over there.' She pointed to the corner.

'Yes, Conor's morning glory.' I laughed again, realising what I'd just said. Thankfully it was lost on her.

Celine's head disappeared behind the wall.

There was something therapeutic about watering flowers. As I moved around the garden making sure not to miss anything, I felt a sense of satisfaction. I held the hose on each flower, watching the petals bend under the spray of water and the leaves bounce back a shade brighter.

'As you can see, people, the garden has been saved thanks to Jojo Swan, not so much Sammie.' Jojo was talking into her fist again.

'Is your surname Swan? That's really nice.'

'Yeah, what's yours?'

'Clancy, well Clancy-Keegan.'

'Okay, yours not so much.'

I was about to make a joke about her real name being Jennifer, but she jumped down saying she had to go.

I moved towards the rockery, spraying the stones as well as the plants. I even gave the gnomes and bird house a quick shower. Lastly, I washed the decking, knowing instinctively it's something Conor would have done. For a moment, standing there on the decking with the hose now trickling at my feet, I thought I could smell him. Conor's musky smell. It was just for a split second but enough for me to notice, for my senses to come alive with the familiarity.

That evening I looked out my back-bedroom window to check on the plants, thinking an aerial view would give me even more job satisfaction. I didn't know what I was expecting, having only watered them once. I noticed Jojo's parents in their kitchen. Her mam was taller than I expected, making her dad look even bigger as he towered over her. He was standing with his back to the dining table and her mam was beside the sink. The outside wall between them, made it look like two TV screens side by side. They were talking, their gestures wide and animated. I found myself leaning closer to the glass, my elbows resting on the windowsill as I watched them, hoping for a clue into the family.

Jojo's dad started to point, jabbing the air with his finger, her mam was throwing her hands up by her sides. I suddenly felt uncomfortable. My eyes scanned the upstairs windows for Jojo or her sister. Everywhere else looked calm and still, a complete contrast to the scene downstairs. Her dad was shouting now, it was like watching a movie with the sound turned off. I could imagine the spit landing on his lip as I saw him swipe his hand across his mouth. I knew I shouldn't have been watching. It was wrong spying on a couple in their own home, but I couldn't look away. Jojo's mam was standing beside the sink, frozen. Anger built up in my stomach as I watched him throw words at her, that had her shrink into herself, like they were physically hurting. He was pacing forward, still shouting, like a dog trying to break free from a leash. Then he broke, disappearing behind the wall. Her face was in her hands and she was crying, her shoulders heaving up and down. I couldn't see anymore of him, only a flash of colour as he stormed out of the kitchen. Alone now at the sink, she was splashing water onto her face and dabbing it with a scrunched-up tea towel. I turned away, feeling more guilty at watching this than the argument itself.

Chapter 18

'What's your favourite food?' asked Jojo, as the smell of charcoal-grilled chicken snaked around us from a nearby barbeque. I had been sitting in my garden for a while now, waiting for Jojo to come so I could ask her about her parents. I had played with the words in my head – do your parents ever fight … because I've a funny story about mine. Or is your dad scary sometimes, adding a joke about my own. I sipped on my wine replaying what I'd say for the tenth time. I knew it was normal for couples to fight, but it was the sight of her mam that was making me uneasy. Now that Jojo was in front of me, I didn't know how to bring them up. It didn't help that she was in great form and I couldn't shut her up talking.

'My favourite food was Gran's coddle. I want to be a vegan now. I looked it up and it's totally the new way forward.'

'Is it? Would your parents let you be vegan?' Jojo shrugged. 'Are your parents good cooks?'

'My gran was the best, she taught me lots.'

I wished my own nana had taught me her conversational skills. Nana Margo had a way of asking questions that didn't come across as intrusive yet told her everything she wanted to know within about five minutes. Her words were like salt drawing out your inner secrets, without you even realising.

'Well … what's your favourite food, Sammie?'

'Cod and chips.' I answered with the first thing that came into my head. Food wasn't part of my life anymore. I ate merely to stop myself from feeling nauseous, which usually had the opposite effect.

'I'm allergic to fish. I get that from my real dad.'

'Your real dad?'

Jojo nodded. 'It's not the only thing I get from him. Seemingly.'

'So, you have a stepdad?'

'Yeah.'

'So, the dad you live with is not your real dad?' I knew I was repeating myself.

'He's still my dad.' There was a bang, making Jojo jump and turn around. I hoped for both our sakes that wasn't him standing behind her.

'Leo is just my dad, not step-dad, that's not a good word. It can hurt feelings.' Jojo picked at her thumbnail.

'Oh, okay. I'm really sorry.' I took a mouthful of wine, needing it.

'A dad is the person who raises you … Who works hard to give you things and I'm very lucky to have him.' She sounded so rehearsed, echoing adult's language, that all I could do was nod and agree. 'I've never seen my other dad – my real dad – and I don't want to. We're just strangers.'

She didn't look sad saying this; it was just like she was stating facts. 'When did your mam and stepdad – sorry I mean your dad – meet?'

'I was only little, like two or something. He took us on.'

'I bet he feels very lucky to have a special daughter like you.'

Jojo scrunched up her nose and looked at me like I was mad. 'I know he feels lucky to not have any allergies, that's for sure. He likes to joke that he's Ironman.'

I held my tongue, not wanting to add that last night he looked more like a bully than a superhero.

'Anyway, I don't think I'd like fish even if I wasn't allergic.' Jojo widened her eyes, sucking her cheeks in to mimic a fish. 'Can you do it?' She was making plopping sounds.

I opened and closed my mouth, accidentally dribbling wine down my chin. And just like that we were back in a world where neither of us had any problems.

Jojo spent the rest of the afternoon chatting about food and she gave me a step-by-step talk on how to make the perfect Knickerbocker Glory, by the end I could almost taste the vanilla ice-cream on my tongue.

By the time I was going inside, I felt hungry. Not belly rumbling hungry but enough that maybe I could face something other than toast. I opened my kitchen cabinets which even though I hadn't been proper food shopping in God knows how long, still had the makings of something. My brain wasn't sharp enough to pull a meal together, so I stood staring, waiting, for some inspiration to jump at me.

Conor had decided to start eating healthier last year. Ironically. Lined up in neat rows were tinned tomatoes, sweetcorn, chickpeas, stock cubes and bags of both brown and white pasta. I'd told him he'd never eat brown pasta and I'd been right. The bag now sat plump in the press as a reminder of how well we'd known each other.

Eventually, I settled on having normal pasta. I ripped open the bag and boiled the kettle. I didn't think pots could get dusty, but mine were covered in a thin layer of grey grime, proof of their neglect. I salted the water and poured in the pasta spirals, stirring the water as it clouded. I turned to fill up my glass, but there was only a drop of wine left in the end of the bottle. I'd have to get more in the shop later and maybe some more food to stock up the presses.

A watched pot never boils, was a quote I remembered from Nana Margo growing up, even though it was more of saying then a quote. She loved throwing it out there if we were being impatient. Of course, it was a load of shite like all quotes and mantras – I'd just put it to the test. And it does – it boils anyway. I'd literally stood watching each bubble rise to the top.

Finally, having practically given myself a facial standing over the steam of the pot, I drained the creamy water down the sink. I shook the pot, tossing the pasta around and filled a bowl. I took out the butter, scooping a knob over the top, and watched as it dribbled golden between the spirals. I think I may have even licked my lips.

I filled a glass of water and sat down at the kitchen table. It felt strange sitting down to eat something other than toast. Before I

167

knew it, the bowl was empty, and I had just rinsed it off and put it in the dishwasher when the phone rang.

'Is Tasha with you?' asked Mam, her voice breathless.

'No, at least I don't think so.' I half laughed, accidentally hitting the glass of water off the phone. 'Shit.' The water splashed onto my lap.

'Are you drinking, Sammie?'

'No, well yeah … water. I made pasta. I ate a full bowl.' I sounded like a proud child telling Mam what I'd made in school.

'You shouldn't be drinking on your own.'

'I had a couple glasses of wine earlier in the garden, anyway it's Friday,' I said, feeling myself getting defensive.

'It's only a quarter past six.'

'What's up with Tasha?' I asked, changing the subject.

'She's missing. She said she was in work, but she left her phone here in Aria's baby bag and the salon called asking her to come in for an hour. I rang Wayne and he thought she was working too.'

'She's hardly missing, Mam. Maybe you misheard her and she has an appointment or something. Was she wearing her work uniform?'

'Yes … I think so, or actually, no, she wasn't. Oh, she was, Sammie, she was.' I could almost hear the wiring in Mam's brain buzzing around, coming up with all sorts. 'Will I go to the Guards?'

'No, she'll be –'

'Oh wait, there's a key in the door. Tasha is that you?' Mam yelled. 'It's her, Sammie – panic over. And where have you been

Natasha Clancy, because you weren't in work?' I could hear Tasha's voice muffled in the background. 'You were getting Wayne's birthday present?' Mam's voice softened. 'Did you hear that, Sammie? She was getting Wayne's birthday present.' I could imagine the smile spreading across Mam's face. The world was okay again.

'Yes, I heard her, Mam. Right, I'm going now.'

'Okay love, sorry for disturbing you. And what did you get him …?' I heard her asking Tasha as she hung up the phone.

I was walking home from the shop, having picked up milk and a couple of bottles of wine that were on offer. I was contemplating ringing Tasha, not really wanting to, but thinking I probably should. I knew she hadn't been out shopping for Wayne's birthday, unless it was a guilt present. An *I'm sorry I kissed someone else* present. She'd been buying Wayne a Chelsea jersey for as long as I could remember, but then again, maybe this year she'd spoil him. I was getting better at deluding myself.

I turned past the curved hedging onto my road, switching my shopping bag to the other hand, and giving my numb fingers a wriggle. When I looked up, I saw my neighbour, the one who'd had the baby before Christmas. The baby looked huge in his pram reminding me that time was still moving on. I tried to quickly think of her name – was it Laura? She looked like a Laura, but I wasn't sure enough to use it.

She looked up, catching my eye, before quickly fiddling with a strap on the side of the pram. If there was a thought bubble over

169

her head, it would read 'Shit, should I cross over?'

I smiled at the baby, who was impressively shoving a whole rusk into his mouth. 'He's gorgeous,' I said, bending down to him. The two bottles of wine clanked together despite being wrapped in paper bags, making him stop chewing and look at me.

'Thanks. He's going mad with his teeth.'

She was even prettier up close with caramel eyes and long black hair that made me want to grow mine immediately. We both stood looking at the baby, while he babbled away with the attention. It was a little awkward seeing as I'd never properly spoken to her before, and I wondered why I'd stopped at all.

'How have you been keeping?' she asked, her voice soft, like a sad song. 'It must be so hard. I can't even imagine.'

I could feel the pity radiating from her. 'I'm good.' I smiled; my jaw clenched. 'I don't miss the mess that's for sure.' My stomach turned at my sad attempt of a joke. Why did I say that? I could feel the panic, my heart fluttering, warning me to say something quick to try and fix it. I wanted to say I didn't mean it. That it was just one of those stupid things you say, to make things less awkward, instead making them worse. I wanted to tell her that even looking at her with her baby, in a house the mirror image of mine, with a husband ... that it rips at my heart. That it makes me think for a second, why me and not her?

Instead, I smiled at the baby and she bent down to him, making a big deal of taking his hands from his mouth as he grunted in protest.

'If you ever need anything –' She looked at me.

'Yeah sure, thanks.'

Back at home, I kept replaying our conversation in my head. I worried what she'd think of me and then berate myself for caring. I opened the wine, each glass dissolving my fear a little more.

It was the middle of the night and I woke to a scream. A muffled scream that sounded both near and far away. I sat up, disoriented, my hair stuck to my neck. Had it come from out the back? I jumped out of bed and ran out to my landing. My ears were ringing now, having moved my body quicker than my brain. I could hear nothing, only the tinny sound inside my head. I went into my back bedroom where my window was lit by an artificial whiteness. My mouth was so dry, it hurt to swallow. Slowly, I drew the blind, afraid to be seen or of what I'd see. The light was from the security light at Jojo's house that switched off as soon as I looked out, plunging the garden into darkness. Everything was still. I was shaking now, rubbing my arms despite the balmy night. I felt I was being watched. Something moving in the tree caught my eye and I leaned closer to see. Two eyes glared at me, shiny green, before shooting further up the tree. My heart sprung into my mouth, bringing a taste of stale wine. The cat jumped from the tree to the wall and I felt my breath steady.

I walked into the bathroom and splashed water on my face. I looked into the mirror, patting my face dry with the hand towel. The image of Jojo's mam with the tea-towel flashed into my mind.

The side of my face was creased with the print of my pillow, telling me that I had been in a deep sleep. Could I have been dreaming? Could I have imagined the scream? But something had woken me up. Had I screamed? Had I drunk too much and given myself nightmares? I went downstairs to get a drink of water and opened the fridge to check for clues. There was still a half bottle of wine left, so I mustn't have been that bad. Knowing I would need the help getting back to sleep, I poured a small glass, just enough to help me settle.

Chapter 19

Over the next couple of days, the grass became dotted with dandelions, making the garden look both ugly and pretty, like a cashmere throw in a dowdy colour. I hadn't seen Jojo but found myself sneaking peeks at her house. There had been nothing more than her mam tidying around the kitchen and her sister playing at the dining table. They both looked normal – happy. I hadn't seen Jojo or her dad. With no distractions from Jojo's place, my focus turned back to my own. The grass needed cutting and I was ready to take on the task.

Like the rest of Dublin, I was taking the clear skies for granted and my recent sunny outlook even more so. I was having moments of thinking that maybe I was going to be okay. I was spending hardly any money, expect for a few essentials, so the need to find a job was slipping further from my mind. I was taking each day, hour even, at a time and it seemed to be working.

Pulling open the patio door, I took a slug of water before setting the glass down on the garden table. My throat felt dry and my head a little muzzy. I had been tempted to have 'the hair of the dog' and run around to the shop to buy wine. Tasha and I used to swear by it, swigging bottles of Fat Frog from under our beds after a night out. We'd been in our late teens and of course Mam and Dad had no idea. Mam had a strict alcohol ban in the house, even though Dad insisted that it wasn't necessary. He would joke that even at his worst, he'd never touch our luminous green concoctions. Mam never laughed, nor took the chance.

The shed door was locked and it took me ages to find the key, trying to think where Conor would have put it. I was just about to give up and forget the whole thing when I saw a small, shiny key hanging among the backdoor set.

I'd always been a bit creeped out by sheds and could feel myself stiffening as I opened the door. It swung back and the sharp smell of varnish and paint hit me. Despite the sun outside, the shed was dim. The plastic window filtered a small amount of light, enough to pick up the silvery cobwebs in each corner. It was neat and tidy, and I had a feeling that was more to do with the previous owner than with Conor.

There were outdoor paint pots stacked along the wall: glossy black and buttercream with congealed lumps stuck around the seal. On a shelf above them was a chipped mug, holding a dozen upturned paint brushes and beside it, a couple of golf tees. I picked one up and rolled it between my fingers, looking around at the unfamiliarity of it. It felt nice being somewhere Conor had been, that had never been disturbed.

I spotted the lawn mower in the corner. It was an ancient looking thing that I'd remembered seeing Conor use in the past. He hadn't wanted to buy an electric one, saying a push lawn mower would be a workout for the arms. My heart flipped a little with the memory and I pushed it aside.

I wrestled the lawn mower through the door, untangling a white plastic bag from one of the wheels. I noticed a pot marked 'shed paint' and instinctively picked it up. If cutting the grass went well, then maybe I could re-paint the shed.

The lawn mower was horrific, and I effed and blinded my way through the lawn, hacking at the grass in patchy clumps.

When I'd finally finished, I was exhausted and flopped onto the garden chair. My t-shirt was stuck to my back and I could get a faint whiff of BO. I closed my eyes and let my arms droop by my sides. The sun swirled pinks and oranges behind my lids. My body felt heavy and I could feel myself drifting off. A sharp clap made me jump, flinging my eyes open.

'Jesus, Jojo. You almost gave me a heart attack.' The words lingered on my tongue.

'You missed a bit.' She smiled, but it didn't reach her eyes.

I sat up in the chair to look at her properly. She was wearing the off-white dress that looked uncomfortably tight and her hair had a sheen that was more from grease than the sun. 'Is everything okay?'

'Eh no, the state of your garden.'

'I didn't mean with the garden, Jojo.'

She tugged on her dress and looked away. There were kids playing nearby; the rattle of scooters and skates filled her silence.

'Why are you not playing with your friends?'

She didn't answer, instead she rubbed her hand over her knee like she was brushing something off.

'Do you have many friends on your road?'

'A few.'

'Did you have a falling out?' I couldn't read her today but there was something up. A sadness surrounded her.

'Is everything okay – at home?'

'Yes! why wouldn't it be?'

'Oh, no, nothing I was just …' Worried I'd upset her, I rattled on trying to bring her around. 'I used to fight with my friends all the time. My sister Tasha was the worst. Every week, her and her friends would make up a different club that would always end in a riot. They'd have to keep breaking up and reforming as something else.'

'What kind of clubs did she have?' Jojo asked, not looking up.

'Well, there was the pony club, even though no one in the club had owned or even seen a real-life pony. There was the Sindy club, which Tasha took it upon herself to state was much cooler than Barbie, and then there was the New Kids on the Block club, which she only set up to rival my Backstreet Boys club. They were both American boybands.'

'They sound weird.'

'Well anyways, the point is, it's normal to fight with your friends, but you'll always make up in the end.'

Jojo looked off into the distance like she was mulling this over.

'It's so important to have friends, Jojo, to get out and have fun.' I was trying not to preach knowing I was in no position to.

'Maybe you need some friends?' She gave me a cheeky grin

that lightened the mood. 'So, are you going to start the shed now?' She pointed to the tin of green paint on the decking.

'Go on then, for the laugh.' I hauled myself up out of the chair. If Jojo was fighting with her friends, then I wanted to cheer her up. I knew only too well what it was like to feel alone. 'Did you hear screaming a few nights ago?' The question slipped out as I tilted the paint pot to pick it up. I'd thought of that night a few times since, trying to make sense of it, trying to protect my sanity. 'At least I'm almost certain it came from out here.' I placed the tin of paint down on the grass.

'I'm a really heavy sleeper.'

'Well, I think you'd have heard this. Maybe I had dreamt it, but I don't think so.' I shook my head trying to forget, again.

'I never hear anything. Ever.'

'Oh, okay.'

Five minutes later and I was having my doubts about painting. 'Do you think it's going to rain?' I looked up at the clear sky.

'Nice try,' said Jojo.

'It's this stupid paint pot. I can't get it open. I wedged the knife in again, and twisted it fuelled with frustration.

'Woohoo,' said Jojo, as the lid popped up.

'It doesn't look the best.' I stirred the paint with the end of the knife. Eventually it settled into a decent consistency, leaving me with no choice but to get on with it.

'Do you want to help?' I asked Jojo. I dipped the brush into the paint and wiped the excess off the side. I started on the door, using small strokes, careful not to paint over the latch. 'You could ask your mam, and just throw an old top over you're dress?'

'No, it's okay.

'Are you sure?' I walked down the garden towards her, holding the paintbrush. 'I can wait while you ask.'

'I said no, Sammie.' Jojo leaned back, moving out of the shadow from the branch above her.

'Jojo. Your face!'

She put her hand to her cheek. 'It's nothing.'

'Let me see – what happened?' She moved again and the bruising was clearer. A half-moon of purple under her cheekbone.'

'I got a slap.'

I gasped, putting my hand over my mouth.

She laughed. 'From a branch – it swung back on me. Did you actually think someone hit me? You're mad.'

'Jojo –.'

'Imagining hearing screams in the night and then, like, child abuse. Cuckoo.' Jojo rolled her eyes and pointed behind me.

I turned to follow her finger, which was pointing to the empty wine bottles lined-up along my back wall.

'Will we count them? One bottle, two bottle, three bottle four … five bot–'

'Jojo, c'mon. What's with you today?'

'I'm only joking. Sorry … It looks bad, doesn't it?' She tilted her head to show her cheek, but it's nothing. Pinkie promise, nobody hit me.' She waved her little finger in the air.

My toes felt wet and I looked down where the paint brush

was dripping green onto my foot.

'Uh oh, you definitely didn't dream that.' Jojo laughed.

I laughed along too, feeling humiliated.

'Why were you going to paint your shed?' asked Tasha again, as I scraped the last of the green paint from my nails. 'Could you not have asked Dad to do it?'

'I wanted to do it, Tasha.' I was already tired of explaining myself. My head was still spinning after Jojo and, as much as I enjoyed her company, she was making me feel unnerved. 'What did you call for anyway? Do you need me to mind the kids or something?'

'No.' Her voice went up a few octaves, and I knew I'd annoyed her. 'I was ringing to see if you're okay. No one's heard from you, and I was reading this thing on delayed depression after bereavement, and –'

'I'm okay, Tasha.' I cut her off. 'I'm enjoying pottering around the garden.'

'Oh god, you sound like Mam – or worse, Nana Margo.'

'Whatever.' I changed the phone to my other ear. 'Anyway, there's a kid who lives in the house behind mine. Her name's Jojo; she's hilarious.' I left out the other stuff, feeling a loyalty to her. 'We've been chatting, and I've just been enjoying a couple of glasses of wine and the weather and that.'

'I hate other people's kids. I go mad when the kids next door pop their heads over our wall.'

'Well, it beats listening to Mam harp on at me about

counselling, or getting a job, or you and bloody Wayne.' The last bit fell out.

Tasha sighed, making me feel bad. 'I'm so sorry, Sammie. I know I've put you in some awkward situations recently.' I heard a buzzer in the background. 'Hold on a sec.' Tasha's voice was muffled. 'Mrs Jenkins, hi. Just take a seat and I'll be with you. I have to go here, Sammie, but I'll chat to you later.'

'Fine,' I said, glad she'd been distracted.

'Just don't close yourself off too much. We're all here for you,' she whispered, unable to resist a final speech before hanging up the phone.

Chapter 20

I held back the curtain just enough so I could watch him. Jojo's stepdad was dressed smartly, in a white shirt and slacks, making me judge him thinking of Jojo in her grubby dress. After five minutes, I'd noticed that he had the same pattern. His phone would light up and he'd hunch over the table, both hands gripping the screen, so that I wondered how he could actually see it. He would then type with both thumbs at an impressive speed. Seconds later, the phone would light up again, he'd fold himself closer over the screen, before punching out another message and so it continued. There was a cup of dark liquid, presumably coffee, beside him on the table, untouched.

I had been staring so long that when he jumped, I jumped too, dropping my phone onto the floor. He flipped his phone face down onto the table. I bent down to pick my one up and looked back to see Jojo's mam now in the kitchen. She turned to open a cupboard and he quickly shoved the phone into his back pocket, before folding his arms across his chest, making him look both aggressive and nervous.

Maybe he was having an affair and she suspected it, driving herself insane with paranoia. Or maybe he was involved in the criminal world and took his anxieties out on his family. I thought of the bruise on Jojo's face, the suspicion alone making my stomach clench.

At that moment, Millie ran in waving a page like a peace flag. It was enough to have her scooped up into the air and tickled by her dad. He held the drawing up, a burst of bright colours, that seemed to diffuse whatever had been brewing. From the side she was his double, her face a smaller, more delicate version of her dad's. He looked like any doting father as he sat down with her on his knee. It was a heart-warming sight, making me want to ignore the fact that I'd never seen Millie in the same clothes twice.

I took a long sip of wine, enjoying the coolness of it compared to the compressed heat in the garden. I was waiting for Jojo, eager to find out more about her stepdad. I was drinking purposely, telling myself I wouldn't usually have one so early, only I was proving a point to this kid. I wouldn't be shamed in my own garden. Although I did take a trip to the bottle bank that morning, but it was more to do with keeping the garden tidy. And the smell. The stench of stale wine in this heat would be enough to turn some people off.

'Hi Sammie,' said Jojo holding a lollipop in her hand. She rolled the stick between her fingers, watching the red glassy ball twist, before taking a big suck. She seemed relaxed, making me relax as I sipped my wine watching her.

'Have you done any fun things this summer?'

Jojo pulled the lolly out of her mouth making a loud pop, she laughed, reminding me she was just a child. 'We haven't done much but I'm sure we will. Dad usually brings us to Bray before school starts back. He's a bus driver, so we get free travel.'

'A bus driver?' I don't know why this surprised me.

'Yeah. He has a jar of coins that he saves in all year; he gives it to us for the slot machines. I've never won anything, but Millie got two teddies last time.'

'Your dad sounds nice,' I said, a little too eagerly, making Jojo raise her eyebrows at me, confused. I smiled, noticing the hue of yellow on her cheek where the bruising had faded. I wanted to ask her if it hurt.

We fell into silence and I sipped on my wine, making the questions about her stepdad slip further down my throat.

'Like my lipstick?' asked Jojo after a few minutes. She pouted her red stained lips. 'Am I gorgeous?'

'Gorgeous.' I laughed as she blew air kisses.

Jojo had a way of distracting me and before I knew it, I'd agreed to another DIY project.

We had got talking about hobbies and I'd told her about my interior design course, how I used to love the idea of doing up pieces of furniture and my dream of putting them into rooms that I'd designed. Her questions filled me with an enthusiasm that managed to stay with me longer than our conversation. I woke up early the following morning, eager to get started and show Jojo how easy it was to turn something old and worn, into something beautiful again.

Outside, I lay an old sheet over the freshly cut grass. The smell of the grass came up to greet me, reminding me of my favourite scented candle, which had been our bestseller in Haven. I took out the chalk paint and wax, which had been given to me by a friend of Dionne's to try out, and I couldn't help but think of her and the shop. I pushed down the sadness threatening to spoil my good mood and moved more quickly, going over each step in my head.

The hall table was light and easy to carry. I tilted it back, so the drawer wouldn't slip out onto the grass. I had bought it a couple of years ago, taking it from our old apartment to the house, with the intention of doing it up. It had a half-moon top with dainty legs that splayed out at the bottom. It would have been perfect, except for the bland oak colour and dated brass drawer handle. I gave it a quick wipe over with a cloth, when an exaggerated fake cough made me jump.

'I can't believe you started without me. How sneaky …' Jojo narrowed her eyes and I couldn't quite make out if she was serious. 'Why's the paint pot upside down?' Jojo pointed to the pot on the grass.

'It's chalk paint; it's used for painting straight onto wood. It needs to mix really well, so you're meant to put it upside down for ten minutes.' I turned the pot over and flipped up the lid.

'Chalk paint sounds cool but the colour's a bit boring.' Jojo watched as I stirred the taupe-coloured paint, trying to get a smooth consistency.

'You should have got a darker one, like proper purple.'

I applied the first coat, knowing she'd be impressed with the silver stencilling later on, if I could still manage to do it. The paint sank into the knots and grooves in the wood, enhancing the shape of the table. My tummy fizzed with the anticipation of seeing something old come to life again.

'Why don't you get people to give you their old furniture and you can do them up?'

'So many people are doing that already,' I said, angling the brush sideways to get the lip of the table.

'But you could do it better.'

'I doubt it. You have to paint in the direction of the grain – that's the trick. See?'

Jojo held her hand up and pretended to jot notes on her palm.

I dipped the brush into the paint and started on the legs, twisting the bristles to fit into each nook.

'It looks easy.' Jojo rested her elbows on her knees, watching me. 'Is that all you have to do?'

'It has to dry overnight before I can apply the wax.' I stopped to examine where I'd missed. 'That wax gives it its shine and protects it. I looked up at the pink tinged sky. 'I think it will be nice tomorrow, I'll get it finished then.'

Although I was enjoying Jojo's company, I felt guilty knowing she should be with kids her own age instead of hanging out with me. The local green was always full, so there was no shortage of them in the area. I tried broaching the subject again, but it just made her go quiet, and then say she was going in shortly after. Maybe she wasn't allowed leave her garden, which would be weird for her age, surely?

Back inside, I'd made myself a sandwich and was tipping the last of a packet of crisps into my mouth when my phone rang.

'What are you up to?' asked Mam, her voice accusing.

I took a second to answer, swallowing down a sharp crumb.
'I'm just out in the garden, well I was, I'm just waiting for the – hey,
get off …' I shouted, banging the glass at a magpie that landed on
the table. 'Stupid birds … what were you saying?' I banged the glass
again, sliding the door open not listening to Mam.

'Samantha.' Mam's voice was stern.

'Sorry, what?' I went back into the kitchen, bringing my
plate to the sink.

'I never thought I'd say this, but have you not had enough
fresh air? You're in that feckin' garden morning, noon and night.'

'I was painting a table and I'm just waiting for it to dry. I'm
trying to keep busy.'

'A table in the garden, like the garden table?'

'No, a hall table. I'm upcycling.'

'Upcycling? I never heard of it, is it a type of tool?' Mam
sounded confused.

'No, it's revamping old stuff. I better go finish it off, I'll ring
you later,' I said, knowing I had no intention of it.

'Would you not give Lydia a ring?' Mam cut me off. 'See if
she has anything for you?'

'She would have rung.'

'Well, she is a blood relative of Wayne, so there's a good
chance she could have gotten the sack and you're waiting around for
a call from her.'

'I'm not waiting around, I'm in the garden.'

'Look, love, you do sound nice and relaxed which I hope is
from the sun and not a liquid sedative, but still, you don't want to be

going into yourself. You don't want to end up like Aunt Winnie.'

'That's a bit harsh.'

'I just mean –'

'You don't want me to turn into a mad widow.'

'Your Aunt Winnie isn't mad. It's just … she's very introverted, would be the word.'

'She's completely nuts, Mam. And it's all since Uncle Ed died. Well, do you know what? I actually have great empathy for her. I can see how losing your soul mate could make someone crazy.'

'Oh, Sammie, I'm sorry love.' Mam's voice wobbled.

'No, I'm sorry. I know you didn't mean it like that.'

'It's just for yourself, love. I worry. I don't mean to underestimate what you're going through.'

'Nana, I'm hungry.' I heard Finn in the background.

'Hang on a minute, pet,' said Mam.

'Can I have a biscuit, Nana, pleeeeeease.'

There was rustling on the other end of the phone.

'Can I have them all?'

'Don't tell your mammy, now go back in and watch the cartoons. Nana be into you in a minute.'

'Did you just give Finn a whole packet of biscuits?'

'There was only half the packet left. Poor mite, he can sense something is up between Tasha and Wayne.'

I looked out the window and there were now two magpies perched on my table and nothing joyful about it. 'Mam, I have to go.' I jumped up, running to the back the door. I stamped my foot on the decking, hanging up on Mam mid-sentence.

The table dried much quicker than I'd expected. I was excited to see it finished, and I got stuck into the stencilling straight away. I placed the swirly patterned stencil along the lip of the table, carefully lining it up straight. Dipping the tip of the brush into the silver paint, I filled in each design, holding my hand as steady as I could. I continued all the way along, feeling my breath settle as I neared the end.

I took the stencil away and couldn't help smiling at my work. I was excited for Jojo to see it. I decided to wait to screw on the new handle, so she could feel part of the finished product. I poured myself a drink and waited for the stencil to dry.

I'd forgotten how rewarding it felt being creative. I imagined a room it would suit – the narrow hall of a Georgian house, with a vase of lilies and a cream vintage phone sitting on top. The more I looked at it, the more I knew it wouldn't suit my hall.

'That's so nice,' said Jojo, admiring the table.

'Do you want to put the handle on?' I held up the crystal ball, which twinkled catching the sunlight.

'No, I want to be surprised.' She put her hands over her eyes.

You'd think I was Picasso with the way we were going on, but Jojo's enthusiasm was infectious and I was surprisingly proud of my small achievement. 'Ta dah,' I said, placing my wine glass on top of the table. 'See, it works.'

'And it doesn't even look granny bangery.'

'Coming from you, Jojo, that's a real compliment.'

I'd decided to put the table into the back bedroom until I found a home for it. No longer distracted by DIY, my mind drifted back to Jojo's family. I walked over to the window, desperately wanting to see her with her parents. To see her with the stepdad she'd described, instead of the man I saw through the window. There was a TV flickering from the top corner above the dining table, kiddie cartoons, that had Millie bouncing around the kitchen. She was twirling, her arms wide, with a carefree look that I'd never seen in Jojo.

Chapter 21

'Just set out the chairs willy-nilly, love, in a sort of semi-circle. Nothing too formal,' said Breda Byrne, dragging a blue plastic chair behind her. Mam was busy talking to a lady called Anna at the top of the room, who she spoke to in whispers, their heads almost touching as they peered into a folder. I was still trying to figure out what it was I was doing there.

Mam had called me that morning in a flap about a group she was helping Fr Brennan to organise in the local Community Centre. She was sketchy about the details but seemingly, Mary Hennessey had let her and Breda down with the organising, and it was of most importance that this group went ahead. So far, all I'd done was stack plastic cups beside the coffee and teapots, and put iced buns and bourbon biscuits out onto plates – well, saucers actually, which meant I needed ten, making the table look like it was set for a child's birthday party.

It was almost six, and I was beginning to wonder if anybody would come. The last time I'd helped Mam in the Community Centre was for a charity bingo night a couple of years back, to help raise money for the local meals on wheels. It had been packed to the rafters with people queueing outside to get in. It felt nothing like this.

At six on the dot, people began to trickle through the door. Nine to be exact (in case Mam asked me for numbers). I had been that long out of work, I was surprisingly keen to be constructive among the public and found myself smiling, gesturing to the empty chairs as they walked in. When everyone was seated, I tried to catch Mam's eye to let her know I was going and needed my car keys, which she'd insisted on keeping 'safe' in her handbag. An old lady's purse had been robbed from the reception three years prior and this was still a cause for immense caution among Mam and her friends when it came to personal belongings. The local Tesco had to order in bum bags specially, to keep up with the demand at the time.

Mam was still having an in-depth conversation with this Anna lady, and I decided to wait it out, rather than have her scold me for interrupting. Surprisingly, she still had that hold over me, the fear of being embarrassed in front of a stranger with a lecture on manners.

I sat down on a chair nearest the door so she could easily spot me. There was a real mixed bag of people in the hall. An elderly man was sitting beside a teenager with a baseball cap. A woman around my age fiddled anxiously with the strap of her handbag, while the blonde woman nearest me, flicked through a Filofax on her lap. There was no clue from looking at them of what sort of group or charity it could be.

'Welcome everyone and thank you so much for coming today.' I looked up at the front of the hall, Anna was speaking and there was no sign of Mam.

'My name is Anna and I'm a trained bereavement counsellor

...' I didn't hear anymore. I stood up. I was fuming. I swear there was smoke billowing from my ears, thick black clouds of it, as I scanned the room looking for Mam. She appeared beside me, pressing a hot cup of coffee into my hand.

'You may as well sit in for a few minutes.'

'You set me up, Mam,' I hissed, through clenched teeth. A couple of people looked around and Anna gave Mam a 'it's okay, take a moment' sort of look.

'I swear on your Nana Margo's grave, Sammie, I didn't set you up. I planned on you being gone by the time everyone got here, just Anna kept me talking.' I sat back down, my anger simmering to a low level of embarrassment and confusion. Mam would never swear on anything, she must be telling the truth. An old man sitting across from us gave me an encouraging nod.

'I would like to thank you all for coming this evening, I hope ...'

As childish as it sounds, I sat there with imaginary earplugs in my ears refusing to listen. What pissed me off most about bereavement counsellors was that, unless they'd been through grief themselves, they'd no clue or right, to dish out advice on it. I reasoned this theory in my head the first time I'd been handed a photocopied booklet in the hospital with a dove on the front cover, and I continued to think about it as Anna harped on. I took to counting the window panels that ran the length of the wall, and then the patches where the yellow paint had curled off, exposing the muggy grey brick. It was only when the man beside me spoke that his thick Wexford accent jolted me back into the room. He introduced himself as Eamon and kept his eyes on the floor.

'My two brothers died in a car crash, a couple year back. They were younger than me, there was only the three of us. We had come up to Dublin to work. We were only here a fortnight, when a truck rear ended the car we were in.' He shifted about in his seat, making the plastic creak under his weight. His hands were like shovels, clamped together as he spoke. 'I don't know how I survived. I don't know why.' He took a deep breath like he'd filled his lungs for a week. There was silence for a moment, while we waited to see if he'd continue.

'And you feel guilty?' asked Anna.

'The guilt eats me up, so it does.'

'Guilt is a common emotion when you've lost a loved one.' Anna looked around the room, allowing Eamon to gather himself. 'Some people can feel guilty because they think they could have done more, or that their last words were in an argument. Others feel guilty for laughing or feeling happy.'

There were nods and low murmurs of agreement.

'Survivor guilt can be a big one. Why wasn't I taken?' She looked directly at Eamon as she said this. 'Why didn't I die instead?'

Eamon nodded, and Anna smiled in acknowledgement. I liked her with that smile, but not enough to tell her my story or to ever come to one of her groups.

'Thank you for sharing your story, Eamon,' she said.

He nodded, his mouth stretching to a tight smile.

The woman across from me was crying into a tissue. The sight of her made a lump swell in the back of my throat. Her pain

193

looked so raw.

'Let it out, Rebecca,' said Anna, which could have sounded cheesy, but was just what she needed to hear by the looks of it. Rebecca nodded, trying to steady her breaths. Her hands trembled as she sipped from a cup of water. The stale smell of alcohol coming from her, made me think she wished it was something more.

'Guilt can have a real effect on us all,' said Anna.

'It's just –' Rebecca stopped herself.

Eamon's eyes were like saucers like he'd never seen grief bigger than his own. The elderly man beside me shifted uncomfortably in his seat.

'It's just –' she tried again, and I thought that maybe a group like this wasn't the best place for her, that perhaps she should be seeing Anna on her own.

Anna walked over and put her hand on Rebecca's shoulder. Rebecca shrugged it off, making Anna step back but her expression didn't change. She looked on, encouraging her with her eyes alone.

Rebecca wiped her eyes and pulled her cardigan tighter around her thin frame. She didn't look much older than me. 'I'm sorry,' she picked up her handbag. 'I thought I was ready to talk. I'll come back again.' Nobody seemed fazed that she was about to make a dash for it. Maybe this was normal, people legging it. Maybe I could just run out and nobody would mind.

Anna nodded looking unconvinced. 'Please. You're welcome anytime.'

Rebecca was gone and Anna, unfazed, looked around for someone else to speak. I studied my shoe.

A woman closest to Anna spoke. 'I lost my son. It was seven years ago, and the pain is still there every day; it doesn't go. It dulls, but time is not a healer, time is just something you try to get through by different means, depending on where your head is at.' She looked around the room. 'Sorry, just ... I wanted to be honest. That's what I'm hoping to be for people.'

Anna cut in. 'Miranda is in the middle of her bereavement counselling training and has been sitting in on a few group sessions.'

'I refused to attend any groups myself years ago,' said Miranda. 'I thought no one could be going through the same pain as me. No one's pain could compare to having their teenage son drop dead at a birthday party, smiling and dancing one minute, lying on the floor the next.'

The old man shook his head, sighing loudly.

'You see, to me it was a competition back then. My pain outweighed everyone's else's. I refused to speak to anyone about it – to me nobody had a clue.' Her voice was very matter of fact, which I think was on purpose. At a quick glance, she was attractive with nice clothes and perfect blonde hair but studying her face now, there were deep lines that told her story without her speaking and a weariness in her eyes. I felt a sense of admiration for her, something I hadn't felt for anyone other than Oprah in my 'Be your best you' days.

Mam was soaking up the woman's words like a sponge, her hand splayed across her chest. She loved a good story, the sadder the better. Her face was contorted, her head no doubt filled with how this poor woman manages to drag herself out of bed each morning. I knew Mam well, and if she dared start to cry, telling this woman how brave she was, I'd up and leave, pulling her with me.

A girl, Shana, in her early twenties was next to speak, her voice barely a whisper. She had lost her mother at eight and spoke about delayed grief. Something the guy in the baseball cap seemed to relate to. He watched her intently from under his cap, his blue eyes mirroring her sadness. If it wasn't bad enough losing a parent so young, you get to experience the grief again at every stage, teenage, young adult, becoming a parent yourself. I felt sorry for her, which I knew was the last thing she wanted, as she said her whole life was spent with people head tilting, telling her how terrible it was that she lost her mammy so young. She made us all laugh, when she said people, especially older women always said 'mammy,' when talking about her mam. Seemingly, if you lose your mam as a child, she's referred to as your 'mammy' forever.

Four out of the nine people put their hand up to speak. The rest of us – I use the term 'us' begrudgingly as I didn't wish to be part of the group, even if life's cruel fate lumped us together, just sat and listened.

Mam sat beside me like a lamb. Breda Byrne stood by the door, holding a clipboard that was no doubt empty because she was holding it upside down, making the black marker dangle between her legs in a compromising position.

I zoned out after the personal stories. Anna was speaking about different techniques to help with panic attacks. I started to shift about in my chair. I wasn't great at sitting still for too long, and I really needed some proper caffeine.

'You're gone a little pale, love. Are you okay?' asked Mam,

leaning over to me.

'I need a coffee, or something.'

'You've had a coffee.' She pointed to the empty cup in my hand.

'I need another one.'

'It's the feckin' AA you'll be needing, and I'm only half joking.'

I ignored Mam, who thought a bottle of wine was the equivalent to a year's worth of alcohol units.

The group ended, and everyone made their way to the table, where the biscuits and coffee were going down a treat.

'Why don't you chat to some people?'

'Don't push it, Mam. You're lucky I stayed put in my chair. 'These people's stories are heart breaking, especially that man from Wexford, he just looks so lost.'

'Pot – kettle,' said Mam raising an eyebrow.

We said our goodbyes and walked out to the carpark, where Mam finally dug out my car keys from her handbag.

'I'm going to walk back with Breda for the bit of exercise.' Mam gave me a hug. 'I really thought this might have been something that could help you.'

'What?' I pulled away. 'So, you did set me up?'

Mam shrugged, holding her hands up.

'But you swore on Nana Margo's grave.'

'Your Nana Margo was cremated, love, remember?'

After the initial shock of Mam's cunning plan, and my own stupidity for not copping it, I drove home feeling like I often did after watching a documentary about a world tragedy. All eager with my bank details ready to do my bit, then the credits roll, and my empathy dilutes, and I fall back into my own life. That's how I felt when I was there listening to their stories. I was lost in their grief with them, but on my own again, I felt no connection and no urge to go back. I just wished Mam would acknowledge that I was doing alright, and that spending time at home and not wanting to talk about Conor with strangers, wasn't a failing on either of our part.

Chapter 22

The weather reached the high twenties, which was impressive for Dublin even in August. Pockets of conversations would carry over from other gardens and just sitting in mine, made me feel part of something. I took pleasure in watering the plants, thinking Conor would be pleased that I'd remembered. I thought of him a lot those days.

In the afternoons, it was too hot to sit outside so instead I stayed indoors in my shorts and t-shirt pyjamas, the set I'd bought for our holiday to Portugal the year before. They still had the faint smell of cocoa butter sunscreen, which triggered memories that threatened to break me.

I slipped my feet into my flip-flops and remembered I'd promised Jojo I'd show her my lemon collection – even in my own head that sounded pathetic! Here I was at thirty, comparing collections like I had done when I was ten with my soaps and fancy paper. I often wondered where my fifty-three different shaped soaps had gone. Something told me Nana Margo had been lifting them each time she came to visit. She always had a thing about soap and asked me too many questions about my collection not to come under suspicion when the numbers were going down.

Upstairs, the spare bedroom at the front of the house was

untouched. It had been a dumping ground for our memories that now sat like monsters behind the door.

I knew all my lemon themed gifts from Conor were in there and, if I wanted to keep my promise to show Jojo and – I hoped – make her laugh, then I'd have to brave it and go in.

I stood clutching the door handle like my hand was glued stuck. I tried telling myself to cop on but it didn't work. I was terrified, and I didn't know why. Slowly, I pushed the door open like it was being held on the other side and I was forcing my way in. As the door swished across the cream carpet I held my breath, my other hand curled into a fist. I didn't know what I was expecting, but the room looked the same. No monsters, just boxes with our names.

The room was painted magnolia, which to most people was bland but in comparison to the rest of the house décor, I'd been grateful when I'd seen it. I had planned on redecorating and turning it into a chic, hotel-style guestroom. I had gotten as far as testing paint samples in different shades of pink, which now looked like little mouths smirking at me.

The only piece of furniture in the room was my vintage white dresser that I couldn't part with. I'd taken it from my old bedroom in my parent's house and it had been the first victim of my upcycling. If I looked closely enough, I could still see the tiny dents in the wood around the mirror, where I'd gone mad with a stapler trying to tack on a silk scarf. I'd also tried sticking pearls along the drawer, convinced that it would turn it into some sort of heirloom. Some of my deluded dreams I could see the humour in. The pin cushioned dresser was one of them.

In the corner were all the boxes, stacked up like a fort. I picked up one from the top with my name scrawled along the side and sat down on the floor to open it. I lifted up the lid and there it was, the card, the one with the lemon tree that had started it all off. I slowly opened it, Conor's handwriting, familiar even in block capitals, each kiss joined together like they were holding hands. I held it to my chest and closed my eyes, trying to pull up the memory of him handing it to me, but it wouldn't come, too tangled among all the other years.

I placed the card on the dresser and continued through the box. There were two ticket stubs from the time we went to see Billy Elliot in London. Conor had moaned the whole way through, saying he didn't think there would be so much singing. I didn't mention I'd seen him wipe his eyes when Billy danced for the first time in front of his dad, or that the word 'musical' under the title should have given the game away.

When my eyes fell on the snow globe, my heart skipped a couple beats. It had softened me to the lemony theme, and I think Conor was surprised when I didn't throw it at him like the rest of the stuff. It looked like something you would find in a cute gift shop in Italy, but Conor had told me he'd bought it on eBay for a fiver.

I picked up the snow globe, wiping the bulb of glass with my sleeve. The dust made my eyes water and I sniffed rubbing my nose. It was more beautiful than I'd remembered with a lemon tree on a hill and a tiny white village in the background. I turned it upside down, and shook it gently, watching the glitter swim around the branches slowly, before settling along the bottom.

After looking through my boxes and putting aside the snow globe and some other bits to show to Jojo, I moved on to Conor's. Opening up his was like turning the handle of a Jack in the Box and my hands trembled as I fiddled with the tape. Inside, his old Man United scarf lay along the top like a blanket keeping the rest of his things safe. I picked up the scarf and instinctively put it around my neck, and tied a knot loosely making the red and whites bleed together. I went through each item and it was like opening a little door inside my head. Memories I'd long forgotten came flooding in, as clear as if they were playing out on a giant screen in front of me.

I must have sat there for a while, looking like a mad woman in my pyjamas and football scarf, and when the room came back into focus it was dark outside. I flicked on the light and with a sea of our memories around my feet, it struck me that I'd looked at everything and felt a happy sad, not the overwhelming heaviness I was used too. I gathered up everything to show Jojo, quickly, almost afraid I was becoming cocky and at any moment I would be struck down into a pit of grief.

I saw Jojo for a few minutes the following day and was delighted to see her wearing different clothes. It settled something inside me, a niggling, that I ended up complimenting her twice with the relief. After showing her my lemon gifts, which were all 'cute' she got talking about holidays.

'I want to go to America and see someone famous. Have you ever been?'

'No, but I've always wanted to go.

'You could go now.'

I just smiled and said, 'maybe.' I didn't want to tell her that I couldn't imagine ever going on a holiday again. Conor and I had planned to travel the world, like most couples do when life is one big adventure and you're in it together. He had loved places steeped in history, while I loved finding the nearest Zara.

'Wanna do some more furniture painting? You could sell them for your plane ticket?' said Jojo, swatting a fly from her arm.

'Maybe tomorrow.'

The thought of money did stick in my head afterwards, and that night I sat down with a glass of wine and logged on to internet banking. Five minutes later I'd managed to lock myself out by putting in the wrong password three times. I wrote 'ring bank' on a post-it for the morning and stuck it to the fridge, feeling I'd achieved something. I rested back, sipping my wine, enjoying the routine I'd become so used to, when my phone rang.

'Lydia knows about Rob,' said Tasha sounding completed panicked. 'She just phoned me, Sammie – fuck!'

'Are you sure?'

'Yes! Her friend saw us that night outside the Bailey. She's threatening to tell Wayne. What will I do?'

There was no talking to Tasha when she was like this and I knew she didn't actually want advice. Instead, she answered the question herself for twenty minutes, giving every possible solution. In that time, I necked two glasses of wine.

By the time Tasha was finished, she was even more wound up. The only sliver of hope she was clinging to, was that she and

Wayne's family were the only ones who knew he'd gotten a suspended sentence a couple of years back. He'd been caught storing stolen car parts for a friend. Lydia knew Wayne would go after Rob if he found out he'd kissed Tasha. She also knew he would go straight to prison if he did, and the chances of her risking that happening to her brother were slim.

Tasha hoped this was enough to stop Lydia from telling him. She ended the call by asking me could I collect Finn from summer camp the following week. She had a hospital appointment with Aria, and Mam was busy with Breda Byrne organising a community trip to Lourdes. I didn't ask questions and quickly agreed, even though I wasn't ready to leave my bubble.

Chapter 23

'So, what you're saying is, you were offered a job to do what you love and you didn't take it? I'm a kid and even I know that's stupid.'

'It was bad timing,' I said, regretting telling Jojo about Audrey's job offer when Haven had closed. She was all talk of careers that morning and what film she would love to star in and how actors, when shooting a movie, like to constantly be in character, something she said she was good at. Seeing as I never knew what Jojo I was going to get – the withdrawn, snappy or upbeat one, I thought acting would suit her perfectly.

'But it's your dream job, duh.'

'That I've no proper experience in,' I said, taking a mouthful of wine. A car drove past leaving us with the strains of a Bruno Mars song that continued playing on in my head.

'So, will you sing in your movies?' I asked Jojo.

'No, Millie is the singer in our family. She's amazing.' She looked sad saying this and I wasn't sure if it was jealousy or something else. 'I wish I could sing, but Millie has the gap in her front teeth and that makes all the difference.'

'Does it? I never knew that.'

'Yeah, so genetically she's already a step ahead. I get the allergies from my dad and she gets the musical genes from hers. Ours.'

I ignored her correction. 'Do you and your sister play together much?'

'She's not really the outdoorsy type. My gran used to call her precious but not in a good way.' I thought of myself and Tasha as kids and how we only played together when we were desperate. 'You've lots of time to practice if you want to be a singer. You're only twelve.'

'And you sound about ninety.'

'I feel about ninety,' I said, flicking a green fly off my arm. 'When I was your age, I had lots of dreams.'

'And what's wrong with you now?'

'Things have changed for me now,' I said, chasing the green fly who was now trying to camp out on my leg.

'But won't you have to do something? You can't just sit around in your pyjamas forever.' She looked down at my sheep t-shirt and I felt self-conscious under her stare. 'Conor be bored watching over you.'

'Watching over me?'

'Yeah, what else will he be doing?'

The green fly flew around my face and I made a big deal of swatting it away, hoping the conversation could change to something lighter. I wasn't sure how a child could have such a grown-up perception on death.

'Just make your own business.'

'It's a bit more complicated than that.' I found myself telling Jojo about our vision board and all the dreams we had together. She listened, and I forgot I was speaking to a child, it was as though our

206

ages had melted together, putting us both at the same point.

'I'm not being bad, but only one of you died. That vision board thingy has both your stuff on it.'

I didn't know if I was insulted or even upset. 'You're very deep, Jojo.'

'Does deep mean thick?'

'No.' I laughed. 'It means a deep thinker, kind of like wise. You're very wise for your age.'

'I'm lethal at maths, ask me anything?'

And I did, for the rest of the afternoon.

Chapter 24

'How's it going, Sammie?' I looked up to see Max waving as I struggled to pull my wheelie bin up the kerb. 'You'd think they'd leave them back by the gates,' he said, crossing over the road. 'It's like an obstacle course around here.' He pointed his keys back at his van, the lights blinking to lock.

'This estate is keeping you busy,' I said, finally winning the battle with the wheelie bin, but not without the lid yawning out a stale stench in my face.

'The best thing I ever did was offer discounts for recommendations, although I don't think I'll get to leave Artane again – not that I'm complaining.' He tipped his head with his finger twice as if not to jinx himself. 'I'm working in Mr Watson's house for the next few weeks.' He pointed to my elderly neighbour's house two doors down. 'He's doing up his conservatory. I'm making bookshelves and that. Bit of a man cave I reckon.'

I laughed at the thought of my seventy-something-year-old neighbour wanting a man cave. John was reversing out of his garden beside us at the pace of a snail. He gave us a wave.

'Are you taking up singing?' Max asked, pointing to my hand.

'Oh, this.' I looked down at the flyer that I'd just found in my letterbox. 'No … it was just in with my post. It's for kid's singing lessons. I was thinking of passing it on to my neighbour.'

'My eldest daughter, Erin, is doing singing lessons a few months now. She's terrible.'

'Really?' I laughed.

'It's not funny. I'll be one of those dads you see on The X Factor, waiting in the wings, while she crows her heart out. Everyone be thinking, why doesn't he just tell her she's crap and save her the humiliation.'

A couple of boys went by on bikes, shouting to each other making us step apart to let them past.

'At least she's not looking in their direction yet.' His eyes followed the boys. 'That's when my real troubles start.'

'How did it go with Carla?' I asked, surprised I'd remembered her name.

His face changed, giving me the answer alone. 'Not too good.'

'Oh.'

'She wanted to meet up to tell me that she's seeing someone. Well, how she put it was that a guy from work had asked her out on a date and she wanted to do the decent thing and tell me first before agreeing. We both know this isn't the case, but I guess pretending to believe the lie is sometimes easier.' He shrugged, looking defeated and I felt a wave of sympathy for him. 'I think they've been seeing each other a while.'

'I'm really sorry, Max.'

'Sure look, it could be worse. At least the girls are happy and I know of the guy. When you've kids, sometimes it's easier to accept someone you know in their lives, than a complete stranger. There's a lot of weirdos out there, and I guess you've to take all the positives you can from a situation.'

My face must have distorted the way Mam's does when she's being told something sad. He looked at me and laughed. 'I bet you wish you never asked?'

'No, it's just sad, that's all.' He rubbed his jaw roughly with the back of his hand, in a nervous way, that made me think he'd regretted saying anything. 'I'm sure it will all work out.' I put my hand on his arm out of instinct. It was a Clancy thing. I could have thrown a few quotes at him a few months ago; I'd ones memorised for every scenario.

I looked up and saw Laura coming out of her house with the baby perched on her hip. She smiled, her look curious, and I felt my cheeks redden. I pulled my hand from Max's arm like I'd just been electrocuted. He didn't realise, he was too busy in his own head, no doubt playing out what he'd just been talking about.

I wanted to shout over that he was upset over his girlfriend, and I was comforting him, but she didn't need to know that, and I was in no position to comfort anyone.

'Anyway, thanks for listening, Sammie.'

'No problem, well I better go. Best of luck with everything and remember, there's plenty more fish in the sea.' I said the last bit loudly, and a little too cheery. I knew I had a quote in me somewhere, even if it was shite.

'The only women in my life now will be my daughters. I'll be steering clear of relationships.'

That makes two of us, I said to myself, walking up my drive

and closing the front door.

Chapter 25

'Singing lessons,' I said, waving the flyer at Jojo. It was a scorcher of a day and, without even realising, I'd turned the flyer into a fan by folding it over and back into a neat little accordion. I'd been thinking about Mr Watson with the sounds of drilling, hammering and Max's voice spilling from every window in the house. I remembered Celine telling me Mr Watson's wife had died a few years ago and his only child, a son, lived in Australia. He went to Celine and John's house every year for Christmas dinner, which didn't surprise me. He always seemed to be busy – pottering in his garden, painting his gate with the teeniest paint brush and thimble of black paint, or walking his two yappy terriers. Maybe that's how he coped? By keeping busy. Maybe keeping busy forever was the answer.

'Singing lessons?' said Jojo.

'Yeah, it's a little crumpled,' I said trying to straighten the page out on my knee and in turn transferring streaks of purple ink onto my palm. 'But you can give it to your parents and see what they say. It's on in the local community centre every Thursday.' I glanced down at the page to be sure. 'Here.' I got up off my chair and walked down the garden, careful not to step on any stones in my bare feet.

'No, it's okay.'

I looked up at Jojo, mid trying not to squish a ladybird that was sauntering across my path.

'– But thanks,' she said, her smile strained.

'Just take it anyway. Sure, one of your friends might even go with you? Will I ask your parents for you?' I stood on my tiptoes trying to see behind her, feeling brave.

'No, please it's fine.' Jojo's voice peaked with panic.

'What's wrong, Jojo?'

'I, they, they'll give out if I bring it home. I'm not allowed do things like that. Activities and stuff.' She looked genuinely terrified, which seemed way over the top, considering I wasn't actually hopping the wall to give it to them myself.

I scrunched up the flyer in my hand, and said, 'No big deal,' while trying to ignore the uneasiness in my stomach. 'I don't want to get you into trouble. They're probably crap anyway, some old biddy banging away on a keyboard making you sing 'Doe a Deer' from *The Sound of Music* – Oh my god these stone are manky,' I said, making a pathetic attempt at changing the subject altogether. 'I'll have to clean them. Maybe washing up liquid and warm water will do it? I might do it now actually –'

'I'm okay, Sammie,' said Jojo, 'it's just … it's like you said, it's complicated.' I saw a flicker of regret in her eyes and realised that dreams can die at any age.

Max was outside Mr Watson's house loading up his van as I was getting out of my car later that evening. I had just bought two tins of paint and was ready to take on my house – well, my living room. Maybe even just the one wall, I'd see how I got on. After Jojo had gone in, I'd sat in my garden surrounded by the noise from Mr

Watson's, which after a while started to speak to me. Not literally, which would mean I was actually insane, rather than just threatening it eighty percent of the time. It was saying 'keep busy' and painting my living room was now the first of my life long 'busy' to-do list.

'Blue, I like it,' said Max, swinging his van door shut. 'And the right shade too.' He patted the bumper sticker on his back window which had a Manchester City crest.

'It's definitely not City's colour,' I said, my voice thick with loyalty for Conor. 'Seeing as we're United fans, but they were all out of red.'

'United.' Max winced. 'Not long left in the transfer window and they haven't signed any big names yet.'

I heard those words so many times before that it gave me shivers, a red flag in the conversation warning me to quickly steer away.

'It's called Cotton Clouds,' I said, holding up the tin to double check the name. 'I'll probably get bored halfway through painting and it'll end up resembling the parting of the sea.'

'Ah, I know the feeling,' said Max, walking over to me. 'Do you need a hand carrying anything in?'

'No thanks, I've just these.' I closed the boot with my elbow and held a paint pot in each hand, like weights helping me to build up strength. I'd panicked in the shop when I was buying them, thinking I couldn't change the house, it would be like I was painting over our memories. Then I thought of Mr Watson and Aunt Winnie and I knew which one I wanted to be. I needed to keep busy, to keep moving even just within the small space around me.

'I hate painting,' said Max. 'Ask me to build anything and I'll gladly do it, but painting all the finicky bits: it drives me mad.'

'What time tomorrow, Sir?' Mr Watson called from his porch door.

'Before 8 a.m., Mr Watson,' Max shouted back.

'Good man.' Mr Watson waved his newspaper as a goodbye and slid the porch door closed.

'Before 8 a.m.? That's early,' I said walking over to my wall to rest the two tins of paint on the brick.

'Bit of a slave driver is Mr Watson, although nothing compared to my girls, Erin and Sophie. They have me driven crazy to do up their bedroom and I haven't a clue where to begin. I bought pink paint and they went mad. They don't want pink or purple, unless it's not a purple, purple, but not blue.' He sighed in a way that made me think he secretly loved their demanding personalities. 'Any ideas?

'I wouldn't have a clue, seeing as my bedroom was every shade of pink growing up. I even wanted to paint our bedroom in this house pink, well salmon, but Conor wasn't having any of it.'

Max laughed, completely at ease with Conor's name, which I'd noticed could be like an allergen to other people making them break out in a mottled rash. 'I wouldn't fancy a pink room myself.'

'What about a chalkboard wall?' I said, remembering we'd talked about them on the interior design course that I'd done. 'It would be nice with white walls and then you could buy a big stencil online or use lots of different purples. Hang on, I'll show you.' I slid the two paint tins further onto the wall, and took my phone out of my pocket, before quickly tapping into Pinterest. 'See.' Max leaned over me, his shadow blocking the sun as he looked at the screen. 'They're just sponges cut into circles.' I pointed at the image, 'and you dip them into the paint.' The skin on my fingertips was peeled from where I'd gnawed down my nails leaving tiny dots of dried blood. I took my hand away, self-conscious, and balanced the phone in my other palm.

'It looks great, the girls would love something like that.'

'You could make any pattern, depending on the size of the room.'

'I took a photo of their room the other day.' He tapped into his phone and swiped his thumb across the screen. 'It's a big enough room.' He showed me the photo in two halves of a cracked screen. 'Don't mind that,' he said flicking a piece of dust from the crack. 'Mr Watson's dog was pulling at my tool bag and the phone was in the side pocket. I don't like to carry my phone in my pocket doing a job, but I will now in future.'

'No way, what did Mr Watson say?' I looked up at him.

'He didn't notice, and I wasn't going to say it to him. He's enough to be worrying about with his man cave design.' He laughed.

'That was very nice of you.'

'Ah sure – what about this wall.' He brushed off the compliment, pointing back to his phone. 'Would you paint that wall as the chalkboard?'

'No, the one opposite the window.' I pointed to the screen too, not caring so much about my nails anymore, 'and the dots over their beds.'

'Don't suppose you want to do it for me?'

'Ehhh, no. But I won't charge you for my ideas. Oh, and I'd suggest bringing them shopping for their own accessories – pillows, lamps, frames and that. Ikea is great. You won't have a clue yourself, and I think they'd like being involved, well, I did when I was young.' I lifted down the two tins of paint which swung heavy in my arms.

'Well, thanks for the – inspo. Is that what they say?'

'Okay, I'm cringing now,' I said, laughing walking up my drive.

Chapter 26

I stood in the middle of my living room, which felt hollow and lifeless. The mud-coloured walls and oatmeal curtains reflected nothing of me and Conor, which, I guess, made it a good place to start. I poured myself a glass of wine and took my time doing the first coat, enjoying the rhythmic swish of the roller against the walls. Each time the nasty gremlins tried to claw their way into my head, dropping rocks into my stream of thoughts – *This will never be a dream house* – *This was meant to be for you both,* I'd take another mouthful of wine and grip the roller tighter, pushing harder against the wall.

Before I knew it, I had painted the whole room and polished off a full bottle of wine. With the smell of fresh paint, along with the warm tingle of alcohol in my veins, I lay on my couch, relaxed enough to close my eyes and fall into a deep sleep. Deep and dreamless. When I woke, I was still in the exact same position with the sun shining golden through the blind, highlighting my work. The walls looked fresh and modern and much warmer than I thought blue could ever be. It was the perfect shade for the room and I thought, *Conor would approve.*

I pulled myself up off the couch and went into the kitchen to make tea. There was only a dribble of milk left in the bottom of the carton. Something I still hadn't mastered was the milk and bread run; it had always been Conor's job. 'FO-ROOM' fear of running out of milk – the TV ad had said, with a bulky man waking up in the middle of the night, the terror of an empty milk carton in a thought cloud above his head. Conor and I had joked that this was most definitely him. We never had less than two litres in the fridge on any given day and I was still getting used to my new responsibility. I quickly ran around to the shop, which in fairness to me, was near enough to a proper run. I'd popped my head into the living room before I left, the blue walls giving me a shot of adrenaline.

Back home, I made myself a cup of tea and heated a croissant that was an impulse buy at the till. The sweet buttery smell had wrapped around my taste buds not letting me leave without buying one. I sat outside on my decking and had the croissant gone in five minutes, savouring the crumbs for a few minutes more. Max had kept his promise to Mr Watson and although it was only a quarter past nine, the work sounded in full swing.

'Papa Smurf or Smurfette? Actually, I'll go with Smurfette, but that bun stuck on your head does look a bit like Papa Smurf's hat.'

I took a sip of tea and tried to rearrange Jojo's words in my head, so they'd make some sort of sense. Her hair was plaited loosely today, with bleached strands that fell around her face as she tilted her head to study me. She looked younger with her hair tied up, which she'd hate to be told. 'What are you on about – Smurfs?'

'Your face,' said Jojo. 'If it's not face paint then you totally have a disease, which by the looks of it could be contagious.' Her eyes scanned me up and down. 'It's not anywhere else is it?'

I put my cup down and pulled myself out of the chair, cursing

219

her for making me move while I was comfortable. I walked over to the patio doors to check my reflection, moving my eyebrows up and down. My skin did feel a bit tight.

'What the –' I ran my hand over my face, over the crusted blue splodges of paint that had even managed to find tiny hairs above my lip to cling to. Tasha would hit the deck if she saw me, out of pure shame alone.

'I was painting my living room yesterday,' I said, looking back at Jojo. 'Goodbye mud-coloured walls, hello cotton clouds.' I pointed to my face.

'You mean blue, and like, how did you not notice? Are you sure it's just tea in that cup?'

I picked the paint off with my nail, ignoring her joke. The flakes were coming away easily, like blue scabs falling around my feet.

'Did you not look in the mirror brushing your teeth this morning? Tell me you still brush your teeth?'

I ran my tongue along the front of my teeth, feeling a thin layer of fuzz. 'Just not today, or maybe last night. But of course I brush my teeth,' I said with enough conviction to let this kid know that I had my shit together. I was re-decorating my house. I was keeping busy.

'Oh, no,' I slapped my hands on my face, peeping at Jojo through my fingers. 'I went to the shop earlier like this.' Kai had been looking at me funny, now that I thought of it. And asked was I a fan of *Avatar*. I launched into a big speech on how Sci-Fi wasn't really my thing, but that the make-up on that movie was amazing, which made him grin even more – ugh, I could kill him.

Jojo only stopped laughing to tell me how great it was that I was doing something with my 'granny banger' house.

'It's bad enough having mouldy teeth, and a blue moustache … but mud-coloured walls? There's no excuse, Sam.'

'Sam.' I repeated the name only Conor had ever called me, making my lips curl into a smile.

'Sam the Man.' Jojo laughed, pointing to my 'tache. I rolled my eyes.

There really weren't any excuses for mud-coloured walls. Apart from wanting to keep busy I now wanted to re-decorate the house for me. I didn't want to think too much about my reasons, only that it was a step in a direction – to where, I had no clue.

Chapter 27

'Is Finn there?' I heard a voice shout, as I carried in a new pair of curtains from my car. Out with the oatmeal curtains and in with the … well, they were still cream but had thick velvet stripes that gave a texture not resembling porridge. I looked around to see Max's daughter Erin waving at me from Mr Watson's garden. Max was carrying a large rectangle of wood into the house as Sophie skipped around him. He looked stressed, his jaw set in a tight line, as he tried to avoid decapitating a skipping Sophie. Erin ran down the garden and swung around the gate towards me.

'Is Finn home? Is he coming out to play?' she asked, pushing her dark fringe from her eyes. They were the same coffee brown as her dad's.

'No, Finn's not here, he lives –'

'Do you share him with your ex?' She interrupted me; her eyes beamed with recognition. 'We were meant to be at our mam's today, but she has to work, horizontally with her new fella says our Dad.'

'No, he's …'

Erin did a little skippy jump thing, distracting me.

'He's my nephew,' I said, adjusting the plastic packaging that was sticking to my arm in the heat.

'Oh.' Erin looked disappointed. 'Is there anyone else to play with, or is it just old people living around here?'

Sophie ran over to us, bumping into her sister almost knocking herself backwards. She had fiery red hair and blue eyes, presumably taking after her mam.

'What's in the bag?' she asked, poking the plastic with her finger.

'That's rude, Sophie.' Erin pulled her arm away.

'Girls.' Max called from the garden. 'I told you both to stay in here.' His face was flushed as he balanced two thick planks of wood on his shoulder. 'Come on, leave Sammie alone.'

I gave him a wave, which he returned with a nod before disappearing inside the house again.

'I think there might be kids in the corner house, but I'm not sure,' I said, looking down the road which was quiet apart from the roar of an aeroplane overhead. The girls were deaf to it, making me think they must live near-by.

Max came back out of Mr Watson's and walked straight towards us. 'Girls, now.' He clapped his hands, which had no effect on them whatsoever.

'We're soooo bored, Dad,' said Sophie, 'and Mr Watson's house smells funny.'

'Don't be rude, Sophie,' said Max in the same tone that Erin had used. 'Now, come on.' He clapped again, this time making me want to laugh. He reminded me of my old geography teacher, Mr Gleeson, who had no control over a class full of girls. At the start of each lesson, we'd pick a random personal question to ask him, which would send him off course for the first ten minutes. When he'd then try to start the lesson, clapping his hands to regain control, we'd just carry on chatting among ourselves.

'Can we see your house, Sammie?' asked Erin.

'Yeah.' Sophie jumped up and down. 'Can we play in your garden. Do you have a trampoline?'

Max rubbed the side of his head, looking at me apologetically. 'Sammie is busy.' The word busy fell like a coin in a slot machine switching my mouth to on and making me speak.

'Yes.' I smiled.

'Yes?' Max repeated like I'd lost my mind. 'They're head wreckers, Sammie.' The girls put their hands together in prayer like two members of a choir. 'That only works on me, not strangers.' They continued by batting their eyelashes.

'Yeah, sure,' I said, switching the curtains to my other arm. 'I've no trampoline but there's a girl who lives in the house behind mine that you can play with, and there's a big tree you can climb.'

'A tree, cool,' said Sophie.

'Yeah, Jojo climbs it all the time.'

'How old is Jo-Jo?' asked Erin, slicing the name like a cake.

'She's twelve.'

'Jojo,' Sophie mouthed the name like she was trying it out on her tongue first. 'Like Jojo bows.'

I'd no clue what she was talking about.

'I'm eight and she's seven,' said Erin, patting Sophie's head like a dog.

I knew that hanging around with younger kids was not a cool thing to do, but seeing as I'd spent most of the summer hanging out with Jojo, she could help me to help Max.

'Can we go, Dad?'

'Sammie, you don't have to.' Max gestured to the curtains in my arms, 'you've your hands full.'

'I can hang curtains anytime. It's fine, honestly.'

'Max,' a young guy shouted from Mr Watson's porch. He was covered in sawdust and dangling a measuring tape like a yoyo. 'It's not fitting, mate.'

'I'm coming,' said Max, tilting his wrist to check his watch. 'Thanks, Sammie. Just send them back down to me when you've had enough.'

The two girls threw their arms around Max's waist giving him a hug as he squeezed them both towards him. It was a sweet sight to watch, the three of them being so affectionate. I grew up with a pat on the head from Dad, or a hair ruffle, if it was meant as a means of comfort. It didn't emotionally scar me – at least I don't think so – but a dad hugging his two daughters, a little triangle of love, was nice to see.

My house came alive with Erin and Sophie: that's how it felt, as their voices boomed off the walls and their feet vibrated down through the floorboards. It was like the house was going to sprout legs and move with them, dancing, hopping and skipping around. I threw the curtains over the sofa and stood watching them explore the downstairs, like two puppies let loose in new surroundings. They disappeared into corners and behind doors like they were on a treasure hunt. For a second, I allowed myself to imagine that this is what it would have been like if I'd had children. My house still alive, having been savaged by a death. Sophie caught me staring, so I quickly turned and plumped up the cushion beside me, not wanting to be all *Hand That Rocks the Cradle*.

'Our mam loves this,' said Erin, picking up the empty wine bottle on the kitchen table and giving it a shake.

'Yeah, she likes all the colours.' Sophie tilted the neck of the bottle and broke into a pop song I didn't recognise.

I opened the kitchen press to see if there was anything, I could offer them. Cheese and Onion crisps, bourbon biscuits … I really was boring.

'This smells like my dad,' said Sophie, with her nose mashed up like a snout against the living room wall. I could feel the anxiety poking me, all my hard work being ruined by two nostril stains of snot.

'It's the smell of paint, Sophie. Did you just paint in here?' Erin looked at me, while rubbing her palms on the wall.

'Yes, just a couple days ago … actually, it's eh, it's probably not even dry yet.' I ushered them both out of the living room with a shaky hand. I eyed the bottle of white wine in the fridge as I poured them both a glass of milk. I'd no juice to offer them and was only short of running down to Max to sign a consent that they weren't dairy intolerant.

'This is like being at Nana's house, isn't it, Sophie?' said Erin, dipping a crisp into her glass of milk. The grease swirled orange around the top, making my throat fill with water.

Sophie was too busy separating my patio blind with her salty fingers and pressing her face against the glass. 'Wow, that's a big tree.'

'Is there a tree house?' Erin ran over beside her sister, the greasy milk threatening to slosh over the side of the glass. 'Can we play out there? Is the girl Jojo there to play with?'

I pulled open the patio door, letting in a blast of warm air.

The three of us sat outside on the decking, which was like a radiator thanks to the sun. The girls insisted on taking their sandals off and wriggling their toes in the warm grass. They talked non-stop, bouncing giddily from one topic to another, as the age gap between them and Jojo swelled even more. Their toenails were painted in a glittery, gold polish, looking like they'd just dipped their feet into sand.

'Who painted your nails? They're really pretty.'

'Our mam,' they both said together. Being with the girls I was suddenly curious about their mam, Carla. The pain she'd caused Max was still etched on his face.

'She did a really good job,' I leaned forward like these twenty glittery splodges were the most amazing thing I'd ever seen. 'They're really sparkly.' I was talking shite and I knew it, not quite sure what I was hoping to achieve.

'She could do your nails if you like, we could ask her?'

'No, it's okay,' I said quickly, feeling like I'd been somehow caught out.

'We're going to wear gold when we're flower girls,' said Erin, flinging her arms in the air and throwing herself over into a cartwheel. Her face disappeared behind her t-shirt before re-emerging puce. I was getting tired just looking at them. 'We're getting gold tiaras.'

'Are you? That's cool. Who's getting married?'

'Our mam.'

'Mam?'

'She has a diamond ring.'

'It's so sparkly.' Sophie wriggled her fingers like she was playing a cello.

'Your mam's getting married?' I asked the question, loaded with so many more that I wanted to say – like, does your dad know?

'Can we climb the tree now?' asked Erin, running down the garden before I could say anything else. She stretched up her arms, tipping a branch that hung lazily over the wall.

'Yes. Yes. Climb the tree,' I said putting on a matronly voice, somehow trying to mask my confusion about something that had nothing to do with me. 'Put your sandals on, so you don't hurt your feet.'

'No, it's okay,' Erin answered me like it was a question.

'But – 'They both climbed the tree like a couple of cats before I could even tell them to be careful. I got the feeling they weren't used to listening anyway.

'Does Jojo live in that house?' asked Erin, ducking her head to look under a branch at the house behind mine.

'Yes,' I said. 'I think you should hold on with both hands, in case you –'

'I can see her in her kitchen.'

'Let me see,' said Sophie, about to stand up on the branch.

'No, no don't stand.' At this rate I'd be meeting Carla in

A&E.

'Oh, I can see Dad. Erin, look,' said Sophie. The two of them waved with both hands setting off a firework in my stomach. I needed a glass of wine – and possibly one of Mam's relaxers – minding these two. They made a heart shape with their fingers, before giggling as he presumably mirrored them. The sight tugged at my own heart, thinking how being apart from them must be incredibly tough, and how he wore the pain of his separation in his eyes.

They soon got bored of the tree, and the garden, and wanted to go back inside. I was in that awkward place of wanting to drop them back to Max, but not wanting to look like I was throwing them out either. I was just about to pour myself a glass of wine, having justified it in my head that their mam obviously drinks in front of them, when the doorbell rang.

'Time to go, girls. Thanks very much, Sammie.' Max's skin was shiny, with a film of dust over his clothes. 'Bit of a disaster in Mr Watson's, we couldn't fit the jacuzzi.'

'Jacuzzi?'

'Your face,' Max laughed. 'I'm joking, the new TV unit.'

'Well, I mean, if he wanted a jacuzzi, who I am to judge?' I shrugged, laughing.

'Thanks for minding us, Sammie,' said Erin. She opened her arms and I bent down to give her a hug. Sophie was next hugging me and telling me she missed me already. They were intense and adorable, and I smiled down the garden after them.

'They really like you,' said Max following my smile with his gaze. 'How's the decorating coming along? Did the painting turn out well?'

'Yeah, it's typical though, when you do one thing to the house, it shows up something else.'

'Try explaining that to Mr Watson.'

'I'm starving, Dad,' shouted Sophie.

'Me too,' said Erin.

'They had crisps.'

'Shh, girls.'

'They – 'Max and I spoke at the same time, both sharing a look of embarrassment.

'Can we get sushi?' asked Erin.

'Sushi?' We both laughed.

'That's those bloggers,' said Max. 'I don't know who Carla lets them watch. Sophie asked me were her eyebrows on fleek yesterday. I thought she said "on fire"! I nearly crashed the van.'

'They will love being flower girls so, getting all dressed up.' I watched Max's face for a reaction, for a sign that he knew the mother of his children was getting married.

'Flower girls?' He repeated, looking at me strangely, like I was suddenly the oddest thing he'd ever seen. My heart rate quickened as I tried to think what to say. I couldn't tell him what the girls had said, but the way he was looking at me, you would think I was standing there in a wedding dress. At that perfect moment Erin ran over and pulled her dad's hand, stretching out the awkwardness between us like an elastic band.

Chapter 28

After waving goodbye to Erin and Sophie, I went straight to the fridge and poured myself wine while walking back to the table. Subconsciously, I was saving myself the journey back and forth. I was drinking the whole bottle without a doubt. It was hot enough in the house, without feeling the intensity of the sun in the garden, so I watched for Jojo through the patio door. I realised how I'd come to rely on her, to dilute the anxiety in my head with her company. Compared to Max's girls, who were fun to be around in an adrenaline rush kind of way – Jojo had a comfort to her, way beyond her years. I also wanted to check she was okay, never taking her happy moods for granted.

I twisted the wine bottle by the base; turning it around, I noticed a lemon on the label. It was tiny, a dot of yellow beside the barcode, but big enough to make my eyes water. I felt vulnerable. I wanted Conor; I wanted my security, my life, so that other people's didn't affect me. I could worry about them without the intensity, trash it out with Conor over dinner. This guy I met, he's so nice but his ex is re-marrying – his kids told me. Can you imagine? Conor would raise his eyebrows, shake his head, offer a few words. Then he'd probably turn back to his phone, we both would, chatting about this and that as we carried on with our own evening.

I drank the whole bottle in one sitting, aiming to get down to the lemon. *By the time I reach the lemon, the tears will stop.* It was like the game I used to play as a kid – if I pare my pencil anti-clockwise then I'll do well in my maths test. If I tie my laces in treble knots, I'll win the race.

I hit the lemon in twenty-five minutes. The dryness in my throat and fuzziness in my head, now masking the hurt in my heart. I pressed my thumb against the lemon like a switch that would make something happen. I didn't believe in signs anymore, but the tiny lemon now made me smile.

Busy, busy, busy – the words floated into my head. I got up and looked for a notepad and pen in the kitchen drawer. It was starting to get dark outside, the lights dimming down on another summer's day. I looked again for Jojo, but two birds were in her place, perched on the branch, their heads bobbing having a chat. She must have gone out and I imagined her at the beach with her parents, her and her sister splashing about in the sea. I knew deep down she was most likely in her bedroom.

I closed the kitchen blinds and turned the light on over the dining table. I probably didn't need it but it helped me to focus, the artificial brightness replacing the fake tiredness from the wine. I was going to make a list of everything that I still intended to do with the house.

The following day I woke up later than usual. A throbbing above my eyes was accelerated by the sound of kids squealing somewhere out the back. Despite feeling like I'd been run over, my curiosity got the better of me and I went to the window hoping to see Jojo.

The grass behind the tree was hidden by a giant princess

bouncy castle. It bobbed up and down with the sides being stretched out by limbs in all directions. My eyes scanned the garden for Jojo, but I couldn't see her or Millie. Jojo's parents were at the kitchen table with another couple and a toddler who was wearing an ice-cream like a balaclava. He bounced up and down on the man's knee as Jojo's dad looked deep in conversation with the woman. Every few minutes, the bouncy castle spat out a child onto the grass. I watched, waiting for Jojo.

There were at least twenty kids in the garden, who, while I quickly ran downstairs to take two painkillers and make tea, had moved into the kitchen to sing 'Happy Birthday' to Millie. My eyes hurt as I squinted to see Jojo. I moved from child to child as I tried to keep track of those who moved behind the kitchen wall only to re-appear seconds later. I knew she had to be there – it was her sister's birthday party after all, but why couldn't I see her?

Chapter 29

Ikea held no memories of Conor. He'd always point blank refused to step foot inside the place. He'd heard horror stories from his mates about following ground arrows for hours and hours, and not even the Swedish meatballs for a euro could entice him to go. I'd only been to Ikea a couple of times, having boycotted it for as long as I possibly could. I'd wanted to hate it for the sake of it, claiming it had no soul – not like Haven Interiors – but, as Tasha had pointed out, 'my' shop didn't have flat pack furniture for the price of a pizza dinner, or a free creche. I couldn't argue with that. At least this time turning into the carpark didn't feel like I was cheating on Haven or Dionne; I could shop around guilt free.

It was a minute to ten when I started walking towards the doors. I thought there had been an evacuation – that the fire alarm had gone off – there was that many people outside. When I realised they were all waiting to go in, I put on my game face and made a mental note to get a coffee table and light fitting. I wasn't leaving without both.

When the doors opened, I made my way straight to the living rooms, to the mock set ups that I had thought were genius the first time I'd come. Walking around I felt at home, not because I was standing in a fake home but because I couldn't get enough. I was filled with inspiration and with it came a wave of longing for my old job. I pushed it down, took a deep breath and reminded myself what I was there for.

'Excuse me,' said a petite older lady, squeezing in beside me to read a tag. We were both looking at the same rectangular coffee table with stumpy legs. 'This is it, it's perfect.' A man appeared behind her, looking equally excited. She ran her finger under the price and gave a quick nod of her head, which was like a signal to him to convert into a human table. He bent over, touching his toes and she filled out the white docket, using his back to lean on.

'Why bother get the coffee table? She could just use him.'

I turned around to see Max and the girls. I must have looked startled because he broke into a laugh. 'Ikea, you said.' He stepped back to reveal a trolley overflowing with everything from multi-coloured lampshades to shaggy rugs and cuddly toys. 'You weren't wrong. And we're going for a rainbow theme, seemingly it's "all in".' He made two bunnies with his fingers like closing quotes, making me laugh.

'Sammie, we're doing the sponge thing you told Dad about. See.' Erin bent down into the trolley, pulling out a pack of yellow sponges. 'We're buying the paint on the way home and going to do it all tomorrow.'

'I said "we'll see," Erin. We might not have time. I've to drop you back to your mam's for eleven in the morning.'

'Wanna sweet?' Sophie shook a half-eaten bag of mini Daims at me.

'I'm okay, thanks.'

'Dad hasn't paid for them,' said Sophie.

'Yeah, he's robbing them,' said Erin.

'I've kept the bag. I'm clearly not robbing them.'

'We're picking stuff for our new bedroom,' said Erin, twisting on her heels, making the fringing on her sundress dance. I noticed Sophie was wearing the same dress and their matching bows had them looking adorable.

'Dad is doing it up for us this weekend.'

'Wanna help us pick stuff?' asked Sophie.

'I think we have enough, girls.'

'But we need photo frames, Dad, for our shelves.'

They both looked at me.

'I was just going to –'

'Sammie is busy,' said Max.

I glanced down at the coffee table and back at the girls.

'I can have a quick look with you, if you like.' I looked at Max, who shrugged.

'Great. You might be able to stop these pair from bankrupting me.'

'Yay, come on! This way everyone,' said Erin, running ahead. 'I saw a sign for more kid's stuff up here.'

'No more cuddly toys, Erin.' Max pulled the trolley back, before turning it around to follow her.

'This shop has the best teddies,' said Sophie, slipping her hand into mine. I looked down at her, but she just continued walking like it was the most normal thing in the world.

'Who needs a mosquito net?' said Max, pointing to a princess canopy.

'Dad, that's for a princess bed.'

Max looked at me, 'Sammie, is that a mosquito net or what?' He put the canopy over his head and looked out through the mesh.

'It has a crown, Dad.' Erin jumped up trying to poke the gold cut out. Max swatted her away.

'See it works. Even on annoying little girls.' He continued swatting, making Sophie burst into giggles.

I laughed along too and stepped backwards to avoid bumping into him. 'Oh, sorry,' I said, still laughing as I accidentally stepped back onto someone's foot. I turned around to apologise again when the words caught in my throat. I took in the eyes, nose, the curved Keegan mouth... assembling them together, the recognition hit like a thunderbolt.

'Samantha.'

'Vivien?'

Vivien looked equally confused, like she wasn't sure if it was me – that I looked strange without her nephew, Conor, standing beside me. 'Samantha, how are you?' Her eyes flicked to Sophie beside me, who's hand, weightless a moment ago, now felt like a brick. I wriggled my fingers trying to let go as Vivien watched, her eyes darting from me to Max and Erin behind us.

'Mum.' We both looked to see Christian, Conor's cousin, walking over to us waving a docket. 'I found the num –' He stopped at the sight of me, the white docket mid-air.

'Sammie. Sammie, Jesus. How are you?' He bent down to

give me a kiss on the cheek oblivious to the giddy seven-year-old beside me, still tugging at my arm.

Max and Erin were still messing about and laughing behind us. Vivien was staring, her eyes taking in the whole scene. She was Conor's godmother, his dad's sister, and possibly the nicest woman you could meet. Her messages and voicemails came flooding back to me in a tsunami of guilt. All unreturned since the funeral.

'I'm doing up the house,' I said, with forced enthusiasm. 'I just popped out for a coffee table and a light. I bumped into –'

'Hi,' said Sophie, waving at Vivien and Christian. 'We're picking out stuff for our bedroom.'

'That's nice,' said Vivien, her smile uneasy, her eyes trying to work out what was going on. She knew Sophie wasn't a relation, or Erin or Max. She knew my whole family as I knew Conor's.

'This is Soph–'

'I'm Sophie. Sammie is our dad's friend and she's helping us pick out things.' Erin was over standing beside us now.

'Can we get the blue colour like in your house, Sammie? Dad said we've to ask you, you're the boss of the decorating.'

I felt sucked out of my body, hovering, weightless, looking down at something I couldn't control. Something that was getting worse by the second.

'Can we?' Erin asked again, her words like darts that I wanted to redirect. These kids were killing me.

'I just bumped into the girls and their dad – here,' I said quickly, feeling the need to explain myself while Christian's expression said it all. He shuffled about uncomfortable like he wanted to be anywhere else but standing in front of me.

'Conor and I had planned on doing the house up. So, I'm going to do it up now, myself, for the two of us.'

'Who's Conor?' asked Sophie. 'Is that your nephew who we feeded the swans with?'

'No, silly. That's Finn,' said Erin.

'Girls.' Max walked over, dragging the trolley behind him. I hated him in that moment. 'Sorry,' he nodded, smiling at Vivien and Christian. 'Girls, leave Sammie alone. We'll see you over at the frames, okay?' He nodded and smiled again, neither of which were returned by Vivien or Christian.

Max and the girls walked off leaving me, Vivien and Christian in a circle of awkwardness. Christian cleared his throat looking at his mam to say something. He was the image of Conor, just younger with the same colouring and dancing blue eyes that made me want to weep.

'I'm, eh, I bought an apartment with my boyfriend Declan, you remember him? Mam is helping me do it up.'

'Make it a bit homely,' said Vivien, her voice soft, calming, something I remembered I'd loved about her.

'I hardly know Max. He's a workman on my road, and I only met his girls a couple of times, and –

'Sammie.' Vivien put her hand up. 'You don't have to explain yourself to us, darling.'

'But I –'

'Please. You have been through a terrible, terrible, thing. Only someone who has walked in your shoes can pass judgement.'

Christian was staring at the ground, either wishing it would swallow him or unable to look at me. I couldn't bare the latter.

It was a shock seeing them both, no matter where it was or with who. Vivien was looking at me now with glassy eyes, and I could tell that I was a reminder for her too. That seeing me alone, highlighted the empty space beside me where Conor usually stood.

Chapter 30

I couldn't explain anymore, there was nothing left to say. We'd looked like the fucking Waltons on a day out – the perfect family – and Vivien and Christian couldn't un-see that. I'd said goodbye to them, exchanged vacant hugs and left straight away. I'd practically ran to my car and drove with a ball of anger so huge I thought my stomach might explode. I was still fuming by the time I got home and had resisted the urge (twice) to stop off to buy wine. The only reason I didn't was because I wanted to make sure I could ring Max with a clear head. I checked the time again; it was almost six. There was no point calling him because he was with the girls for the night.

I was in the kitchen boiling the kettle, even though I wasn't in the humour for tea. I could see Jojo in the tree from the window. She was playing with a spinner thing, tipping the edge making it light up – yellows, pinks and purples bounced off the leaves. I abandoned the kettle and poured myself a glass of water instead.

'What's that?' I asked Jojo, stepping out into the garden.

'A fidget spinner.' I sat down and watched her spinning, her lips pursed in concentration.

'That's all it does is spin?'

'Pretty much,' she said, not looking up.

'I didn't see you at the party?'

'What party?' Jojo stopped to look at me.

'Millie's. I saw the bouncy castle from my back window. The

party looked great.'

'You were watching from your window?'

'No, well, yes – just for a minute or two.' I'd no idea how long I'd been watching, minutes fused together when I was hungover. 'It looked like a lot of fun, the bouncy castle had caught my eye and then I saw your family, well, your parents and Millie.'

Jojo looked genuinely freaked out.

'I didn't see you, that was all.'

'You're such a weirdo, Sammie. Stalking me. Of course, I was at my sister's party.'

She lifted the fidget spinner again, tipping it, making her face light as it spun. I had been hungover that morning, she'd obviously been there and I'd just missed her. I regretted mentioning it, leaving a new awkwardness between us.

My thoughts soon went back to Max, the anger pinching at me again.

'Are you okay?' asked Jojo after a few minutes.

'Sure?' I sat up in the chair and shrugged. 'I'm fine.'

I watched her for a few moments, sipping my water, trying to ignore the urge to divulge my whole Ikea saga to a twelve-year-old. I could hear Celine over the wall, humming all chirpy, like birds were flying around her head and she was skipping about with a broom – realistically she was probably hanging washing.

Jojo glanced up at me over the lights. 'What's wrong?'

I took a long slug of water, a little too enthusiastically making the ice clatter off my teeth. 'Me? There's nothing wrong with me.'

'You're like the worse liar, Sammie.'

'I am a pretty bad liar, to be fair.' I ended up telling Jojo the whole thing, a child friendly version with no cursing and less emotions.'

'Erin and Sophie sound like head wreckers.'

'They're actually lovely, it was just … well, I suppose it wasn't their fault, now that I think about it.'

Jojo was holding the fidget spinner flat in her palm, the lights still flickering; it looked like a mini-UFO about to take flight.

'It's just Conor. I felt bad hanging out with them – with Max. I wouldn't ever do that to –'

'To Conor?'

I nodded, feeling an unexpected lump rise in my throat.

'How can you do anything to Conor, he's … well, he's ye know.'

'Yes. Jojo. I know Conor is … He's in heaven.' I said the word 'heaven' through gritted teeth, wanting to shout 'dead', 'but I would never replace him.'

'You can't replace anyone.' She was off again with the fidget thing, spinning it between her thumb and forefinger making my eyes unwillingly follow. 'Mrs Addison always says that we're all different. We got, like, ten different worksheets to fill in and colour on it. If there's one thing school has thought me it's that nobody is the same.'

'You can be a little wreck-the-head sometimes.'

She was laughing and I had to take a sip of my drink so as not to swear.

'Just saying, Conor is Conor and Max is Max.'

'This is silly speaking to you about it. I'm sorry, Jojo. You're just, well, I'm an adult and I shouldn't be talking about such adulty stuff.'

'You just said the word "adulty."' She arched her eyebrow.

'Anyway.' I ignored the dig. 'How was your day? Did you do anything fun with your friends?'

'No, Sammie – I didn't. Did you do anything fun with yours? Oh, yes, you went to Ikea.'

'I went to Ikea on my own. I met Max there.'

'So Max is your friend?'

'No, and I'm not speaking to you about this. Can I have a turn of your fidgety spin thing?' I asked, trying to change the subject.

'No.' She clasped her hand around it, smiling.

'Okayyy.' I laughed at the randomness of it all, and she joined in.

'FYI Sammie. You're, like, obsessed with me having friends, when you have none yourself. I think Conor would like you to have a friend, to have a Max.'

My smile faded. 'It's different, Jojo. You don't understand.'

'I think you're the one that doesn't understand.'

After Jojo went, I sat out for a while longer. The anger was still there, laying low, waiting to be raised by the thought of Max. I still needed to clear things up, in case … well, in case I'd given him the wrong idea about our friendship, or whatever it was.

I remembered Conor and I talking about one of us dying. We weren't together long, perhaps a year, and it was one of those morbid conversations that are romantic at the time. I'd told him I wouldn't care if he met someone else, but that I'd haunt them, which looking back didn't make much sense. We had the same conversation again just before we'd bought our house. We were signing mortgage protection forms in a stuffy cubicle in the bank. I wasn't listening, I'd just wanted to go pick out furniture and talking about one of us dying, or getting critically ill, wasn't really on my radar. When the bank lady left us to go photocopy stuff, Conor had mistaken my silence for me being freaked out. 'This is all routine, Sam. Nothing will happen to either of us.' He took my hand and I nodded, enjoying the sweet moment, which had been rare amidst the stress of buying a house. 'And if anything happens to me, if you bump me off to clear the mortgage,' he squeezed my hand, smiling, 'I would want you to meet someone. I wouldn't want you lonely, or afraid on your own.' This was back when the thought of staying in a house on my own, would have been the equivalent of a Bushtucker Trial. The bank lady had come back, and that was the end of our conversation.

Conor had been right. I was lonely, and scared was an understatement, but I was only lonely for him. It was him that I missed and no decorating or keeping busy was going to ease that yearning. And especially not another man. The thought of Max ignited the anger again, and I picked up my phone, no longer caring if the girls were with him.

I didn't have his number. I was standing in my kitchen with the phone like a stress ball, squeezed in my palm, ready to give him a piece of my mind and I didn't have his bloody number. Without thinking or caring and blinded by frustration, I punched a message out to Rob asking for Max's number 'for a neighbour looking for an extension'. I had to stop myself going into more details, pretending it was John and Celine wanting a sunroom. That's how irrational my thoughts were, I was paranoid. He replied straight away, and I tapped on the number highlighted in the message. I wasn't going to save it.

'Max, it's Sammie,' I said when he answered the phone, as sharp and formal as I could.

'Sammie, before you say anything, I'm terribly sorry about earlier. I went mad at the girls afterwards.'

'You did?' I said, his apology knocking me off kilter.

'I've told them before about speaking out of turn. The amount of times they've made a show of me in front of people saying … well, it doesn't matter now, but today was serious. They told me what they'd said, and I know how that could have come across to your friends.'

'To Conor's family.'

'Really, his family? Aw, Jesus.'

'Yes, aw Jesus.'

'I'm so sorry –'

'Look, Max, I think you're a nice guy, but I don't like you like that. I love Conor, and I –'

'Whoa, Sammie, hold you horses.'

'Hold you horses?' I couldn't help but laugh. 'Who the hell says that.'

'Me,' said Max. I could tell he was trying not to laugh too. 'Sammie, we hardly know each other.'

'I know,' I said feeling a bit ridiculous now.

'I'm not really sure where this has all come from. You've been though a lot and I never for a second thought of us as anything more than, well, if friends would be okay to say? Look, as much as Carla does my absolute head in, I still love her. I wish I didn't, but sure, it is what it is. I can't see myself with anyone else either. I compare everyone to her.'

'Is she, ehm … the girls mentioned something about her getting married?' I winced waiting for him to break down crying, he needed to know if he didn't already.

'Ah, the big diamond ring? It's a promise ring or some bollocks like that. She told the girls not to tell me, which was pretty stupid seeing as they can't keep their mouths shut – being kids and all. Anyway, it's nothing, but if she does – when she does get engaged for real, I'll just have to deal with that when the time comes.'

'I didn't know you still loved her?'

'It took me a self-help book to figure that one out. Don't laugh. I picked it up online. Seemingly there's a fine line between love and hate, and if you feel hate for someone, you're still feeling so ye know, bottom line I love and hate her.'

I felt my shoulders drop with relief as he said that.

'Now it doesn't help that every time I'm collecting the girls,

247

she has herself done up like a dog's dinner, even though she's with her fella. So, I get to see the best physical version of Carla every Wednesday and Friday.'

'I'm sorry, Max. I didn't think.'

'No, I'm sorry. Your head must be wrecked now over Conor's family.'

'Yes, it is. It really is, I'd hate them to think I'd forget about him and move on just like that.'

'Anyone in a ten-mile radius can see you love Conor.'

I felt my eyes prickle with tears.

'Hopefully one day though I can stop loving Carla.'

'When you catch her off guard and she's in bits.'

'Exactly.' We both laughed.

'I hope we can be friends, Sammie?'

'Can a boy and girl ever just be friends?' I joked.

'They can. I read about that in my book. You may at times find me attractive and wonder what if? But you should be able to restrain yourself for the sake of our friendship.'

'I'll try to control myself.' I laughed.

'Do. Now I gotta go and get these two motor mouths to bed. I'll chat to you soon.'

His words had washed away my anxiety, and I felt physically lighter hanging up the phone. I didn't care what anyone else thought. I knew how I felt, and whatever way Vivien or Christian perceived it was their own business. I was going to drink to that.

Chapter 31

The next few days passed in a murky heat wave. The air was tight and the sun relentless. I hadn't seen Jojo but I'd found myself sneaking peeks at her house. Her dad had looked up at me once, holding eye contact long enough for me to panic, and pretend I was opening my window. He was dressed in a sharp grey suit, which seemed odd for a bus driver. At least, I was almost certain Jojo had said he was a bus driver. I was doubting myself on everything.

I'd seen Max a couple of times on my way to the shop; the second time he was packing up, having finally finished Mr Watson's house. The old man stood beaming from his porch, obviously delighted with the transformation.

Mam was full on harassing me, texting me to go for walks, even though it was twenty-six degrees. Then a string of – Are you okay? What are you doing with yourself? Fancy a night out? I had replied each time, telling her I would call around at the weekend, but that wasn't enough. Breda and Jim were having an anniversary party, or 'do' as she liked to call it, and she was adamant I should go. As her text had said – 'to get out and be sociable'. I'd politely declined three times; the third time I'd written 'fuck off', before deleting it and again sending, 'no thanks'. So, by the time my phone rang that evening I had no doubt it was Mam asking me again was I going. I was ready to lose it.

'Well, are you coming tomorrow night?'

I had the phone wedged between my shoulder and ear, drying a pot. I'd just made pasta that I'd ended up throwing out, it was too hot for food. 'Like I've said already in my last three text messages, I'm not going, Mam. But thanks for the invite. Again.'

'But –'

'I'm not being bad, but I've no desire to go to a forty-seventh wedding anniversary party. Who even has parties for those anyway?' I placed the lid upside down on the pot and opened the press, stacking it in on top of the others.

'Of course, sure what was I thinking?' said Mam, her voice rising. 'You don't want to be celebrating wedding anniversaries. It was insensitive of me to ask.'

I rolled my eyes, wiping down the draining board, and folding the cloth by the tap. The smell from the sink seemed a lot better – or maybe I was just getting used to it. 'It wasn't insensitive, Mam. Don't be silly. It has nothing to do with Conor, even if he was here, I still wouldn't want to go.'

Mam paused, waiting for me to say more to ramble on with my excuse, so she could pick a loophole. I stood firm, quite literally with my back against the sink watching the hands of the kitchen clock jut around.

'Right, so … I guess I'll go along with just your dad. He won't want to stay long, obviously, with him on the mineral water. Hmm, I might have to ask Tasha to come too. Breda is my very best friend, and I can't just run out after the cake. Do you know she hired someone to make the cake? Chocolate biscuit: she's gone all modern. Personally, I think a celebratory cake should be fresh cream and sponge.'

'I'm sure Tasha would love to go,' I said, interrupting Mam's bitch fest about her very best friend.

'Right, well if you change your mind, love, you know where we'll be.'

The next conversation I had with my mam was like a weird dream. The phone rang the following morning and I groaned at the sight of her name. She'd always been suffocating, but this was getting ridiculous. I presumed she was ringing to give me the low down on the party. What the food was like, the turn out, if Dad was in good form. I'd had a few glasses of wine the night before and had fallen into a deep sleep. It took a couple of moments to get my bearings and digest what she was saying to me.

'So, let me get this straight, Mam. A neighbour of mine has told you that I'm drinking too much. And that they're concerned? That's actually what you're saying to me?'

'They said that – you're – drinking – quite – regularly.' She said the words slowly, like she was teaching me a new language.

'Right sorry, quite regularly.' I spat out a laugh.

'This is serious, Samantha.'

'Serious? Too bloody right it is. The cheek of them,' I said, sitting up in the bed.

'Well, technically it's not a "them", it's only one person who said it.'

'Great.'

'Look, love.' Mam's voice was soft now, angering me more.

'They're just concerned – '

'I have a glass of wine in my back garden when it's sunny out, for god's sake.'

'You don't need to get defensive.'

'I'm not. I'm not getting defensive. This is ridiculous.' I sighed heavily, trying my best to keep my cool.

'They're just concerned about you.'

'Ha. Concerned?' I almost choked on the word. 'The nosy bastards.'

'Samantha Clancy.'

'Mam, don't. I mean it. I'm not in the mood. I'm thirty years of age. Jesus, if I can't have a lousy drink in my garden then what the hell can I do?'

'It doesn't matter, just forget I said anything.'

'Did Tasha go last night? Was he or she talking to Tasha too?'

'No, it was just me. Tasha stayed at home.'

'Who was it? I don't know any of my neighbours that drink in the Railway pub. In fact, I don't know any of my neighbours, full stop. Except John and Celine, who were home last night, because I could hear their TV. Was it Laura? Or at least I think that's her name. She's around my age with long black hair?'

'Look, love, please … try and calm down. Maybe they got it wrong and confused you with someone else. It's an easy mistake to make.'

'You're a shit liar, Mam.'

'Well, that's something I pride myself on.'

We both stayed silent, my breath ragged like a fighting dog.

'Just maybe try cut back on the wine, that's all. People for some reason think wine is not like other drink, it's not a spirit so it's more acceptable, but it's not. Alcohol is alcohol, no matter how fancy.'

I couldn't believe we were having this conversation. I actually blinked a couple of times, squeezing my eyes tight, thinking I might wake up. 'I don't over drink, Mam. I have a couple of glasses in the evenings. It's no different to a sedative or whatever you're always trying to ram down my neck.'

I was fuming by the time I got off the phone and was tempted to have a bottle of wine instead of tea with my breakfast. Mam knew lots of people through the Community Centre, especially old busy bodies. It could have been any one of the curtain twitchers on my road, watching me coming back from the shop. Maybe they'd seen a bottle of wine sticking out of my carrier bag and discarded the rest – the bread, the milk, the tampons!

I was tempted to knock on every door and ask them out straight, but I'd seen enough movies to know that would make me look insane. I felt restless for most of the day, like an electric current was running through my body. I couldn't sit still. I tried channelling my frustrations into cleaning. I scrubbed the floors, the tiles, and rammed the hoover around every room. I was exhausted by the time the sun went down taking the temperature with it. Despite it all, it took me forever to fall asleep.

Chapter 32

The following day, I woke up angry. It was like Mam's words had grown roots overnight leaving me paranoid. I drew the blinds in the living room, craning my neck in every direction. The road was quiet as usual. I pulled on my dressing gown to check the post box, taking my time, feeling for nothing. The only person I saw was an elderly neighbour walking back from the shops with a newspaper. He looked frail, aided by a walking stick, and when I waved, he didn't notice, making me eliminate him on poor vision alone. The blinds were down in Laura's house and there were no cars in the drive, making me think they'd gone away. I felt relief about this but wasn't sure why.

Back inside my phone beeped with a message from Tasha and a couple of missed calls from Mam. I turned on the radio in the kitchen, something I'd never done even when Conor was alive. I never got the whole kitchen radio thing and only ever listened to it in the car.

There was a breakfast show on, a woman giving out about parking outside her house. The presenter was egging her on, using her first name at the end of each sentence, building up a rapport. 'They park the boot of their cars over my driveway, and I'd have to be driving a scooter to get out, Pete. It's extremely inconsiderate, and I've done up signs.' I wondered for a moment did she live on

Tasha's road.

'You're dead right, Angela. If you bumped off their car, sure wouldn't it be you that would have to pay out …' The conversation went on, and I found myself glad that even if I did have neighbours who made up lies, at least I didn't have Angela living beside me.

Tasha used to love listening to talk shows. I spent my teenage years falling asleep to the tinny sound of her radio through the bedroom wall – joyriding was a big topic in the nineties and seemed to be always featured. So, when she rang later on that afternoon, I answered eager to give her laugh about aul Angela and the talk show.

'I can't fucking believe you forgot him.' Tasha's voice burst down the phone.

'Forgot who – what?'

'I sent you a message, Sammie. I texted you this morning to remind you to collect Finn. The summer camp rang me; he was sobbing. I'd told him you'd be there.'

'But today is Tuesday. You asked me to collect Finn on Thursday.'

'I said Tuesday.' Tasha's voice was more a growl.

I scrambled through my brain for the conversation, for the day. I was adamant. 'I feel terrible that Finn was upset, but –'

'So, you should.'

'… But you said Thursday, Tasha. You definitely did. I have a reminder set on my phone for it.'

'I told you Tuesday. You were probably fucking drunk.' She mumbled the last bit, making me ask her to repeat it.

'You heard me, Sammie. You were probably drunk.'

I felt my face burn. 'Don't even think about turning this around on me. It was your mix up.'

'You're turning into a dipso, Sammie.'

'And you're turning into a slapper.'

I could hear Mam's voice in the background. A rush of anger shot through me. How could Tasha pull me up in front of Mam? This was all I needed.

We hung up and I was tempted to ring Mam and tell her that her precious Natasha was not the poor tolerant wifey she painted herself as. For a split second, I wanted to tell Mam about Rob. I wanted to hurt Tasha back.

After my anger subsided, I was left in a pool of confusion. Had I made a mistake? Had I mixed up the day? I knew I hadn't and for that reason they could all piss off.

'Are you thinking about Conor?' asked Jojo. She settled back against the tree bark, tucking one knee under her chin.

'No,' I said, squinting to look at her. The sun was settling behind her, lighting her hair with an orange crown.

'You look really sad and I thought nothing could be sadder than someone dying.'

I was only half listening to Jojo, instead replaying Tasha's words in my head. I took a sip of tea. I'd replaced the wine to prove a point. I could tell Mam about the loan shark. I could tell her Tasha's finances were fucked, along with her relationship. I was being nasty, and I knew it, revelling in my toxic thoughts.

'Sammie!' Jojo waved, breaking me from my daze. She wrapped an arm around her knees.

'Sorry, I was thinking about my sister.'

'Is she okay?' asked Jojo looking genuinely worried. As Jojo spoke, I noticed a raised bubble on her forearm. It was bright red and glowed angrily under the sun.

'What's that on your arm?'

Jojo looked around her.

'On your arm, Jojo.' I knew my tone was accusing but Tasha had left me with little patience. 'It's looks nasty, let me see.' I got up and walked towards her.

'It's nothing.' Jojo cupped her hand over the mark 'It doesn't hurt.'

I stood beneath her, realising it was the closest I'd ever been.

'I spilled beans on it – they kind of exploded in the microwave.' Jojo removed her hand and turned her forearm towards me. 'There was orange mush everywhere.'

I shielded my eyes from the sun that had found my face through the branches. Up close her arm was worse, covered in a wet gloss like it had been weeping.

'I think you should have it covered, Jojo. It could get infected.'

'It's fine.' Jojo rolled her eyes. 'You sound just like my dad. He always over-reacts.'

The comment threw me. I surprised myself by doubting that he'd care. 'It's just, it looks really sore.'

'Well, it's not.' Jojo's eyes anchored on mine.

Something shifted between us, the repressed anger in Jojo's voice. She was looking at me different and I wanted to ignore it. I sat back down and started up a conversation about her favourite TV shows, but the burn kept catching my eye. Even in the shade, it was glowing, fighting for my attention.

Chapter 33

'How are you getting on, Dad?' I asked, bending down to try and see what he was doing. Dad's legs were poking out from under my kitchen sink, his t-shirt leaving a smile of pasty belly. 'I can just call a plumber if you can't fix it. It honestly doesn't bother me anymore, and I was only thinking the other day, that the smell isn't so bad lately.'

'No, all good, love … just tightening her up.'

This was only the second time my dad had ever been in my house, and we both knew it wasn't just to do odd jobs. After he finished fixing the sink, I made us both a cup of tea, and we sat facing each other at the kitchen table. I left the patio door ajar, the sounds of outside diluting the new awkwardness.

'You've been busy with the garden anyway, and the house is looking lovely … fair play.' Dad took a swig of tea, looking around him.

'Thanks, I've had plenty of time on my hands.'

'Just keep an eye on that sink. I cleared a mountain of shite out of it, so it should be grand now.'

'Thanks, Dad.'

'You should get one of those stoppers with the grids on them.' Dad gestured making a claw with his hands. 'They catch the food in the sink for ye. If I see one, I'll pick it up.'

'Thanks Dad, one of them would be handy alright.'

Silence fell again, leaving us both staring into our mugs.

'Sammie'

'Yeah, Dad.'

'I don't want to get all mushy on ye, you'll be throwing me out the door in a minute, but I want to tell ye, I'm proud. I'm really proud of you, Samantha.' His use of my full name made the hairs on my neck stand up. I sipped my tea, hoping he wouldn't steer the conversation into territories we were both uncomfortable in.

'You know your mam's worried. When is she ever not? says you. But she's honestly getting herself into a twist altogether.'

I shifted about in my seat. I knew what was coming.

'She told me you both had words.' He fiddled with the handle of the mug. 'I think, it's just with your Aunt Winnie –'

'I'm not Aunt Winnie. I'm nothing like her.'

'I know … I know.' He took a deep breath and tried again.

'What you've been through is unimaginable, Sammie. I mean, Jesus …' He shook his head, and I swore I saw the glint of a tear in his eye. 'I can't even think of the chap. I can't even say his name and it rips at me. It really bloody does.'

I put my hand on Dad's arm and he slid it back by his side. He wasn't one for emotional outbursts.

'You never cease to amaze me with your strength. Even as a kid you were tough. You went around in your pink frocks and what nots without a hair out of place, and those bow things your mam had yis wear – but you were fearless. It was always in you. You were different, even me … I was never fearless, and then there was the drinking.'

'Dad, don't …' I hung my head and gnawed the inside of my cheek. We'd never discussed Dad's drinking. It'd never affected me or Tasha. We were shielded, we felt we'd no right to bring it up.

'The drinking was probably the only time I'd stepped outside the lines.' He half laughed. 'I stayed in the same job because it was safe. The same area, the same everything. I was afraid of what I didn't know, but you never were. I don't think I could have been as strong as you've been, Sammie. I know you don't like when people say you're strong. See, I know that about you, love. But I'm just so proud of you …' He choked on his words and had to cough to compose himself. I never saw my dad like this, and it was making me anxious.

'Dad, it's okay. I know what you're trying to say. I'm okay, honest. I'm doing fine.' I smiled, my jaw tight.

'My life's been pretty uneventful for a man of sixty-three.'

I opened my mouth to speak again, but he put his hand up to stop me.

'Ye see, I had a grand start out, a great childhood. My da had a good job and in Dublin back in the fifties that was all that mattered. There was food on the table and we'd shoes on our feet. I had good mates and a gang of siblings. I was never lonely. Then when I was a teenager – well, about fifteen, back then that was a fully-grown man. I was working and handing me ma and da up a wage, when it all went wrong. Your Granda Jack did his back in. He fell on wet leaves on the footpath – that fall changed our whole lives.' My dad was looking at me, his eyes locked into mine.

'It started with just a few pints in the afternoons. Me ma used to send him – she felt sorry for him hanging around the house all day. He'd always been a worker; he was going out of his mind with the boredom. But it was like he put his foot on a slide and couldn't get back off. Within weeks, he was coming home drunk every day. Our house was turned upside down. It affected Winnie the worst, being the only girl. She was always a daddy's girl. The drink took a hold of him and messed everything up. Then it was my turn. It came out of nowhere, Sammie. I swear to God, one minute I was enjoying a couple of pints with the workmates. The next thing I had your mam and your Nana Margo crying in my face, begging me to stop. I'd never seen it coming. I hadn't seen where I'd ended up.' He paused, and I realised my heart was racing, my pulse galloping in my ears.

'Looking back, I'd been feeling off. I'd had it all, but something in my head switched, and I enjoyed a drink more cause it took me somewhere. It took me on a journey where what I was feeling didn't matter. I was an alcoholic, Sammie. I still can't believe I was an alcoholic. I'll always be a recovering one. I'll never shake the label. It's part of who I am. I still have to go to meetings, and I do a bit of mentoring, trying to help others who want to quit. There ye are now,' he winked. 'Not just a pretty face.'

I sat up, straightening my cup on the coaster. I was glad he was opening up to me, but there was no comparison.

'You thinking you're above this conversation is what's worrying me, love. No-one thinks they're above this kind of story, unless they can see themselves in it.

'Do you think I'm an alcoholic, Dad? Do you think I'm like

Granda Jack or Aunt Winnie, or even you?'

He shook his head. 'No. But I am saying it started out small and snowballed that's what happens. You think it's helping, but it grips ye.'

'It does help. It helps me sleep and relax just enough to be okay.'

'It runs in families, Sammie.'

'Alcoholism?'

'As true as anything, it rips though generations.'

'Do you think you're okay now?' I wanted to ask him about John seeing him in the pub, but I couldn't get the words right in my head.

'How do you mean?'

I shrugged, unsure now myself.

'Do you mean do I ever want a drink?' I felt my cheeks redden and I wished I'd never asked. 'If that's what you mean, then no. Your mam can't understand that; she thinks I don't trust myself when actually it's her that doesn't trust me. I know I won't drink again, but do I miss the pub? Yes. I miss the company and the banter.'

'Do you ever go in?'

'Sometimes, to my old mates, and I'm not the only one drinking mineral water.'

'John next door saw you and I was wondering –'

'Wondering if I'd fallen off the wagon?' He laughed.

'Well, kinda, not really.'

'It's terrible, isn't it? The worry of someone drinking.' Dad said no more but his point had been made. It left me confused, I wasn't sure what I was. Maybe I was relying on the wine too much?

'I'll cut back, Dad.' I looked him straight in the eyes and the words seemed to satisfy him, relaxing his mouth into a smile.

'Come here to me, love.' Dad held his arms out and I leaned into them, wishing for the first time, that he was still the only man I'd ever loved.

That evening there was no sign of Jojo. I had sat in my garden with two cans of fizzy orange, like a kid waiting for her friend to turn up. I pulled back the metal ring and the bubbles hissed, spilling orange around the rim. The smell brought with it, happy memories of my childhood. I took small sips, hoping Jojo would come soon. I wanted to offer her the other can so I could see her arm – a stupid plan, but it was the best I could think of. I don't know why I needed to see it, it's not like the burn would have healed or I expected there to be more. My brain cramped with Conor, Tasha and now Jojo. I didn't know if I was building things up in my head or missing red flags, like maybe I had with my drinking. Even sober, there was no sharpness to my thoughts. They would swarm in, blur together, leaving me to pull out what I knew for sure. Which was nothing.

The garden went from peach to grey, leaving me under a nail clipping of moon. I picked up the two cans and went inside, throwing one into the bin and putting the other in the fridge for Jojo tomorrow. What if I didn't see her? If that was it – I'd annoyed her with my questions. The thought made me anxious.

Upstairs, I looked out the back window. Their kitchen was lit up like a white box in the dusky surroundings. As I leaned against the windowsill, I could see the double doors open behind the dining table. A pair of black socked feet poked out across the living room, presumably her dad sitting down. I could see glimpses of pink, flick back and forth across the gap, either Millie or Jojo dancing. I was so close to the window my breath made a foggy screen on the glass. I desperately wanted it to be Jojo.

I wiped the window with my sleeve, leaving damp streaks, making me move over so I could still see. Jojo's mam appeared at the back door and pushed it open, stepping outside. It was the clearest I'd ever seen her. She looked different to what I'd built up in my head. Her face was pinched. That looked like her natural expression, giving her a harshness I hadn't imagined. She shouted in to someone behind her, before rubbing the side of her face looking agitated. As she stepped outside, she stopped to look up at the sky and I instinctively moved back so she wouldn't see me. Behind the curtain now, I could see her walk to the side entrance and glance down it, before stamping her foot at what I imagined was a cat.

She walked back to the patio door and I thought she was going in. Instead she closed the door and walked again to the side entrance. She patted her jeans pocket and pulled out a small box. A packet of cigarettes, glossy and unopened. She ripped the side of the box with her teeth and spat the plastic wrapping onto the ground. Flicking a lighter, she stood back into the darkness. My stomach tensed as I watched the small, round glow move from her mouth to her side, back and forth, back and forth. Glowing red and angry in the dark.

Chapter 34

I woke the following morning and went straight to the window to look at Jojo's house. I hadn't slept well. Each time I closed my eyes I saw Jojo's arm, the burn haunting my sleep. All the blinds were pulled down and the house looked still. My phone buzzed in my pocket.

'Sammie, are you in?' Wayne's voice was sombre and I knew instantly my sister had told him about Rob.

'Yeah, call around.'

Half an hour later, I was sitting in my living room with Wayne on the sofa opposite. He looked slimmer; the dark circles under his eyes made me think he'd known for a few days. He was rubbing his hands together like he was trying to spark a fire. The sight of him pulled at my conscience and I felt guilty for being so mad at Tasha, for regurgitating her words in my head and lining up more come backs to fire at her. By the looks of it, she'd had enough going on.

'Tasha will kill me if she finds out I called into you.'

'Don't worry, although I'm sure she'll have guessed. Do you want tea, or something to drink?'

His shoulders were slouched, his body moulded into a giant ball. I was surprised I felt sorry for him.

'Tasha told me about Rob, about the – I can't even say it. It makes me feel like I'm gonna burst.'

I stayed quiet. I didn't know how much Tasha had told him, if she'd even mentioned having feelings for Rob.

'She told me last night. We weren't even arguing, she just sort of said it.'

The famous words – 'and how does that make you feel?' sat on the tip of my tongue. I nodded, not giving anything away.

'I didn't sleep a wink. I couldn't even go to work 'cause my head was all over the place. I keep seeing them together and I'm thinking all sorts, like was it just a kiss? Or has she been messing about with him for months behind my back?' He spat the last words, wiping his mouth with the back of his hand. 'I'm a mess, Sammie. I can't say it to my family. They'll go mental on her and my mates would think I'm a mug.'

I guessed he didn't know Lydia knew, but I didn't dare ask.

'I'm sorry to be here.' He looked down at his hands. His eyes watered and for a second I thought he was going to cry. Please don't start crying, I thought. As much as I felt sorry for him, I could never in a million years comfort Wayne when it came to my sister. There was too much history between them, too many times he was awful to her.

'It was just a kiss, Wayne.' I heard myself say. 'A stupid kiss and Tasha was drunk. She loves you and I know she's sorry.'

'She didn't say that?'

'She didn't?' Oh crap 'What did she say then?'

'She told me she wanted to kiss him. That she knew what she was doing, and because things between us haven't been good in so long, it felt right.'

267

What the hell was Tasha on? I tried to not let the shock show on my face. 'Did she say all this last night?'

He nodded his head. 'She was as calm as anything. She just said it like she was telling me she'd been shopping, or she was talking about one of the ditzes that she works with.'

I wanted to pull him up on calling her work friends thick, especially when he knew it pissed her off. Him saying this made his victim mask slip – and made me feel a little more comfortable that I could see glimpses of the Wayne I knew.

'She said things weren't right even before we had Aria, and if it wasn't for the kids, we wouldn't be together. I didn't know any of this, Sammie.' He jabbed his chest with his thumb. 'I'd no bleedin' clue.'

'Look, I know it must be really tough having Tasha say all this to you. And well, the Rob thing – the kiss.' I corrected myself so we all knew where we stood. 'It's a shock for you but, in all honesty, you and Tasha have been at each other's throats for years. Surely, you can see she isn't happy? I'm not saying that it's okay to kiss someone else – it isn't. But it hasn't just come out of nowhere.'

'My ma and da fought my whole life, that doesn't mean anything.'

'But you're not them. And the way you speak to her, Wayne. The way you have Finn speaking to her: he's learning from you and that kills Tasha.'

He looked down at his hands, kneading his thumb into his palm. I didn't want to be too harsh with him and had to stop myself from mentioning the whole loan shark mess that she'd been dealing with on her own.

'She talks down to me too.'

'Yeah, but come on, you know how nasty you can be to her – and it goes further than banter, it's chipping away at her all the time.'

Wayne was staring at the floor, his expression unreadable.

'Tasha is far from perfect, but she is an amazing mother and works hard for you all. She always puts the kids and you before herself.'

'I could be better, yeah, I get that,' he mumbled at the knot in the floorboard.

'Do you want to make things work?'

He shrugged, still looking at the floor.

'If you want to make things work, give her some time. Think of what you both need to do, to make things right.'

'Not wear the head off someone else for start.'

'And not constantly put someone down, not be a lazy bastard and not take someone for granted for eleven years.'

He looked up and half smiled. 'I knew you were being too nice.'

'Even if she wasn't my sister, I'd be telling you this. What she did was wrong and it wasn't your fault that she did it, but, well …'

'I do love her. I don't know what I'd do without her. Eleven years is a long time and I don't want to be with anyone else. It's not all bad.' He looked at me like I might not believe him. 'We do have good times too.'

'Well then maybe you need to remind her of them.'

After Wayne had gone to his friend's house for the night (as suggested by Tasha) I gave her a ring. We did the equivalent of what we did growing up, like asking the other if they wanted a cup of tea after a fight, and let the recent tensions between us dissipate.

'Is he gone?' asked Tasha.

'Yeah. He was quiet upset in fairness.'

'Well imagine if he knew I'd slept with Rob?'

'You didn't, Tasha?'

'I did. We met up to discuss the kiss and, well, one thing led to another. So, I'm the slapper you said I am.'

'Tasha –'

'I don't regret it, Sammie. I don't,' she said, trying to convince me or herself.

'Do you love him?'

'Who Rob?' She laughed. 'No. But I did spend an unhealthy amount of time imagining us together over the years. Unfortunately, he hasn't grown much since we were kids. If you get what I mean?'

Stupidly, I said, 'no.'

'Wayne has a lot of flaws, but he's great in bed and would give a twelve-inch Subway a run for its money.'

'Enough details, Tasha, please. I'm going to be sick.'

'Well, what I'm saying is, the connection I thought I'd have with Rob wasn't there and I'm glad I found that out now, rather than imaging it and building it up in my head. Me and Wayne, aren't a match made in heaven. I don't even know if we'll always stay together, but for now I want us to try and work things out.'

'He looked really upset.'

'And? So have I been, hundreds of times over the years. I didn't even tell you half the times he had me tears, putting me down and making me feel worthless. Not to mention being a waster. I may as well have been a single mother trying to raise the kids.'

'But what if he goes after Rob? He'll be locked up!'

'I told him if he does and he ends up in prison, that the kids will be traumatised. To be honest, I think he'd be more traumatised. He's not as tough as he makes out, and I think him being insecure has a lot to do with how he acts.'

'I've never heard you talk like this before, Tasha. You're so calm about it all.'

'I know. It's just I never in a million years thought I'd cheat on Wayne. I despised cheats, but what happened, happened, and I think it happened for a reason.'

'You're not just staying with him for the kids, are you?'

'No, I couldn't. I'm going to try again for me too.'

'Did you tell him about the loan shark?'

'No, for some reason telling him I wore the face of Rob Campbell seemed easier than telling him I owe thousands to a psycho.'

'He's going to find out, Tasha. It's only a matter of time, and it will be a lot worse when he does.'

'I think he's had enough home truths for one week.'

When I hung up, my thoughts bounced back to Jojo. I needed to see her and when I did, I would ask her out straight, all the questions I had pushed back over the weeks. I would ask her everything and be her safe place. Clear, sober, I wouldn't let myself be distracted.

Chapter 35

It was the first of September and I woke under a cloud. A dense grey one that swelled to every inch of my bedroom. I couldn't shift it and it followed me around all morning. It stopped me from washing my face, dressing and even attempting to make breakfast. The first of September even left me with a half cup of cold morning tea, practically unheard of in my family.

There was no outlet for how I felt. No palpitations, no sweating, the terror inside me had nowhere to go. It was caught within me. I felt numb and sad all at the same time and I couldn't shift it, no matter how much I tried.

Every step forward I'd taken seemed minuscule, compared to where I'd planned to be. It was nine days to our wedding anniversary, to what would have been the second part of our journey together. Maybe I would have been pregnant? We'd be discussing baby names and I'd be designing our nursery. I'd pick lemons and greys and farm animals and clouds. We'd go on holiday, just the two of us – one last blowout before our lives would change forever. We would spend hours talking about our future, about our excitement with all that was to come.

I missed Conor so much, it felt raw again. Like the months he'd been gone had evaporated and I was thrown back to the very beginning. I spent the rest of the day trapped inside my head, wandering aimlessly around the house looking for comfort or distraction.

I found myself in the back bedroom, a fist of anger in my stomach. I wanted to find the vision board. I wanted to rip apart every piece of hope we'd ever had. I wanted everything gone from the house, to start afresh, in what was the reality of my new world.

The rain was beating against the window, the wind whistling a harsh tune through the vent. I turned on the bedroom light and walked to the window to pull the blind. For a second, I thought I was imagining it. I squinted to see better, pressing my nose against the glass. The rain was rolling in zig zags down the window, but it was her, it was Jojo sitting alone in the tree. She'd no coat, just her grubby denim dress and she was shaking. I banged on the window trying to catch her attention, it was useless with the wind. I saw a flicker of movement by the kitchen patio. The light was dim, but I could see her mam sitting at the table drinking from a cup. Her face was stern and when she took the cup from her mouth, putting it on the table, I could see her lips set in a straight line. From here, even through the rain, I could see she was angry.

Millie was in the kitchen too, her ponytail poking over the windowsill like a shark's fin. Her mam turned to speak to her, before Millie skipped over, getting pulled into a hug. I banged on the window again, this time harder. I wanted Jojo to see me and her mother to catch my eye, to be embarrassed and ashamed, leaving one daughter outside in that weather, while she snuggled the other. Could things be that bad at home for Jojo, that she'd rather sit in the rain than be inside? Jojo looked like she was talking to herself. My heart ached watching her as she wrapped her arms around her body for comfort. I looked around me for the window key, my hands shaking. Anger bubbled. How dare this woman treat her child like this. How dare she do this to Jojo. I ran into my bedroom, remembering the same key opened all the windows upstairs. I grabbed the key but by the time I got back, Jojo was gone. They all were. Only the cup remained on the kitchen table, letting me know I hadn't imagined it. I wanted to call around and tell her mam what I'd seen, and that it wasn't right. I wanted Jojo to know it wasn't right.

'What a psycho bitch, Tasha, just sitting there all cosy in her kitchen like nothing was wrong. I felt sick looking at Jojo.'

'It's not a big deal for kids to get wet, Sammie,' said Tasha, the phoneline cracking. 'The kids on my road play out in the rain all the time.'

'But she wasn't playing, she was sitting, getting soaked and her mam just looked on like she didn't care.'

'Hmm, has Jojo ever mentioned anything to you about her?'

'No, well I mean, I was so caught up trying to find out about her stepdad that I never really thought that much about her mam. I often heard her calling Jojo and she doesn't sound like the sweetest mother in the world –'

'Who does when they're calling their kids in?' Tasha interrupted.

'Yeah, I know, but she makes Jojo flinch.'

'Has she come out and said that something bad is going on? Has she confided in you at all?'

'No. She talks about her family in a whole different way to

how they look when I'm watching them from the window.'

'You're watching her family from your window? For fuck's sake, Sammie, that's it. You need to get out of the house. You're going insane, like proper weird. I'm sorry!'

'It's not as weird as it sounds.' I sighed. 'Ugh, maybe I am imagining it all. I dunno. Jojo tells me funny stories about her family, they sound normal enough when she's talking about them.'

'There you go then; it could be anything. She could have begged to go out to play and her mam was like "Right, go, get wet, see if I care." Kids are complete head fucks; sometimes you just break and let them do what the hell they want.'

I was silent for a moment, trying to take comfort in my sister's words. Something was still unsettling me, a gut instinct that nudged me harder the more I tried to ignore it.

'She wasn't crying, was she?'

'Well, it was hard to tell with the torrential rain and all, Tasha, but yeah, I think so.'

'Still, it sounds like a normal mother-daughter standoff. That'll be me in a few years with Aria. I'll be standing at the window, shouting – I told you it's freezing out, you can stay out there now. And some neighbour will be looking at me thinking I'm a cruel cow.'

'Yeah … I guess.'

'Say it to Jojo when you see her the next time, in a breezy way, and then see what she says. If she's seems upset, then maybe you could do something, but if she seems normal then forget about it.'

'The bruising.' My heart stung with the memory. 'Tasha, she had bruising on her arm and face and I thought I'd heard her mam slap her once, it was weeks ago. But I can't be sure, it could have been something else. I should have asked her more about everything …'

'I think you're over-reacting, Sammie. Finn goes around black and blue. Kids get bruising, especially ones who climb trees on a regular basis. You need to start concentrating on yourself.'

'But I should have asked her about it again. She also had a burn: she said she was making beans.'

'Well, you can ask her the next time. She's not going anywhere, she lives in the house behind you, Sammie. You'll probably see her tomorrow.'

'I hope so,' I said, feeling like tomorrow was too far away.

It rained for the next couple of days and I felt anxious not getting the chance to talk to Jojo. I watched her house, examining it, but there was nothing to see. I was over thinking everything that I had seen, pulling and twisting at it, until it became completely distorted. I really wanted to believe Tasha, that it was all normal kid stuff, something I had no clue about.

But then all the dots would try to join inside my head – the bruise, the burn, her stepdad's temper, her mam. The pure sadness that would creep into Jojo's eyes. Out of fear I pushed them back, scattering them around my mind, afraid of what they could all mean together. It was all I could do until I saw her again.

Chapter 36

I yanked at the crooked tower of shopping baskets stacked inside the shop door and looked up to see Kai laughing at me. It was his last week before starting back at college. I narrowed my eyes at him as I wrestled with a basket handle. The weather had cleared the past few days, and I'd spent most of my time watching the back garden to see if Jojo was there. I didn't know what I wanted to say to her – nothing, going on Tasha's advice.

Having finally freed a basket and sticking a middle finger up at Kai, I walked down past the newspapers and magazines stand, towards the fridges along the back of the shop. I hadn't drunk wine since my chat with Dad, not that I hadn't wanted to. It was more to prove a point. I was still convinced that I hadn't become dependent on it. I just enjoyed it, that was all – or maybe that was the problem. Either way I kept on walking, picking up milk, ham and butter and placing them neatly into my basket, maintaining control. I turned onto the sauce aisle as a short cut to the tills and stopped still.

It was her. It was Jojo's mam. She was standing with a basket full of groceries and a scowl that could sour every milk carton in the shop. She glanced at me before turning back to the jar of white sauce in her hand. She was reading the label, running her finger along the side. I took in the sight of her, the woman who'd intrigued me for so long. She looked older up close with dark greasy roots that bled into yellow hair. She was wearing a grey t-shirt and cut off denim shorts

– the dowdy frayed type that stopped just below the knee. Realising I was staring, I quickly turned towards the shelf and looked at the soups. Tomato, chicken noodle, country vegetable. I could feel the heat of her beside me like she radiated anger. I wasn't sure what to do. Should I go over? But what could I say? I scanned the packets in front of me, the words now foreign staring back. Picking one up, I watched her from the corner of my eye. She put the jar back on the shelf and sighed, rubbing the side of her face, like choosing a jar of sauce was the most stressful decision to make. Maybe they were struggling financially, and it was causing a strain on the whole family – or she was depressed, and her moods reflected onto Jojo. She picked up a packet of something and flung it into her basket before turning to walk away.

'Excuse me,' I shouted, shocking myself with my voice.

She turned to look at me.

'Ehm … excuse me, hi.' I walked over to her bouncing the basket off my knees with each step.

'Hi … my name is Sammie; I live in the house at the back of yours.' She looked at me with narrow blue eyes that were a darker shade than Jojo's. 'I chat to your daughter over the garden wall and –'

'You chat to Jennifer?'

'Yes.' I nodded, hoping we'd found some common ground. 'She's the funniest girl, she loves a chat, and well, over the past couple of months while chatting, she seems a little –'

The woman turned her whole body to face me, lowering her eyebrows. 'Sorry, what's your name again?'

'Sammie.' I felt my face redden, hoping she hadn't seen me watching her house from my window.

'Sammie.' She repeated it like it was the silliest word she'd ever heard. 'Sammie. You're telling me you've been talking to my daughter Jennifer for months?'

'With the nice weather, I've been in my garden and she chats to me in the tree.' I was feeling more like a weirdo by the second. I changed the basket to my other hand, the handle now slippery in my wet palms. She tilted her head, looking at me like she was trying to figure out if I was deranged. I needed to just come out and say it. 'As I said, she is a lovely girl, and, well I'm a little concerned to be honest. She hasn't said anything to me about it, but I think maybe she's falling out with her friends, or there is … I don't know, something going on at home that's causing her to worry.' I chewed my lip.

'Excuse me.' She spat the words out, startling me. 'Who on earth do you think you are?'

'I was ehm … just concerned, I'm sorry to upset you.'

'Upset me? You haven't upset me. There is nothing wrong with my Jennifer.' She turned around calling Jennifer over her shoulder. 'Jennifer, come here.' She shouted louder in the tone I recognised. 'Do you speak to this woman?'

The girl who rounded the corner wasn't Jojo. It was her sister, the girl I'd seen in the kitchen. She was holding a box of multi-coloured cereal. 'These are the ones I want to try, Mum.' She put the box in the basket.

'Do you know this woman, Jennifer?'

The girl looked at me and shook her head.

'Sorry no, not this daughter,' I said, waving my hand, eager to clear up the misunderstanding. 'I meant your other daughter, Jojo. I presumed Jojo's name was short for Jennifer.' I gave a laugh that was more nervous than intended.

She put her hand on her hip. 'I don't have a daughter Jojo. I only have one daughter and you're looking at her.'

'But Jojo, she climbs the tree at the end of your garden. Over the summer, we've been chatting and well I just presumed that she lived in your house.'

'Well, she doesn't.' She turned to her daughter. 'I told you before Jennifer about closing the side gate when you're coming in.'

'I do, Mum. I close it after me all the time.'

'Well obviously not, if this woman is right and there's some street rat hanging around our back garden. And you wonder how your scooter and good tennis racket got stolen?'

'But –' She put her hand up, making Jennifer stop and snap her mouth shut like a puppet.
'I suppose living on a corner doesn't help, it's easy for anyone to climb over the wall. I'll be hiring someone to build it up now, maybe put those spikes things on top of it.'

'I'm sorry,' I said begrudging the apology. 'I just thought she lived in your house. She was in your garden when it was raining and –'

'Well, she doesn't.' She grabbed her daughter's hand. 'I presume you don't have children of your own?'

'No.' I shook my head.

'I thought as much, befriending random kids. You would want to watch you don't get a name for yourself. And, just so you know, mothers don't like to have their parenting questioned, especially not by strangers.'

'I'm sorry.' I heard myself say again as they turned and walked away. 'I'm very sorry for the confusion.'

After the initial sting of her words, all I was left with was confusion.

'You okay?' asked Kai, walking past me with a pile of boxes.

'I don't know.' I said, putting the basket on the floor and walking out of the shop. 'I don't know anything anymore.'

My mind raced as I drove to Tasha's house. Where was Jojo? Was she in real trouble? Had I been drunk talking to her most of the time? Had I mixed up everything she'd told me about herself, or did she tell me that was her house? The questions kept coming and coming shovelling more fear onto my chest. By the time I pulled up outside Tasha's house I was in a state.

'What's wrong?' My sister's face dropped at the sight of me.

I burst into tears. Tasha led me into her kitchen, sitting me down at the table. 'What's happened?' She sat beside me. 'Is it because of your anniversary?' I shook my head, trying to catch my breath between sobs. Slowly, I explained everything.

'Sammie, relax.' Tasha straightened up in her chair. 'I know things have been a bit crazy these past few weeks, and you've been drinking more than usual, but still, you're not mental or like a raging alcoholic. I think you're right. I think this girl is in trouble.'

My stomach turned at the thought. How had I been so bloody stupid? Jojo was obviously in trouble and I chose to ignore it. I was too busy talking about myself to a twelve-year-old, to even notice that she needed proper help. What kind of an idiot was I?

There was a thud behind us, and I turned to see Aria wedged sideways in her walker in the door frame. Wayne appeared behind her. It hadn't dawned on me that anyone else was in the house.

'Come on, Ari.' Wayne bent down, manoeuvring the walker, before pulling it backwards with his foot. Aria squealed looking up at him.

'Sorry.' He looked at Tasha and me. 'I'll bring the kids down to the park, give you two some time to talk.'

It's funny how in moments of craziness, you can still notice small things. Like after Conor died, I'd noticed the size of that doctor's engagement ring. In that moment, I noticed how my sister looked at Wayne. It was a look I hadn't seen before. Maybe it was gratitude or maybe it was something more.

'Sammie's just a bit worried about something; we need to figure a few things out.'

'We'll take our time at the park.' He looked at me and smiled, before turning to leave. Tasha made us both a cup of tea as we waited for Wayne to get the kids out the door.

'Okay, so maybe this kid lives on a different road?' said Tasha, sitting back down with two cups of builder's tea, meaning she thought this was serious even if she wasn't saying as much. 'Your estate is kid central. Did that woman say she knew a Jojo at all?'

'No, she'd no clue. No wonder Jojo used to jump when she'd

shout, she was probably afraid in case she saw her in her garden.'

'So Jojo never actually said she was her mam?'

'Well, no. I just presumed she was, obviously, as she was in her garden.'

'Did the woman say she saw her that day in the rain?'

'I didn't get a chance to ask her, but maybe not; it was lashing out and the tree would have hidden her. Maybe she'd nowhere else to go?' I felt my eyes fill again and quickly grabbed a tissue. 'Why didn't she just call into me.' My voice broke off.

'It's okay, come on we need to think.' I nodded, swallowing hard, pushing my heart back down to my chest. 'I'll ring Vanessa Shannon,' said Tasha, taking a mouthful of tea. 'She knows everyone from here to Wicklow. She'll know who owns Jojo.'

I watched as my sister scrolled through her phone, looking for her client's number. 'I only had Vanessa in the salon yesterday getting her nails done.' Tasha put her phone to her ear. 'She's going away but not until the weekend, thank God – Hiya Van …' Tasha's voice trailed off.

Tasha had a habit of walking around as she talked on the phone. It used to drive us all mad at home, especially if we were watching TV. She would drift in and out blocking the screen, oblivious to whoever was there. I caught snippets of her conversation as she got up and walked between the kitchen and hall. For the most part I zoned out, lost in utter confusion as to what was going on.

Tasha walked back in and put the phone on the table. 'Vanessa hasn't heard of her. She was on the bus into town; it was a bit noisy. She says she knows a Georgia, not a Jojo. She's not sure of her surname, but the kid has brown hair, not blonde.

'What if she's in real trouble, Tasha? She was probably dying to open up to me.'

'Did she ever ask you for food or money?'

I shook my head, feeling an overwhelming sadness with just the thought. I wiped my cheeks with the back of my hand trying to catch the tears, now unstoppable, spilling, making dark blobs on my t-shirt.

'Come on, it's okay.' Tasha rubbed my arm. 'We'll find her. And when we do, we'll do everything we can to help her. I promise.'

The sick feeling in my stomach made me pray that we would find her, and soon. Tasha's phone rang making us both jump.

'Vanessa? Yeah, hi.'

I put my hand on Tasha's arm to stop her from getting up and walking around.

'Yes, okay ... Joanna Sommers?' Tasha raised her eyebrows, looking at me. 'She's blonde, around eleven or twelve. Yeah, I know Leah too. Okay ... yeah ... okay ...'

My heart thumped in my chest. Tasha hung up and looked at me. 'I think we know who she is.'

'We do?'

'Vanessa's sister is with her and said her neighbour's little one had a run in with a girl a few years back and her name was Joanna Sommers. Her nickname is Jojo. The neighbour had called into the parent's house and the dad practically went for her.'

'But Jojo would never –'

Tasha put her hand up to shush me. 'Turns out there was lots going on at home, social services got involved and the girl was fostered out along with her younger sister. She was a good kid, just her home life was mental. Anyway, the woman who fostered her is Leah Blake. She used to work with me and there's a photo of Jojo at a birthday party on Facebook.' Tasha was already searching through her phone, trying to find Leah's Facebook page as I tried to digest what she was saying.

'Tasha, stop – wait,' I said putting my hand out. 'Jojo said her surname was Swan.'

'Oh my god. I can't believe it.'

My stomach twisted.

'Leah unfriended me. Her page is private. I'm morto …'

'Tasha!'

'What?' Tasha looked at me. 'Sorry, I just can't believe she'd unfriend me. The cheek of her.'

'It's not her, Tasha. Jojo's surname isn't Sommers. It's Swan.'

'Her name is Jojo Swan? And you don't think she could be lying about that?'

'She isn't, that's definitely her name. Well, obviously Jojo could be short for Joanne or something.'

'But Swan? Jojo Swan, really?'

'Yeah.' I nodded. 'She definitely said Swan.'

'Right well, who am I to judge with an Aria Reddy. Anyway, we could try find her online. The surname Swan is unusual. Maybe her mam or dad have pictures on their Facebook page, or maybe she has her own page.'

'She said she didn't.'

'In all fairness, we can't really trust much that she's said.'

I wanted to defend Jojo. She'd helped me so much. I didn't want to think of her as a liar. I didn't want to taint the bond we had.

Tasha went upstairs to grab her laptop, insisting we needed a full screen and not a phone for such an important investigation. Her using the term 'investigation' along with taking out her leopard print notebook and matching pen, made me worry that she was getting caught up in the drama. I couldn't think straight anyway, so maybe her sensationalising things was what we needed.

As the laptop hummed and beeped into action, Tasha assured me again that we'd get to the bottom of it. I had already given us an hour in my head before I was phoning the guards.

Tasha started with Facebook and Instagram, typing in the surname Swan, and searching for Dublin.

There was nothing.

'What are you doing?' I asked, as she hit the exit tab and clicked into Google.

'I'm going to Google her.'

'This is ridiculous, Tasha.' I picked up my cup, taking a sip of tea. 'You can't Google search a kid. I mean, what on earth would you find?'

Tasha nudged me, still staring at the screen. The name Joelle Swan was in thick, black, bold on the screen, with the name Jojo highlighted further down in the article.

I didn't see the words around it, I just kept focusing on her name. Could her name be Joelle? I'd never heard of the name before. It was a cute name. What I saw next, nothing could have prepared me for.

'Jesus Christ,' said Tasha, putting her hand over her mouth.

Joelle Swan (10) died following a car accident near her home in Artane. Described by her mother, Rebecca, as a fun-loving child with a big heart and a smile for everyone. She will be deeply missed by her parents, siblings, grandparents, family and friends.

'It's not her.'

'Well, obviously it's not her,' said Tasha.

Tasha scrolled down the screen, and there was a photo: a young girl stood smiling, looking directly at the camera.

'It's her.'

'What?'

It was Jojo. I moved closer, my nose touching the static off the screen. I blinked. She was still there. I blinked again. Still there. I moved back.

'Are you sure?'

I nodded my head, slowly, still staring at the screen.

If I hadn't had Tasha beside me, keeping the whole situation firmly in the real world, I would have thought I was dreaming. Or that I'd lapsed into insanity. I turned and looked my sister straight in the eyes. 'Has Mam been spiking me with tablets?'

'I swear, Sammie.' Tasha held her hands up. 'She wanted to

in the beginning, but me and Dad talked her out of it.'

'Are you positive, Tasha? Remember with Aunt Carole? Mam was so quick, there were three relaxers in her tea, before she'd even finished stirring the milk in.'

Tasha raised her eyebrows questioning if I was serious.

'This would all make sense to me then. I would have been imaging my conversations with this girl – I would have been tripping or whatever it is you do on those tablets. So, what do you think, was I spiked?'

'I bloody well doubt it. You would have gone the opposite way for a start. You wouldn't have been able to lift your head off the pillow, let alone imagine conversations with a kid every day.'

'Do you think I was drunk?' My voice quivered. 'Do you think I was sitting in my back garden, locked out of my head and imagining all sorts? That maybe I'd read this article a while back and it was playing in my subconscious and I –'

'Try to calm down, Sammie,' said Tasha, turning back to the computer screen.

Tasha read the rest of the article quickly, her voice thick with disbelief. I was waiting for the punch line, for something that said all this wasn't real. Her words floated off leaving me to catch them seconds later, 'accident – bubbly – full of life – a real character'.

Tasha looked at me. 'She had a twin.'

Chapter 37

'Okay, so Jojo isn't a ghost, which is a good thing, I guess.'

'She still could be, you don't know who you were talking to, Sammie.'

'Tasha, stop!'

'I'm being serious. You don't just die and that's it ...', Tasha clicked her fingers, 'your caput. We're all energy, energy can't die.'

I thought of my grandfather who I'd seen when I was ten – a definite ghost, I shook my head. 'Tasha cop on. Jojo is living and having lost her twin sister. Oh my god, the poor little thing.' I pushed back the urge to raid Tasha's presses for a drink. A real one.

'There's another article here,' said Tasha, scrolling down. 'It says she had a younger sister too – Millie'

'Yes, Jojo spoke about her.'

'And a twin sister Jodie.'

'Jodie?'

'That's what it says here. Jodie, the name Jojo is in brackets, so it's obviously her nick-name.'

'Jodie?' I repeated the name slowly. 'That's so weird.'

'Out of all this, that's what you think is weird?'

'Does it say where they live?' I leaned over to read for myself.

'Just says Artane.'

'But they don't live in that house behind mine. I need to find her, Tasha.' I felt the anxiety rising again. 'I need to know that she is okay, because clearly she hasn't been. Something is going on. And her parents, they are obviously grieving themselves. I just need to know she's –' My voice broke.

'C'mon, Sammie.' Tasha rubbed my arm. 'Take a few deep breaths, this is a lot to take in. Jojo will be back, she doesn't know that you've found out any of this. You can talk to her properly when you see her again.'

I nodded, unable to speak.

Reluctantly I went back home and, as Tasha advised, tried to sleep on it. On top of it all, I was starting to worry that maybe I did have a drink problem. All I could think of was necking a bottle of wine – to get to sleep more than anything, and to settle down the noise inside my head. The guilt for not trying to help Jojo, that she had been grieving too, just felt too much to bear. I was so angry with myself.

Finally, having mentally beaten myself for long enough, I went to bed. But not before checking out the window for Jojo. The tree was empty, its branches full, holding nothing.

The following morning, I woke to shouting. Sober and alert there was no questioning it this time. I quickly realised that the voices were coming from out the back. I jumped out of bed and ran into my back bedroom to look out the window. It was the woman from the house behind mine and she was shouting at Jojo.

'Hey, hey you, little madam.' She shouted from her back door.

I quickly ran down the stairs and out into my garden. 'Jojo.' She looked at me, her eyes wide with fear.

'Jojo, come here, jump down to me.'

The woman was still shouting, her voice nearing as she came down her garden. 'Did you steal a scooter from here, you little thief?'

Jojo looked from me to the woman, her face etched with panic.

'Jojo, come here – please. I know about your twin sister.' I held my arms out and she jumped, falling onto the rockery, her foot landing awkwardly on Wayne the Buddha's head.

The woman appeared over the wall, her face puce as she glared at me. 'Is this the girl you were talking about?'

'No, no, this is my niece. Sorry, I let her climb up on the wall. We hit a frisbee into your tree. I'm really sorry –'

Both Jojo and the woman looked at me. The woman tutted and shook her head before disappearing back into her garden. 'Get back inside the house, Jennifer – and keep that side gate closed. Bloody weirdos living around here.'

'A frisbee? What am I, a dog?' said Jojo.

I laughed. We both did. Forgetting for a moment that anything had changed.

'Is your foot okay?' I asked Jojo as she bent down to rub it. 'Come sit down with me over here for a minute. I led her back towards my house so we could sit on the decking. I could tell she was nervous, her eyes scanning mine perhaps for clues to what I was thinking.

Sitting beside Jojo felt surreal. She was elf like, delicate and beautiful with a sadness that was more evident up close. I wanted to hug her. To tell her I was sorry for her loss, to say all the cliché things that I myself hated.

'Will I ring your parents?' I asked, 'and let them know where you are.'

Jojo shook her head, staring down at her lap.

'I'm so sorry about your twin sister, I –'

'Please don't.' Jojo looked at me properly for the first time. 'Please don't be all sad with me. You're the only person in the world I can speak to, without all the sadness.'

I smiled, understanding. We both sat in silence for a few moments, the questions I wanted to ask, hanging over us like deflating balloons.

'So, your full name is Jodie?' I asked eventually, unable to wait any longer. I was almost afraid of her saying no. Thinking if she lied to me about something so basic as her name, it would hurt more than anything.

Jojo nodded. 'My sister, Millie, couldn't say Jodie when she was really little, and so she called me Jojo. It just kinda stuck.'

'It suits you.'

'That's our home,' said Jojo, looking straight down the garden at the house behind.

'Jojo, I know you don't live there. You don't have to lie anymore.'

'I never lied.' She looked hurt. 'You never asked me if I lived there, you just thought that I did and I never corrected you.

For the first time, I felt weary of her. An uneasiness settling over me, perhaps fuelled by my dinted ego. How had I been tricked by a kid. As if sensing it, she continued.

'My family lived there for three years before Joelle died. That was our back garden and mine and Joelle's tree.'

She was talking so matter of fact, that I didn't know where to go with it. I think I had presumed that my own experience with grief would somehow make me a pro.

'I always climbed that tree with Joelle.' Jojo smiled like she was remembering, making my heart physically hurt for someone other than Conor. 'She still feels alive, you know. I can feel her with me. It might sound silly.' She raised her eyebrows as if daring me to challenge her. 'But I can. Maybe it's a twin thing?' She shrugged, 'but I don't think so.'

'I don't think so either.'

'I think when I'm happy, that's when I know Joelle's with me most. She never liked to see me crying, it used to make her sad too.'

'I saw you sitting in the rain last week. Were you upset then?'

Jojo nodded. 'I thought Joelle might come back – just for a bit. I was talking to her, telling her to meet me by the tree. The rain wasn't going to stop me from seeing my sister. Then when she didn't show … I'd waited ages.' Jojo looked down at her hands and I could feel her disappointment, a weight that made her curl over, into herself.

'Can you talk to your mam or dad about Joelle?'

'Not really, my mam … well, she doesn't talk much to anyone anymore.'

'You could have spoken to me, Jojo. You helped me so much.'

'Helped you?' She looked at me, confused.

'You did. You've motivated me to do what I love, upcycling furniture and doing interiors, you –'

'You're going all weird, Sammie. Were you drinking your special juice?' She made rabbit ears with her fingers, making my cheeks go warm.

'No actually, not for a while.' It felt surprisingly good to say that out loud, even if Jojo didn't look like she was listening. She was staring straight ahead now.

'I miss our house as much as Joelle – that sounds bad, doesn't it?' She looked at me. 'But everything was normal there, we were happy in that house. When someone dies, everything good doesn't have to die with them.'

I put my hand to my mouth trying to hide my chin that was now caving, causing my lip to quiver like a strained tight rope.

'I didn't cry when you told me about your husband being dead. So, don't start crying for me.'

'Sorry.' I took my hand away. 'I'm really sorry. It's different though, you're so young and your sister was so young. It's okay to – '

'… not be okay? That quote was stuck up in my school. I

know them all.' She rolled her eyes.

I smiled, wiping my eyes. 'I know you do.'

We chatted for a few minutes more. Jojo spoke about her sister as if she was alive, unfazed, retelling stories but the mention of her parents, especially her mam, had her quiet again.'

'Where do you live now?' I asked when she'd fallen silent again. 'Is it nearby?' I hoped the answer was yes, and that she hadn't run away, like Tasha and I had thought.

'We live across from the shopping centre in an apartment the size of a kennel. It's all we could get after we'd to leave our house.'

'Why did you have to leave?'

'Our landlord was selling, but Mam wanted to leave anyway. She couldn't stay in it after Joelle died. Dad said we were lucky, that there's families living in hotels. I wouldn't really call us lucky, and when he said it … I didn't blame Mam going ballistic, that time.' Jojo looked away, picking at something on the arm of the chair.

'Is everything okay at home, I mean, obviously not, because your sister –' I stuttered over my words.

'It – is – fine.'

'But the bruise on your face?'

'I told you what happened.'

'And the burn? It's just … you can tell me if there is anything –'

'You sound just like her.' Jojo shouted, standing up. 'You sound just like Bea. Why can't everyone just leave us alone.'

'Bea?'

'Stupid busybodies. The lot of you.' Tears sprang into her

eyes and she scrunched her fists to wipe them roughly.

'Jojo, please. I'm sorry.' The sight of her upset was too much for me.

'Nobody's taking me away!' She ran around to the side gate.

'Jojo, wait –' I ran across the garden after her, but she was over the side gate in seconds. I wrestled with the rusty bolt, trying to slide it across with a shaking hand. By the time I opened it, she was gone. As I stood in the side entrance her words fell around me like stones. It was Bea, Beatrice Lyons. I just knew it.

Back inside my house, I phoned Tasha, choking back the tears as I retold her my conversation with Jojo.

'The poor kid.'

I nodded, afraid to speak, in case I started blubbering again. Which I knew would have my sister guilt ridden and running over to me – out of her normal life and into my chaotic one, again.

'So at least you know what was wrong with her, and it's not like she can hang around your garden forever. All good things must come to an end.'

'But Beatrice has to be Jojo's social worker.'

'You don't know that. Bea could be anyone.'

'There is definitely more to it …'

'Ah for fuck's sake, Sammie. I think you're just bored now. The kid lost her twin sister, that's what's been wrong with her. Yeah, she's okay generally, but obviously she's going to have her moments. She is only human – thank god. Remember, we could've been dealing with a whole *Sixth Sense* thing here. You need to just focus on yourself, you've been through so much –'

I could hear Finn calling Tasha in the background and Aria starting to cry.

'Yeah, you're right, Tasha. I'm just glad I got to talk to her properly before saying goodbye.'

'Exactly. Now onwards and sideways. You still need to find a job.'

'Yeah grand, I'll start thinking about all that tomorrow. I hung up, knowing that tomorrow I would have something much more important to do.

Chapter 38

I looked up at the apartment block opposite the shopping centre, my eyes scanning each tiny square of glass for a hint of Jojo. The apartments were grim to be fair, state of the art a good fifteen years ago. There were thirty altogether, each number faded on a piece of card next to a tarnished buzzer. I would have to go through each one I thought as the apartment door suddenly opened. An elderly man came out, cane first, swinging it wildly in my direction.

'Sorry, excuse me.' I quickly moved left, missing a wallop. 'Do you know which number the Swan family live in, please?'

'Sorry, Miss?' He tapped his earlobe with a thick crooked finger.

'The Swan family,' I said louder. 'Do you know which number their apartment is?'

'Are ye having me on. Did you try the park?' He laughed shaking his head and muttering something about junkies.

I reached for the door as he walked past, but it clicked shut before I could grab it. 'Shit.' I muttered to myself. The thought flitted into my mind that Jojo could have been lying about where she lived, not wanting me to meet her parents.

I looked around hoping to see someone else, preferably Jojo. There was a cafe across the carpark, beside the main entrance to the shopping centre. I could sit in there and wait to see her. 'Conor, please help me.' I heard myself whispering under my breath. I turned to walk back towards the shopping centre, when I saw Jojo. She stopped still, a look of panic shooting across her face.

'Jojo, hi.' I tried my best to sound calm. 'I just wanted to make sure that you were okay.'

'I am. Now you have to go.'

'But I just want to –'

'Go, Sammie. Please.'

'Jodie!'

We both looked in the direction of the voice, that followed up with a hysterical laugh.

'Jojo – honey pieeee …' The woman put her arms out making her handbag swing wildly down her arm. The clumsiness of how she fixed it, the slow jerky awkwardness of her grappling with the strap, told me everything I needed to know.

'Mam.' Jojo pushed me, jolting me from the scene that I was taking in. 'You need to go, Sammie.' I watched as the woman, Jojo's mother, walked towards us, her blackout sunglasses slipping down her nose.

I opened my mouth to speak, but she walked past me like I wasn't even there. I don't think she even noticed that I was. I looked at Jojo who was chewing her nail, her face serious. Her mam tiptoed up the steps, impressively for someone who was clearly drunk, and fumbled with the door key.

'I'll get that.' Jojo ran up beside her, easing the key out of her mam's hand. Her mam looked at her, rubbed her face, and went inside.

'Jojo.' I called, afraid she would go inside and that would be that.

Jojo ran back down the steps to me. 'My mam likes a drink, Sammie. She'll be okay after she has a sleep.'

'Is your dad home?'

'No, but he'll be back soon.'

'I'll wait with you until he gets back.' I smiled, hoping it would be enough to convince her. I'd forgotten who I was dealing with.

'I am fine, my mam will be fine. This happens most days, okay. I'm used to it.'

'It's just, I think if I waited a bit, we could –'

'Her daughter is dead, Sammie. I think my mam can have a drink, some of that juice that you like, if she wants to. Don't you?' Jojo turned and ran up the steps, she rang the buzzer beside number eight, twice, before punching in a code to let herself in. Reluctantly I walked away, but not before noting each digit.

I sat in the café across the road, hunched under the menu stuck to the window, waiting. I figured Millie hadn't been left on her own in the apartment and that if I saw a mini Jojo with a man going inside, then I could approach him. I could tell him I was concerned, which was a complete understatement.

I drained my second mug of tea, thinking best to not have any more in case I needed to use the toilet. I couldn't risk missing them. I looked up at the clock on the café wall, the large painted knife and fork told me that two hours had passed. That Jojo had been with her mam, on her own, for all that time. The thought alone made me anxious. She was only a child, however grown up she liked to act. She had been there for me at my lowest, when I'd turned my back on my whole family. I needed to be there for her, even if she didn't know it.

I picked up my bag and walked across the road to the apartment block. My heart was thumping in my ears and again I found myself mumbling to Conor for help. I could feel him with me, like how Jojo had described it with her sister. It seemed that the more I accepted he was gone, the more I realised he never would be.

I made my way across the carpark, trying to get the words right in my head. I had no idea what I was going to say. When I reached the main door, I quickly punched in the access code that I'd memorised and followed the wall sign to number eight. The corridor was narrow with a sticky, yellowed flooring that made my runners squelch with each step. Voices carried through each keyhole, babies' cries, toddlers' tantrums, and foreign languages I couldn't make out. The smell of fried fish would have been tantalising, if it hadn't been mixed with stew.

I turned left at the end of the corridor and found myself standing directly outside number eight. The paint was peeling off the door, the shiny red showing gashes of brown, like a half-eaten chocolate bar. I knocked gently, a meek tap, a reflex of my anxiety. The door swung open quicker than I'd expected with my hand still mid-air.

Jojo was standing in front of me. 'Oh. It's you.'

'I just called to see –'

She turned and walked away, leaving the front door open. I could tell she'd been crying.

'Jojo.' I quickly followed her, not waiting for an invitation.

The smell inside was pungent. A mixture of cigarette smoke and urine. I stifled a cough in my sleeve and followed her, past bulging black bags and clothes strewn each side of the hall. The apartment was small, much smaller than I'd expected. Jojo's mam was sitting at a round dining table beside a couch that was covered in everything from slippers to sweet papers. I pulled my eyes away from it, not wanting Jojo to see my horror. Her mam was hunched over the table, scrolling through her phone, her blonde hair covering half her face.

I cleared my throat. 'Sorry to disturb you, I'm Sa–'

'It's okay, Jodie, honey pie. I'll ring your dad. He'll be back soon with Millie to see you.' Her words were slurred. She looked up at me and smiled a wobbly smile with jittery eyes, before letting her head drop down to her phone.

'He's not coming back, Mam. Either is Millie or Joelle. Everyone is gone, it's just us. Why can't you remember that!' Jojo shouted the last bit making me jump. Her mam didn't flinch, she seemed to have not heard a word. She continued to scroll through her phone, her eyes squinted in concentration as she swayed.

'I'll make it better, honey pie, I promise. I will.' She looked at me.

Me, a stranger, standing in her home didn't mean anything. She spoke like it was perfectly normal for me to be standing there in the middle of her living room. I recognised her. She smiled at me and shrugged, pouring the last dribble of gin into a Disney tumbler.

It was Rebecca from the bereavement group, the woman who had got upset and ran out. My heart opened. I felt a swell of pain just watching her holding her drink, as she jabbed at her phone. I bit the inside of my cheek, willing myself not to cry. I was out of my depth.

'This is us, Sammie,' said Jojo, swinging her arms open. 'Just me and my mam, who is usually like this. Now you know everything.'

Rebecca pulled a cigarette from the handbag in front of her, her fingers scratching around for a lighter.

'Mam, no! Not, when you're drinking.' Jojo grabbed the cigarette from her hand. 'This isn't how I got the burn, so you can stop staring at us with your mouth open.' Jojo looked at me. 'My mam would never hurt me.'

Like a child, Rebecca did what she was told and put the packet back on the table. She hiccupped and drained the dribble of gin in the bottom of her tumbler, sucking at it longer than necessary, like a new-born desperate for milk. Jojo slumped into the chair opposite her and put her head in her hands.

I needed to do something. Fuck, I had no clue. 'Tea? Will I make us a cup of tea? It's okay if I use your kitchen, Rebecca, isn't it?' Rebecca shrugged and Jojo raised her head looking puzzled.

The kitchen was a health hazard. Crusted foods stuck to the counter tops, dirty delph was piled high in the sink and a bin over-flowed in the corner. I could see remnants of the beans explosion on the microwave door. My hands trembled as I filled the white plastic kettle, spilling water down the sides. Maybe I should call someone to help – like Tasha or even the guards. The kettle seemed to take forever to boil and as it rattled on the counter, I worried about Rebecca suddenly sobering up and kicking me out of her home, and Jojo. Poor Jojo, who at twelve, thinks she has to act like an adult, that she has to always be mature. I opened the fridge, relieved to find milk but not much else. A couple of cheese slices curled at the edges and a half jar of jam.

After what felt like an hour, the kettle finally clicked, and I quickly made tea – and an extra strong coffee for Rebecca. I walked back out into the living area, where she had fallen asleep face down on the table. Her gentle snores the sounds of her escapism.

'She falls asleep like that all the time,' said Jojo, who now looked exhausted too. 'She says that's why she drinks, to go asleep, and I guess it works.'

'Will she stay like that for the night?'

'I usually find her on the couch in the morning,' said Jojo, getting up and draping a pink blanket over her mam's shoulders, making her look like a defeated superhero. She rooted through her mam's handbag and pulled out the rest of the cigarettes and a lighter. For a second, I thought she was going to smoke one.

'As if,' said Jojo, reading my mind. 'I've to hide them with all the others in case she lights one during the night. She nearly killed us a few weeks ago.' Jojo lifted up a sofa cushion to reveal a large, scorched hole. My stomach churned.

'I know the place looks bad. I do try and clean up. And the smell.' Jojo looked at me. 'Mam hasn't had a chance to wash the bedsheets.' Her cheeks reddened.

'I hadn't noticed.' I tried to smile but it was so bloody hard.

Jojo walked past me into the kitchen and I followed her with the two cups that I'd forgotten I was still holding. Everything felt surreal. Seeing Jojo somewhere other than sitting in a tree was strange for a start, but now knowing that this was where she came home to every day was horrific.

'Why did you come here anyway?' asked Jojo.

'I wanted to make sure you were okay.'

'Well, I am.' She picked a lump of congealed Weetabix off the counter. 'I'm going to do a big clean at the weekend; we both will.'

I placed the cups beside the sink. 'Where's your dad, Jojo?'

'I don't want to talk about it.'

Jojo took a bowl down from the kitchen press, her spindly legs quivering on her tip toes. She reached across me for the box of Sugar Puffs, shaking them out into a mound of gold.

'But your mam – you can't be here on your own.'

'My mam is okay or she will be in the morning anyway. She will be fine for the first few hours, and after that I just go out.'

'But Jojo –'

'She's my responsibility.' Jojo poured the milk until it splashed over the edges, making creamy puddles on the countertop.

'I have to go to bed after this,' said Jojo. 'If my mam sees I'm still awake when she wakes, she'll get confused and think it's daytime. She'll try to wander out and anyway I have to lock the front door when you go, so ...' Jojo raised her eyebrows as a 'see ya later,' but I wasn't going anywhere.

'I know to you this may be normal, but it isn't, Jojo. Your mam being drunk like this and you being in charge of both of you, it's not right. I need to speak to her when she wakes up.'

In that moment, looking at Jojo with a dribble of milk on her chin, standing in her bare feet holding a bowl of cereal, she looked all of her twelve years, a child.

'Is Bea your social worker?'

'Bea is a bitch, is what she is.'

'Please just tell me.'

'Yes, okay she is. Some goodie two shoes neighbour thought she was doing a good deed and reported us to the social. Can you actually believe that? My sister is dead and someone reported us because my mam likes to have a drink and our place smells a bit. This whole apartment block smells.' She threw her arms wide. 'It's a dump.'

I held my arms out to her, an instinct to comfort, but she turned away.

'I want to help.'

'We don't need help. We need Joelle back. We need our old, normal life back. Unless you can make any of that happen then there is nothing you can do.'

'Jojo –'

'I'm not being bad, Sammie, but your life isn't perfect, you know. You should probably try fix yourself.' She looked down after saying it and I knew she felt bad.

'I have a few emails to catch up on.' I took my phone out of my bag. 'I'll just sit here at the table and you can go on to bed. When your mam wakes up, I can have a quick chat with her and then I'll go.'

'Whatever.' Jojo put the bowl on the table and walked out to her bedroom. 'If you think you can fix us, go right ahead.'

'It's not like that.'

'Yeah, whatever.' She closed the door.

Rebecca was still snoring, and I could hear Jojo opening and closing drawers in her bedroom, before the flick of a light switch made the room go silent. I punched a text out to Tasha –

I'm in Jojo's. Found out where she lives. I think her mam has a drink problem, no sign of dad or sis. Just waiting for her mam to wake up x

Were you drinking with her Sammie ... like WTF???

Will explain tomorrow x

I liked you better as a recluse!

Just as I was trying to find an eyeroll emoji to send back to Tasha, Rebecca began to stir. I sat rigid, turning the phone over to hide the light. If she woke now, she'd still be drunk, which would be useless. She rubbed her eyes making mascara bleed into the creases above her cheeks. She turned over, burying her head further into her arms that made a nest on the table.

Chapter 39

The minutes rolled into hours and if I hadn't been sitting in someone else's home, thankfully with my phone as a distraction, I'm certain I would have dozed off too. I itched to tidy around, to scrub the kitchen and wash the dishes but I was afraid I would wake Rebecca. Instead, I rehearsed what I was going to say, but when she did eventually wake, slowly, before sitting up to look straight at me, I just smiled.

'Who are you?' Her voice was gravelly and she coughed to clear her throat.

'I'm Sammie, I ehm, I know Jojo. I also met you at the bereavement group in Artane.'

Rebecca blinked as if trying to focus.

'I just dropped by to see how Jojo was doing, and then –'

She rubbed her eyes roughly, before standing up and walking into the kitchen. I didn't know what to do, so I just sat there, waiting for her to come back.

When she walked back in, she had a glass of water. She sat down and sipped it with trembling hands like the first time I'd saw her. She looked at me, confused. 'Sorry, Sandy, is it?'

'No, Sammie.'

She narrowed her eyes. 'Are you a social worker. You are, aren't you?'

'No, no, I'm not.'

'I'm so stupid. How did I not know – you coming here, watching me.'

Jojo came out of her room.

'I'm not a social worker. I promise you.'

'She's not, Mam. It's just Sammie, I know her. It's okay.'

Rebecca looked at me unsure.

'I'll make you a coffee, Mam, sit down.' Rebecca sat back down still staring at me.

'I know that look,' said Rebecca after Jojo went into the kitchen.

'Sorry, ehm, what?'

'That pity look, the judgement.'

'Oh, no, no I'm not –'

Rebecca looked down and closed her eyes, squeezing them tight with her a finger on each temple. She looked exhausted, like she was drowning in pain.

Jojo came out with the coffee and Rebecca reached out to hug her. 'I'll be okay today, sweetie. Promise.'

'Yeh, sure, Mam.' Jojo smiled but it didn't meet her eyes.

'I'll go,' I said standing up, 'and if it's okay, I'll come back later?'

'Please don't,' said Jojo, 'There's literally nothing you can do.'

I ignored her and looked at Rebecca who just shrugged. I could hear her asking Jojo who I was again as I closed the door.

Back home, I went between busying myself around the house, trying to forget what I'd seen, to sitting down wracking my brain about what I could do to help. A few hours had passed and I still hadn't decided if I should go back. But as I left my house to go for a walk, I followed my gut right back to their front door.

'Ugh,' said Jojo rolling her eyes as she answered.

'Can I speak with your mam? Please Jojo.'

'You're such a stalker, Sammie.'

'I know.' I smiled, trying to light the old spark of banter between us.

'You've about an hour before she starts drinking again. I'm going out.'

I walked into the living area, not knowing what to expect.

Rebecca was sitting at the kitchen table, just staring at nothing on the wall, a place I'd found myself so many times since Conor died. Her hair was wrapped in a towel with damp strands framing her face.

'I'm so sorry to bother you again.'

She blinked, her trance broken.

'Is it okay if I sit down?' I took her silence as a yes. 'I just wanted to see if you're okay, I don't want to intrude.'

'Jodie told me about you, after you left.' She smiled, the faintest twitch of her mouth that made my breathing settle a bit. 'I'm not great when I've just woken up, after – well, you know. I didn't catch what you were saying earlier. So, if you want to start again.'

And I did. Slowly at first, then when I realised that she was sober, I told her everything. Explaining about Conor, and how Jojo had helped me over the summer, and how I'd been worrying that something was wrong with her. And that I'd foolishly been watching another family all this time.

'So, Jodie's been going back to our old house every day? She forgot to mention that.'

'To the garden just – please don't be mad with her.'

'I'd no idea, I mean …' She rubbed her face looking bewildered.

'It wasn't every day –'

She stared at the wall above my shoulder. 'When Joelle died – it was my fault you know. I killed my own daughter.'

'Sorry, what?' I leaned forward, knowing I must have misheard her.

Rebecca reached down into her slipper, pulled out a cigarette and lighter, and lit it up. She inhaled deeply, the blue smoke swirling around her face.

'It was my fault Joelle died. I can't tell Jodie that. She'd never forgive me, not that I can ever forgive myself.'

I tried to think had I miss-read the article. Had I missed the part where she was a murderer, but she couldn't be a murderer, she'd be locked away.

'I was in a really bad place,' said Rebecca, reaching across me to grab the plastic ashtray. She flicked the bent ash onto a piece of chewed gum. 'I was in the depths of depression; I'd never experienced anything like it. The darkness to each day.'

I was afraid to move in case she stopped talking.

'Three beautiful daughters, a good husband, a successful job and yet I couldn't get out of the fog. I used to laugh at people with depression, women like myself. Isn't that awful? I'd say, I don't have time to be depressed.' She laughed, a hollow laugh. 'It's funny, isn't it? how karma works. How what we put out, is what we get back.' She waved her hand, leaving an ironic halo of smoke around her head. 'How this is all my own fault.'

I shifted in my chair, not wanting to look uncomfortable, but unable to hide it either. She looked at me, her eyes pooled with pain.

'What happened to Joelle?'

She looked down and I regretted asking. 'My youngest daughter, Millie, had a singing competition. My husband Leo and Jodie were going, but I couldn't. I just wanted to shut myself away, stay in bed. They rarely tell you that about depression, that it's not just all in your head, that it can be physical too. I could barely move.'

I nodded finding a thread of familiarity in her story.

'Out of the three girls Joelle was the most attached to me.' She sucked the last of her cigarette, before crushing it against the side of the ashtray. 'She said she wanted to stay at home to mind me.' She slowed each word down, like it was the only way she could get them out. 'My skin was crawling, you know, like I wanted to tear it off my bones, and I'd a headache, a deep throbbing over my eye.' She tapped her forehead with a chewed nail. 'They were only gone a few minutes but I just wanted to be left alone. I told Joelle to get out, get out and play. To just get away from me. I'm not sure if she heard the last bit, she was already running out the door and down the garden path. Minutes later she was hit by a car.'

I exhaled not realising I'd been holding my breath. I wanted to cry.

'I don't know why I'm telling you all this, I'm sure you think I'm a monster. I wouldn't blame you. If I hadn't of shouted at her to get out, she'd be still here now.'

'But you can't think it was your fault, surely? It was an accident.'

Rebecca stood up, ignoring me, and walked over to a side table against the wall. She opened the drawer and took out a paper bag, inside was a bottle of pills. 'I've to take these in the mornings.' She held the bottle up and gave it a shake. 'The doctor said take one as you need. I would go full on tranquilisers, but I still need to be a mam. I need to be able to function. She shook out a pill and popped it into her mouth, swallowing it like air. 'Take one as you need.' She said again. 'I don't know how I'm not rattling when I walk.'

She walked back over to the table and sat down, and I watched in awe as she moved with her grief, like physical chains wrapped around her. 'I'm sorry for rambling on, you probably need to get going. Thank you for chatting to Jodie and keeping her company. She needed that. Leo has gone to stay with his parents for a bit with Millie and she misses them both. She's herself convinced they won't come back like Joelle –'

'So, it's just you and Jojo here?'

Rebecca straightened up. 'Yes, why?'

'Nothing, it's just –' My eyes fell to the empty bottle on the table.

'I like to have a drink. Have you ever liked a drink after your husband died?'

I nodded, understanding, even though I wasn't responsible for a child, so it wasn't really the same thing.

'I am doing okay with Jodie. I'll get on top of all this.' She looked around the room. 'We moved from a three-bedroom house into a box, we've stuff everywhere. It looks a lot worse than it is, plus a broken washing machine ...'

So that's why Jojo always wore the same clothes, I thought to myself not wanting to shame her by saying it aloud. Although there was something I couldn't keep to myself. 'Jojo had some bruising on her face. I know it's none of my business but when it comes to a child, any child, I guess it's everyone's business.'

Rebecca took a deep breath and I felt my stomach tighten. 'It was a complete accident, one that eats me up.' She wiped the tears that began to fall. 'I tripped on the steps just outside. I swung my arm and caught Jodie's cheek. Thankfully a neighbour saw and knew it wasn't intentional, but I'd had a couple drinks, so she called the social services who haven't left me alone since. Understandably, look I'm not stupid. But at the end of the day I love my daughters I would never, ever, lay a hand on them. The thought alone makes me ill.'

I nodded, feeling an understandable sadness looking at this woman.

'It must be hard on your whole family?'

'Leo's left; he's suffering too. Says that he should have made Joelle go with him that day. That if he hadn't been such a walkover with the girls and insisted she went with him, then she'd still be alive. He has always spoilt the twins, making up for the fact that he's not their biological father.'

'You're dealing with so much. Have you talked to anyone?'

'Have you?' She raised her eyebrows.

'No.' We both smiled.

'My mam tricked me into going to that bereavement group, Anna's one. I saw you there,' I said.

'I was a nervous wreck before I even went in, and I'd only gone to it for Jodie and Millie.' She twisted the empty tumbler in front of her. 'The drink isn't helping, not really. I know it's not good for the girls either. Even though Millie is with Leo she will be back with me soon. I just feel so broken. It's bad enough losing a child, without knowing that it's my fault, that I somehow deserved it … that I made it happen.' Her voice quivered. 'There's other stuff too – it's just a mess.'

'But Joelle dying, it wasn't your fault, Rebecca. It was a tragic accident and you're not to blame.'

'I'm not so sure,' said Rebecca, as if already accepting her fate.

'I do know how you feel about bringing it on yourself. I felt the same after Conor died. Like I'd done something terrible to deserve it. It didn't help that I'd been reading all these positive thinking books, the ones that harp on about how you create your own experiences with your thoughts. I never thought about Conor dropping dead. I didn't create this …' It was the first time I'd said the words aloud, making the vice around me chest loosen, slightly. 'It just happened for a reason I'll never know.'

'And so did this, Mam.'

'Jodie.' Rebecca's hand shot to her mouth.

'I heard everything.'

'Oh, Jodie –'

'It's okay, Mam. I already knew.'

'You did, how?'

'You and Dad used to shout loud enough about it.'

'Oh sweetheart, come here.' Rebecca held her arms out and Jojo walked into them. Allowing herself to be rocked like a baby on her mam's lap.

Rebecca was crying, making Jojo lean back and look at me, her face worried. 'I'm sorry, Jodie. I'm so, so sorry.' She was sobbing now, and I didn't know what to do. Running to make tea didn't seem like the right thing.

Jojo jumped up and grabbed some tissues from the box on the windowsill. 'Mam, here. It's okay.' She ran into the kitchen and came back a few seconds later with a glass of water. I felt useless, sitting, watching as she took over.

We both sat side by side with my hand on top of Jojo's and watched Rebecca cry. It felt like the right thing to do. That us just being there for her at arm's length was what she needed. Eventually, her gulps melted to sobs and then into gentle sniffs, where she looked at us puffy eyed and smiled. I could tell she was only smiling for Jojo's benefit, but it was a good place to start.

Rebecca lifted the bottle of gin off the table and turned it over. 'I've another two of these in the fridge and I think I'm going to want them.'

'Will I pour them down the toilet, Mam?' asked Jojo, her eyes eager, making a bubble of pity rise inside me.

'No, darling, I don't think that will do it. But good idea,' said Rebecca, as if they were talking about a topic for a school project.

'I'm starving, I'm going to make toast.' We both watched Jojo as she walked into the kitchen.

'I want to stop drinking, Sammie. Not for me, but for Jodie and Millie. I know I need to want to for me too, but right now that's a starting point.'

'I get it, I really do. Wanting to drink it all away – to sleep, to feel better. I did it too. It doesn't help things though. It just takes away the pain for a bit but passes it on to those around you.'

'Leo doesn't know how bad I've gotten.'

'Is he gone for good?' I asked, regretting how I phrased the question instantly. 'I mean –'

Rebecca shrugged. 'He took Millie to his parents down the country. She will be back for school. Whether Leo stays in Dublin too … I don't know. Part of me hopes so. I want what family I have left all together. But with Joelle gone, we'll never be a whole family again and …' She sighed. 'Mine and Leo's relationship is probably the last thing I've the energy to fix. I need to sort this out.' She tapped on the side of her empty tumbler.

'My dad was an alcoholic.' For the first time the words didn't sound like a betrayal but a label of bravery. 'He still goes to meetings; he swears by them. You could have a chat with him, he helps people. He helped me.'

'I don't know. It's hard to open up; this is the most I've spoken to anyone and I don't know why. I think you caught me off guard!' She half-laughed.

'I understand, I do. But I really believe my dad can help you.'

She smiled. A proper smile. 'Thank you. Not only for today, but for being there for Jodie.'

I reached across and gave her a hug.

'And I'm sorry for your loss; losing your husband so young – that's awful.'

I shrugged.

'There's no hierarchy with grief, Sammie. I know that much.'

'Thanks.' I smiled as Jojo plonked herself down between us waving a triangle of toast.

'I better get going,' I said, putting my phone into my handbag. 'Can I help you tidy up?'

'I'm ashamed of how bad this place has gotten. I used to have OCD. Can you believe that?'

'I'll help you clean, Mam.' Jojo put her arms around her, making Rebecca pull her in close.

'Is it okay if I still visit Sammie, Mam?'

Rebecca looked at me. 'Only if it's okay with Sammie, and if you stay away from our old house. This place isn't forever, Jodie. We will get a bigger place again, I promise. But that's not our home anymore and it's not fair on the people living there.'

'Yeah, I'll knock on your door, Sammie, like a proper guest.'

'You're welcome anytime.'

'Maybe I'll climb the tree though one last time – for closure.'

'Closure?' said Rebecca and me at the same time.

'And to annoy the old hag who lives there.'

'Jodie Swan.' Rebecca raised her eyebrows making Jojo mumble, 'Sorry, Mam.'

For the first time I caught a glimpse of how it must have been. Rebecca the responsible parent and Jojo the cheeky kid. It was clear the roles had been blurred and swapped at times, but the love between them was still strong.

'You said a lot worse about Bea.'

Rebecca's face turned serious and she looked at Jojo. 'Don't mention her okay, I'm dealing with it.'

'But –'

'I mean it, Jodie, please.'

'Okay.' Jojo chewed her lip and snuggled into her.

Before leaving, Rebecca and I swapped numbers so we could arrange Jojo's visit. I also gave her my dad's number, knowing it would be up to her to contact him when the time was right. It felt like I had been there days, and at the same time, all of ten minutes. Rebecca gave me a hug, before Jojo threw her arms around us both. There was more than Jojo that linked us now, we had bonded through our grief and a shared hope of clawing our way through it.

As the door clicked shut behind me, I felt my body deflate. I was exhausted. I stood outside in the hallway and took a deep breath. I believed Rebecca when she said she wanted to stop drinking and hoped she could fight the urge, that would no doubt start surfacing again, as the day went on. I was under no illusions when it came to facing demons. I knew how close I'd been myself to that slippery slide Dad had talked about.

Chapter 40

Over the next couple of days, I tried to relax and just focus on myself, but I couldn't get Rebecca out of my head. She had been so open and honest with me, yet there was still something she was holding back, 'other stuff' going on, as she'd said herself. I knew it was to do with the social worker. I could still see the fearful look in Jojo's eyes at the mention of Bea's name. Maybe there was something I could do?

Her phone answered on the first ring.

'Hello, Beatrice Hyde speaking.'

'Hi, ehm … Beatrice Lyons?'

'Yes, Beatrice Hyde nee Lyons, who is this?'

'It's Samantha Clancy. We went to school together, I ehm, found your number online. I hope you don't mind.' I cringed hearing myself.

'No, not at all, Sammie.' Her voice relaxed. 'I was so sorry to hear about your husband; my brother played football with him.'

'Oh, I didn't know that.'

'Yes, they were on different teams, but played for the same club. I've thought of you a lot since I heard.'

'Thank you.'

'Is everything okay? I mean –'

'What am I calling you for?' I laughed.

She laughed too, a light giggle, which I remembered as a trait. 'Is there anything I can help you with?'

'Yes, well, I'm hoping so. I'm calling you about a little girl, Jodie Swan.'

'Okay …' I could sense her discomfort. 'How do you know Jodie?'

'She lives nearby, and she's kind of a family friend.' I couldn't think of a better way to describe us. 'She mentioned you're her social worker.'

'Look, before we go any further, Sammie. I'm really sorry, but I won't be able to discuss an individual case.'

'Of course, sure, I understand,' I said, hoping I could convince her to bend the rules.

'Do you have anything you would like to report, any concerns about her welfare?'

'No, no, quite the opposite actually. I met her mam Rebecca only recently, and I know she is having a tough time of it –'

'It's not as straight forward as it seems, I'm afraid.'

'I know her daughter Joelle died tragically and –'

'Yes.'

'I had concerns too, I had eh –' I quickly stopped myself not knowing what was okay to say. 'I thought something may be up, nothing big or bad or anything really, just I went to visit them.' I knew I was making little sense, the words scrambling in my mouth.

'Okay …'

'And she opened up to me about her daughter. And Jojo, she is such a lovely girl.'

'That's one word for her alright.'

'I know she can be a bit lippy.'

'And the rest.'

I held back, wanting to tell her not to speak badly about Jojo.

'I can't go into details, Sammie. But what I can say is that we are closely monitoring the family. Rebecca in particular, not all is at it seems.'

'Oh.' She caught me off guard, making my stomach knot.

'Yes, so as I said, it's not straight forward.'

I needed to find out more. Beatrice had always been prone to exaggeration. I wondered if that was still the same. 'So, how are things with you anyway?'

'Great, yeah good.' Her voice sounded lighter, relieved. 'I'm due my first baby next month, so I'll be heading off on maternity leave soon, thank god.' She laughed, again the same laugh.

I ignored the tiniest splinter of envy, refusing to draw it out, knowing it would always be there, something I'd learn to live with. 'That's amazing, congratulations.'

'Thanks. I'm as big as a house, waddling around like a penguin, but I just can't wait to meet him or her.'

'I can only imagine.'

There was a silence, no doubt her filling with pity for me. I felt awful too with what I was about to do with it – but this was for Jojo.

'I've just been lonely, with you know … everything.' I couldn't bring myself to use Conor's name. 'Jojo has been like a niece to me, really, she's made me smile these past few weeks, when clearly she hasn't had much to smile about. I know you can't tell me anything, Beatrice, I completely respect that. It's just her mam Rebecca. Oh my god does she love that little girl. I know she has problems, who wouldn't after what has happened to her daughter Joelle.'

'I know.' Beatrice sighed. 'It's absolutely horrific and we are supporting Rebecca as best we can or she'll allow at the minute.'

'Jojo thinks you're going to take her away.

Beatrice stayed silent.

329

'Obviously you're not. You don't actually take kids off their parents unless it's really serious, do you? Like jeez, I don't know, sexual abuse or drug addiction or violence.'

Beatrice cleared her throat.

'I know about the accident on the steps when Rebecca fell. There isn't anything terrible though is there? I know you can't tell me, but now I'm worrying,' I could hear my voice quiver. I swallowed trying to get it together. 'I've become close to them, to Jojo, and I want to help. I just really, really care and I thought if you could just reassure Jojo that no-one is going to take her away.'

'I appreciate you want to help and so do I, believe me.' Beatrice sighed.

'A mother is struggling grieving her child, what more could there be.'

It was more of a statement than a question, so I held my breath not quite believing when she answered.

'Look, the twins' father, their biological father, he's never been in their lives by choice. Rebecca contacted him of course after Joelle died and he came over from England for the funeral. He behaved terribly, picking fights and all sorts. Then Rebecca found out he'd started a 'Go Help Me' page to fund his trip back to Ireland, which I think included a lot of sight-seeing, a fancy hotel and not much grieving.

'That is awful.'

'When he'd called to their home out of the blue demanding to see Jodie, Rebecca went ballistic and assaulted him.'

'I can't say I blame her.'

'The fact is she did it. So, of course he reported her, saying she's violent and an unfit mother and now wants custody of Jodie, to take her back with him to the UK.'

'What, no, but he can't, surely?'

'We don't think he's serious. He's just reacting out of anger. Of course, he has a right to be in his daughter's life, but not full custody. To be honest, it's bloody ridiculous. A bit of digging across the pond and he doesn't have the best record himself. Petty crimes and of course fraud with the charity page is enough to get a case against him.'

'He sounds absolutely horrible.'

'I met him once, he insisted on meeting with me to try and build-up a case against Rebecca. He's a real creep.'

'She won't go to prison, will she?'

'I think, given the circumstances, no. But there are still problems there. I'm sure if you are anyway close to them you can see that?'

I couldn't lie, it wasn't perfect.

'Rebecca needs to be making an effort, Sammie. She needs to seek help for her addiction to alcohol and she needs to get her home in order. She knows what she has to do.'

'She will get help, she is. I'll make sure of it.'

'I really hope so; she's a good person. I know she's ashamed of the assault charge. She has closed herself off a lot, so maybe having someone like you as a friend will be good. She needs all the support she can get.'

'I will help her. If you can sort out Jojo's dad, I can help Rebecca.'

'I'm hoping to take a career break after I have the baby, and I don't plan on coming back for a couple of years at least. So, I won't be looking after their case. But I will pass all this on to my colleague who is taking over. And if she is happy with Rebecca's progress, and it has to be good progress going forward, then I can't see Jojo going anywhere. It's the absolute last resort that we would separate a child from their mother.'

'Thank you, Beatrice. Thank you telling me all this and giving me, and them, the opportunity to do better. Best of luck to you and your baby.'

'Take care of yourself, Sammie.'

I hung up and, although I was shocked to hear about Rebecca's assault charge, the facts remained. She loved her daughters; she was grieving her child and she was ready to accept help.

I walked with no purpose, other than to clear my head and digest what Beatrice had told me. It felt good to walk and file my thoughts.

Please give me a sign that everything will be okay for them, I said, realising I was asking Conor for help again. I walked past the corner shop and turned onto the path by the main road. I laughed out loud as a thick white feather fell right in front of my face, then another and another. It was like standing in a snow globe as the feathers tumbled around me.

'You're a dirty bastard, Trevor.'

I looked up to see a woman beating a pillow off the side of an apartment balcony. 'And in our bed too! Well, she can have you.'

I turned to see a man, his face the same colour as the feathers, stood beside me in a pile of boxer shorts, clothes and a busted open gym bag.

'Will you calm down, Rachel.'

'Calm down? The mattress is coming next, Trev, but it'll be on fucking fire so you better run.'

I turned and walked away trying my best not to laugh. Could I still take the feathers as a sign? Did it matter that I'd seen where they'd come from? As I walked home, I realised that they would mean what I wanted them to. And to me I was taking them as an, everything would be okay.

That evening, I phoned Dad and told him everything. About Jojo and how she'd helped me and about Rebecca's dependency on drink. Dad said he was only too happy to speak with Rebecca and that they'd go from there. He also offered to fix her washing machine, bragging he was a man of many talents. I felt proud that he was my dad and his struggle and knowledge could help someone else. I got into bed that night feeling the closest I'd been to contentment since Conor died. It was at the fringes, waving at me, as I fell asleep.

Chapter 41

'Do you want seconds, love?' Mam waved a bowl of roast potatoes under my nose. After taking a few days to relax, I'd decided to call over to my parents' house without having to be asked first.

'Don't push it, Lil,' said Dad, taking the bowl from Mam's hand.

We'd decided to tell Mam a diluted version of Jojo and Rebecca's story, brushing over the part about Rebecca's drinking and Beatrice. She simply couldn't be trusted not to blab Rebecca's business to Breda and every other old biddy in the community centre. After Dad had told me that Rebecca had contacted him, I was beaming. He did say that she'd have a long way to go, but with the right support, she'd get there.

Mam kept watching me the whole time, her motherly instincts flaring with every laugh or joke I made. She even asked me if I'd met a new 'friend,' making Tasha snap at her, telling her not to be so insensitive. I'd said it was okay, but my heart was full up with Conor that I'd no room for anyone else.

I did have some other news for Mam that I knew she would like.

'You know how much you enjoyed our afternoon tea at the Shelbourne? Well, I've booked you and Dad a weekend stay there.'

'Do ye hear that, Lil, a dirty weekend away.'

'I told you he'd say that,' said Tasha, pretending to gag. I had phoned Tasha earlier to tell her that I'd booked it.

'Ye might get to be a big sister yet, Tasha.' Dad laughed.

Mam threw her eyes up at Dad. 'Sammie love, I don't know what to say.'

'I'm not sure I've told you, but I really appreciate you both. You deserve a treat.'

'No, you definitely haven't told us that.' Dad joked.

'Oh, right – maybe I was off my face these past few months.' I laughed, and they joined in on the first drink related joke in, well, forever.

'A posh weekend stay, Gerry. The style of us. This calls for some nice cake,' said Mam. 'I have a lovely Victoria cream sponge that I bought earlier. Maybe it was a premonition, a sign that there'd be a nice surprise.'

Tasha raised her eyebrows at me. 'Sammie doesn't believe in any of that anymore. Don't you not, Sammie?'

'Hmm … I think I may have changed my mind.'

We all sat around the table, digging into large rectangles of cream cake.

'That must have cost you a fortune, Sammie,' said Mam, waving a piece of kitchen roll at Dad. 'Me and your dad will go halves.'

'We will?' asked Dad, wiping his chin.

'My running away fund, Gerry.'

'Jesus, Lil. Where had ye planned on running to? You could catch a flight to the moon with the amount you have.'

I'd noticed Tasha had gone quiet.

'I've still a bit left, love, don't be worrying,' Mam put her hand on Tasha's, and turned to me. 'I know about Tasha's debt.'

'Her ehm, what?'

'Don't give me that what, Samantha Clancy. You two are as thick as thieves, always have been. I know, you know, about the loan shark.'

I could see Tasha shrink with Mam's words.

'Oh, right.' I glanced at Tasha.

'Mam gave me a loan, and I'm paying her back every penny.'

'Stop that now, Tasha, I told you I don't want it back. I've paid off your man, the scummy aul fecker, and you've learned your lesson. Haven't you?'

Tasha nodded her head like a scolded child.

'Do you hear Mammy Warbucks here, putting out fires all over the place,' said Dad.

'I've definitely learned my lesson. And it is a loan. I'm not letting you use your inheritance paying off my debt. Our debt, Wayne says he's going to pay it back too. He felt awful when I told him the truth about it.'

'Inheritance?'

'Nana Margo's,' said Tasha.

'I thought we spent that?' Dad looked at Mam.

'No. I kept a bit aside for a rainy day, along with my own little savings. I'm very good with money.'

'Well, I can see that, Lil. Or should I say, I can't see it, seen as you have it all squirreled away.'

'I was actually thinking about getting a job,' I said, quickly changing the subject. 'I might ring Dionne to ask about working in her café.'

'Café. Really?' said Dad, his voice a little high. 'I thought you're into the bit of housey business.'

'I am, I definitely want to work in interiors, but the café could tide me over.'

'They have interior stuff in your old shop. I went past there yesterday. You wouldn't recognise it. It looks completely different to Haven,' said Mam. 'I didn't let on who I was, she seems nice enough though, the new owner.'

'Wasn't it great all the same, getting the boot from there,' said Dad. 'It doesn't do any good staying in the same place forever. Sometimes you need to step outside the comfort zone.'

'Do you hear him?' said Mam, nodding towards Dad. 'We all know what happened the last time you stepped out of your comfort zone, Gerry.'

Dad smiled at me and we both knew what he meant.

'You should pop into the shop,' said Tasha. 'It might be good to see it all changed.'

'Yeah, maybe.'

'The clothes are muck, mind,' said Mam. 'Very trashy looking, altogether.'

Chapter 42

I swept my fingers along the bottom of my handbag, feeling for loose change. I never had to worry about parking meters when I worked in Haven. I'd had a swipe card, a little plastic piece of heaven that exempted me from the dreaded parking fees. After begrudgingly feeding the meter, I took my time walking around to the front of the shopping precinct, each step setting off more butterflies in my stomach. I still hadn't decided if I would go into the shop yet, although I knew deep down that I needed to see the changes, I needed to see them to move on. I was no different to Jojo in how she'd been holding onto her old house. I too needed closure from Haven.

As it turned out, the changes were evident enough from the street. Jaclyn's boutique stood out more than Haven ever had: her shop sign was three-dimensional, for a start, and outlined in white flashing bulbs. The sight of it took me by surprise, pulling at my heart and making me feel sad and intrigued all at once. I would just walk past I decided, unnoticed, and get the closure I needed without having to actually go inside. This was possible as she had a window display that would give Brown Thomas a run for its money. I stopped a few feet away, my eyeballs practically licking the glass. It was like a scene plucked from a roof top bar in Manhattan; it looked busy and vibrant with clever use of silhouettes. It covered every inch of the window and I felt a sting remembering her complimenting mine, which had looked pathetic in comparison.

'Sammie, oh my god! Hi!' I turned to see Jaclyn crossing the road towards me, carrying a coffee cup and paper bag, in what was possibly the world's worst timing, ever. 'How have you been keeping?'

I pretended I'd no clue who she was, tilting my head and squinting like I was trying to place her. I could never have pulled it off, only I'd figured in that nanosecond that it was the lesser of two embarrassing evils, the latter being caught gawking at the window.

'Jaclyn.' She pointed to herself and then the shop with the paper bag swinging in her hand. 'I bought the shop from Dionne. We met once before, remember?'

'Oh, yes, Jaclyn. Yes, sorry, I was miles away there.' I forced out a laugh that I didn't know I possessed.

'Come on, come on in.' She walked over to the shop door and turned around, hooshing it open with her bum. Before I could even think about it, I was following her, stretching my mouth into a smile.

'I'm so glad you came by. You know, everyone still asks after you.' She walked over to the counter, putting her cup and bag down. I stood inside the shop door, waiting for the longing to hit. But there was nothing. The shop had changed so much, it was as though Haven had never existed.

In between the thick rails of clothes, I could see slivers of gold textured wallpaper that had replaced our duck-egg blue walls. A chunky chandelier and black frayed curtains that hung like false eyelashes each side of the fitting rooms, distanced me further from any sense of familiarity. It was good. I was glad.

'This is Alison,' said Jaclyn.

'Hiya.' A cheery looking girl with a brown, swishy ponytail had appeared from the back room. She gave me a wave, her smile big and eager. She was me ten years ago.

'I'd be lost without Ali. Wouldn't I?' The girl beamed with the compliment. 'Sammie used to run the interior shop that was here.'

'Oh, cool,' said Ali, sounding genuinely impressed.

I spent the next ten minutes walking around the shop with Jaclyn, who's enthusiasm made it feel twice its size. She was so passionate and looked at me with the intensity that I'd mistaken for recognition the first time I'd met her. I chatted easily with her and Alison, complimenting pieces of clothes that I'd loved to have tried on. Mam had been her usual loyal self when she'd said they were muck.

'I'm still looking to take someone else on – a managerial role,' Jaclyn whispered, while Alison was on the phone. 'I also want to incorporate more homewares, but super classic with a twist. I know how creative you are, having seen what you did with Haven. I think we could work well together.' Before I could say anything, she continued on. 'I'm looking at another property too. I'm planning on opening up a chain of stores – it's always been a dream of mine. So, you would have full reign of this place eventually, if you jumped on board.'

'Excuse me, Jaclyn,' said Alison, 'that was the delivery guy.

There's tailbacks on the quays and he won't get here until just before closing.'

Jaclyn rolled her eyes. 'Bloody typical.' She turned back to me. 'So, what do you say, Sammie?' She smiled, her eyes expectant.

My head shook from side to side before the words even left my mouth. 'No thanks, Jaclyn.'

'Oh. You can take some time to think about it if you like?'

'No, I'm sure.' I could almost hear the elastic bands snapping from around me, releasing me from the shop. There was no going back. 'But thanks so much for the offer, it's really nice of you. I think I've worked in retail long enough. I fancy a change.'

She looked genuinely disappointed, which gave me a shot of confidence. 'Anyway, I'll leave you guys to it. The place looks really great by the way.'

'Thanks, Sammie. And be sure to pop in to see us again.' I waved, both to them and the shop. I knew I'd never be back.

Outside the sky was deep navy, a sign of colder days to come. There was a change in the air, people slotting back into routines of school runs and activities. I knew I'd have to find a job before the dark nights fell upon me. I couldn't work for Jaclyn in the shop, but if I got a job in Dionne's café it would be something different, and I could keep my interior stuff as a hobby for the time being. Maybe even brainstorm my ideas with Dionne. I got into my car and had just put it into reverse, when my phone rang.

'Sammie, it's Audrey Wallace. Sorry to call you out of the blue.'

'Audrey, hi!' I turned the key, cutting the engine off so I could concentrate.

'The last time I spoke to you probably wasn't the best time to offer you a job. Your head must have been all over the place. And after your poor husband passing, well, I can only think of when Trixie, my little fur baby died. The last thing I wanted to do was motivate myself.'

I couldn't help but smile at her comparison.

'Anyhoo, I couldn't stop thinking of you recently. I've taken on a property in Malahide: this house is unreal, Sammie. The owner is some reality star. I can't remember her name and her husband is a football player – more money than sense, you know the kind. They're living in an apartment and won't move into the house until it's perfect. Sammie, sweetie – I'm fooked. I'm up to my eyes with a dozen other properties. I spoke to two designers, who won't touch it. She has a bit of a reputation … I know you don't take any crap, and you're good, Sammie.'

'But I –'

'You can have fun with it. She can't ruin your name because you don't have one in the business yet, and if she doesn't like your ideas – fook it, you can walk away. What do you think?'

'To doing the interior design?'

'No, to styling her hair, sweetie … yes, of course the interior design!'

I looked around me, like a camera crew was going to leap out from behind the wall and tell me this was some kind of joke. A young guy walked past and bleeped open the car beside me. He caught my eye and then quickly glanced over his shoulder, my look of confusion obviously making him paranoid. 'But I wouldn't know what I was doing, Audrey.'

'Nonsense. Now will you have a think about it, at least? I'll text you the address and you can Google the property, mail me a few ideas. I'll pay you for your time.'

Two job offers in one day, my head was spinning.

'Sometimes you have to just take the bull by the horns, Sammie. What have you got lose?' I knew the answer to that one. Absolutely nothing.

Chapter 43

Turns out, I spent my wedding anniversary with Audrey in Malahide. I was in my element, walking from room to room, seeing my ideas come to life. The house heaved with activity, with workmen, Audrey, her assistant and me – not quite sure how I was pulling it all off but loving every minute of it. Audrey had told me to get business cards made up, and she'd pass them out to her contacts – she had plenty. I felt terrified and it felt good. She told me to 'Fake it, until I make it', a quote I used to say to myself and again, that I'd learn best on the job. The funny thing was it didn't feel like a job. It gave me a purpose and made me feel like I was living again.

'Are you sure you've tested out this paint, Sammie?' asked Audrey, stepping back to look at the wall surrounding the fireplace.

'Yeah, it looks like someone sneezed,' Max shouted from down the hall. There was an echo of laughter from the other work lads with him.

'Do you hear them?' I turned to Audrey. 'Not a bit of creative vision between them. And as for you, Max, that's the last time I'll be recommending you for a job.'

'Isn't that terrible, Audrey,' said Max, 'and me a single father.'

'She's the boss.' Audrey winked at me. 'Seriously though, Sammie, this colour – it is a bit bodily fluid-ish?'

'Not you too, Audrey. You're meant to be the design queen.' I smiled at her. 'It'll be perfect when it dries, promise.'

Audrey smiled, crossing her arms. 'Well, I've every faith in you.'

And for the first time in a long time, I had every faith in me too.

That night, I ordered a Chinese take-away for myself and Conor. I ordered our usual with a can of 7up for Conor and Diet Coke for me. I thought back to this time two years ago, to when we were finishing up our wedding meal about to have our first dance. I never in a billion years would have imagined that this is where I'd be, and I certainly couldn't have imagined getting through it.

Before the memory could swallow me, I focused on what I was doing now, knowing I'd have to take the good days with the bad and try to stay hopeful for more good ones.

I was just about to eat when Amy texted, saying her and Mark were thinking of me and would I be up for a night out the following weekend. I replied 'yes' straight away. I knew Jojo would be delighted to hear that I'd be needing some fashion advice. Rebecca had called around a couple of times to visit and Jojo had been quick to make herself at home. Rebecca had seemed a lot more relaxed having had a better meeting with Beatrice before her maternity leave, who'd said she was really pleased with her progress. Jojo still said she hated her, but sure you can't win them all.

I put my phone on the coffee table and sat back into the couch, pointing the remote at the TV. Ed Sheeran's voice filled the room, making me stop open mouthed, with my fork raining rice onto my lap. *Thinking out loud,* our wedding song. I knew it was a sign. I knew it was Conor's anniversary gift to me.

I looked up at our vision board at where we had both written our goals. I'd ticked a couple of his off, and with a shaking hand, added some new ones of my own. This was my gift to him; to keep dreaming, to keep living for myself and to enjoy the adventure. Time wasn't a healer, but I knew it would pass anyway, so I was going to make it count.

Printed in Great Britain
by Amazon

69138944R00208